S0-BJI-932

A Beastly Confrontation–

"Stand where you are!" hissed a voice from an alleyway, **"Compose yourselves, for you're about to meet your Maker!"**

Mav leaped between me and the vicious brace of eye-blades which slithered around the corner. We retreated, step by step, as a daunting figure emerged from the alleyway, a darkly-pelted lam of giant stature, his furry covering shirred in many places with ancient badly healed scars. Much taller than my companion and of incomparably greater bulk, his glittering swordpoints made tiny, menacing circles in the air before us.

"Remsi vy' by onsen, nrdeikaz!" he gestured with his empty middle hand, **"By reban yat ot me avima!"** We'd backed ourselves nearly to the curbing-edge, Mav reaching beneath his cloak, when a Fodduan voice behind the sailor warned:

"My friend says stand where you are—nothing can save you!" I let my bag slide a little from my shoulder, ready to swing it with all the energy at my command, for I was determined that neither of our accosters should buy our lives as cheaply as they apparently expected.

Also by L. Neil Smith
Published by Ballantine Books:

THE PROBABILITY BROACH

THE VENUS BELT

Their Majesties' Bucketeers

L. Neil Smith

A Del Rey Book

BALLANTINE BOOKS • NEW YORK

TO OWEN, for the kindest cut

A Del Rey Book
Published by Ballantine Books

Copyright © 1981 by L. Neil Smith

All rights reserved under International and Pan-American
Copyright Conventions. Published in the United States by
Ballantine Books, a division of Random House, Inc., New York,
and simultaneously in Canada by Random House of Canada,
Limited, Toronto, Canada.

Library of Congress Catalog Card Number:

ISBN 0-345-29244-8

Manufactured in the United States of America

First Edition: August 1981

Cover art by Ralph Brillhart

Contents

Pasje, uai nrytu wesoh lixxu lenoh oj-niiwaav!
—The Book of Pah

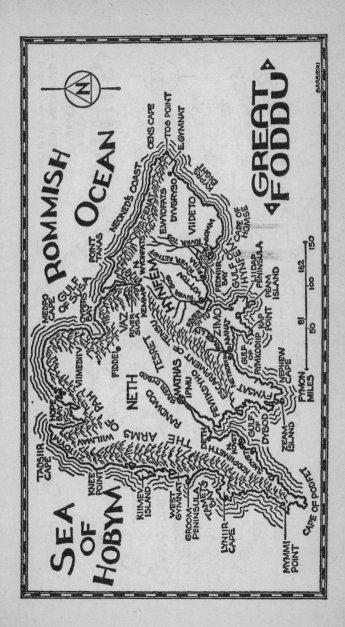

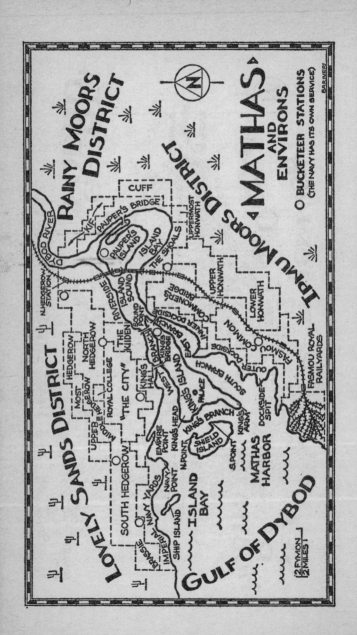

Prologue

The Solar Confederacy's discovery of the lamviin of Sodde Lydfe is recounted elsewhere. It well deserves to be, representing, as it does, the historic first contact by humans, simians, and cetaceans with an alien intelligence.

What we have here, instead, is a sort of diary, kept by a member of that species over a few days some twenty-five years before the coming of *Tom Paine Maru*, a highly personal adventure, set in a period now regarded nostalgically. It would hold no greater significance except that it revolves about the same Agot Edmoot *Mav* who figures so highly in our initial relations, and provides a preview of the desperate circumstances leading to our still-controversial intrusion.

By way of introduction, the lamviin are a race of furry pseudocrustaceans approximately forty inches tall, trilaterally symmetrical. Set around the carapace between the large dark eyes are three major limbs used for both locomotion and manipulation. About halfway down, each of these "legs" branches once again into three "arms," which terminate in deft, three-fingered hands. Lamviin are, of course, trilaterally *sexual* as well, but it is *far* beyond the scope (and capacity) of this brief Prologue to so much as touch on the complexities of that!

Sodde Lydfe is frequently described as "roughly Earthlike." *Very* roughly: unmercifully hot (though, naturally, it doesn't seem so to the lamviin) and arid to the point of indescribability. Its gravity, about two-thirds standard, retains three rather large, bright, natural satellites.

That perverse minority of readers with a taste for figures and statistics may content itself with the official record of *Tom Paine Maru*'s interstellar travels and undertakings. Mymy's story, told in *rher* (yes, that's the pronoun) own words, gives a much more satisfying feeling of what life was all about in the Empire of Great Foddu while

1

Mav was busy making himself into the kind of person we were damned lucky to find there, *waiting for us.*

In some respects, it's a familiar story, filled with all those life-distorting attitudes and customs one invariably encounters where political and military power have supplanted individual reason and voluntary exchange as the bases for civilization. That Mav began, so long before we met him, to recognize and try to alter these circumstances is what makes him remarkable to us.

And to Mymy, by all indications, as well.

So imagine Sodde Lydfe as first we saw it, as we would have seen it had we arrived a quarter-century earlier: the second planet of an orange dwarf called Pah, small and slightly cooler than our own primary. From space the surface is a wild, cloudless swirl of brown and orange-yellow, the seas a brilliant scarlet. The inhabitants . . . well, let Mymy tell you about them.

And rherself.

EdWina Olson-Bear
Chief Culturologist, *Tom Paine Maru*
October 23, 276 A.L.

I: Ungentlelamly Remonstrations

Agot Edmoot *Mav*, Extraordinary Inquirer for Their Majesties' Bucketeers, trod down the well-worn steps of North Hedgerow Precinct in a visible state of agitation, practically onto the cobbled pavement of Kevod Lane before he realized that he was being followed.

I could scarcely blame him in this: there seemed little he was aware of at the moment save that unbearable frustration that our immediate superior's reactionism never failed to inspire in him. To be blandly informed that Bucketeers attired as civilians might very well find apprehending criminals easier, but that such an expedient was *unsporting*, and on this principle unthinkable . . .

The fur stood out upon Mav's carapace in ill-tempered spikes as he commenced inhaling deeply after the fashion of his *Resre* masters—another "foreign affectation" disapproved of by Battalion Chief Waad Hifk *Tis*—a subtle but efficacious aid to a gentlelam's composure. Breath whistled quietly in turn through the nostril on either side of the bases of his limbs, which appendages he alternately tensed and relaxed, regaining mastery of his public disposition.

In my esteem, Mav was the very specimen of mature Fodduan lamviinhood, tall, symmetrical, ordinarily of restrained and courteous demeanor befitting the station to which he had been born, and of a tawny-golden coloration typical of the Imperial race, shading to a darker hue at the extremities. A manicured and shapely three-fingered hand equipped each of the arms that served him with inherent grace whether they supported his weight upon the ground, or—in exercise of that singular ability which, with certain other attributes, distinguishes us from speechless beasts— were held erect, displaying a strength that often came as a surprise to the resisting felon (and to many an enamored female and surmale, if one credited the least of Department innuendo, in my presence he was invariably the

3

model of moral exactitude, although whether this was wholly to be desired I could never then quite decide).

Where each triad of arms joined together, a crisp measure of carefully selected shirt cuff set off the lower edge of his aristocratically tailored uniform sleeve. The limbs above these joints (one would assume) were proportionately well-turned—although in one of them a lingering indisposition from a savage arrow taken during brief and, rumor has it, notorious service in some colonial war, occasioned traces of a limp that he artfully concealed by carrying his duty weapon strapped there, rather than regulation-style from the underside of his carapace.

This contrivance, of seasoned ajot-leather, I knew to be one of Mav's several minor inventions, some of which— despite the most strenuous of official resistance—were in everyday use in the Department. It is difficult for even the highest public servant to argue against apparatus that regularly saves lives.

Manifesting satisfaction, the detective now examined the quiescent texture of his fur as I, the accidental witness to this ordeal of self-containment. *Mymysiir* Offe Woom, a surmale paracauterist and Mav's admirer and friend, clattered out through the high glass-paned triangular Precinct doors to join him.

"Another altercation with our governor?" My own pelt must have betrayed a riffle of amused sympathy. As a determinedly independent representative of my gender, I confess that Mav's exertions on behalf of Departmental progress seemed strikingly to parallel my own. "I daresay we could hear the two of you through solid stone in the infirmary below!"

My companion cast a sardonic eye my way as he watched with the remaining pair for a break in the afternoon traffic rattling busily between him and his apparent objective, the Hose & Springbow. "My dear Mymy, do not compound impertinence with prevarication. Will you deny it was *your* silhouette I saw just now, outside the frosted glass of Tis's office door?" With this he stepped across the curb but was forced to retreat as a heavy waggon bearing Myfin's Celebrated Remedy—*for ague and the dampening of carapace and limbs*—rumbled into his path, drawn by an ill-matched trine of watun.

I would not dignify this accusation of his, not wishing our conversation to digress. "Dear Mav, more patience

4

upon your part might have an agreeable effect on our employer's health. It's been less than a year since you persuaded him—"

"Persuaded?" He produced from a pocket on his jacket-leg a small embellished silver tube and tiny matching flask of the aromatic distillates especially blended for him in the King's High Road. A drop or two fell into an aperture at the end of the cylinder; he waited as the volatile saturated its felt lining, then thrust it into one nostril. "Our venerable Battalion Chief had virtually to be compelled at pistol-point to concede that scientific criminal investigation might someday become practicable, provided I were to begin—"

"And *begun* you have, Inquirer sir, with considerable enhancement of your own professional status in the bargain. No longer is the estimable Mav obliged to pursue the common ruffian when a fellow Bucketeer sounds trumpet in some darkened alley. Nor does the *enviable* Mav march his appointed rounds at odd hours of the evening in every sort of disagreeable weather, and speaking of disagreeable"—I indicated his pipe; its fumes were causing me to blink—"that is a filthy habit; it will be the death of you, someday."

"Not," he replied evenly, "if I can get across this thrice-accursed street to entertain an even filthier one." He took my instrument bag. "Coming, paracauterist?"

At last watun and waggons had consented to let us pass. We approached that familiar after-hours haunt, an establishment nicknamed, from affection and ancient usage, the Bucket & Truncheon. Mav swung the door aside to the saloon bar where the landlord greeted us, a surly expression in his hair.

"Here now, none of *your* kind allowed!"

Despite a natural trepidation, I looked through him icily: "Pray, innkeeper, is this not a *Bucketeers'* tavern?" Rhetorical to say the least; the scars and scorchings of a thousand city fires were plain upon the fellow's body. His bristling exterior softened at my words to a sort of dull-witted perplexity.

"You know it is, Missur Mymy, why do you ask when you know it's so?" He wiped a grimy trio of hands on the apron hanging between his legs.

"Well, good Tamet," I declared, pointing to the insignia upon my cap and sleeves, "am *I* not a Bucketeer, then?" We'd been through this disheartening charade uncountable

5

times, yet it was always difficult accosting the old veteran thus.

The male habitués were staring at me as I stood partway through the door, half my walking hands still resting on the pavement outside. Each fiber on my carapace stirred with ill-concealed embarrassment and dawning anger.

"Aye, Mymy, but you're also a—"

"A paracauterist? Why, I see several: there's Nrydmou over there, and hallo, Zihu!" I refrained from pointing out that these were, of course, the only *male* paracauterists left in North Hedgerow Precinct.

"But, Missur, I can't . . . I mean, in twenty-seven nonades, there ain't *never* been permitted no—"

"*Surmale*, Tamet? That same three octaries ago, there weren't any *peace-keeping* Bucketeers, either. But there, as you might put it, 'plain as th' jaws on yer head,' sit Dapod and Em, juicing it up just like regular firefighters. How is it, fellows?" Our somewhat less progressive colleagues ignored my greeting.

Mav's coat was fairly curling with amusement now, though I believe it was not at *my* discomfiture. "Mymy, come with me. I'll sit with you in the public bar." He took my arm to lead me out the door where we walked another few paces along the street.

The public, or "family," portion of the Hose & Springbow was furnished much as the saloon that had always been forbidden me, in dark and ancient seasoned cactus plank and with yellow sand spread generously upon the footworn flagging. Streaks and splotches among the rafters attested to the age of the place, where tallow first and gaslamps afterward had left their sooty signatures. Now there were strung the glassy envelopes of electric candles, affixed to the copper mountings and reflectors of their predecessors. This illuminatory revolution, accomplished in my grandparents' day, had done much in Mathas to reduce the relative importance of the firefighting branch of our Service. As yet, the bureaucratic structure of its organization had not been appropriately adjusted.

Tamet met us again, addressing my companion: "Awrr, it just ain't *lamly* you should take yer current with th' ladies an' th' lurries, Cap'n." Giving signs of unbearable spiritual pain, he added, "C'mon back th' saloon an' have a jolter on th' house."

Observing Mav, I let my other eyes wander briefly over

the "ladies" present, reflecting how scandalized my family might feel had they known what I was seeing. The neighborhood of the Precinct was the intersection of three distinctly different districts, and, as such, had never quite settled on a character of its own. There was fashionable and wealthy North Hedgerow, where my parents made their home and I, myself, overcoming their most strenuous objections, had managed to establish independent lodgings—admittedly selected and well supervised by my mother. There was The City, where respectable businesses flourished by day, among them my surfather's professional offices for the practice of medicine. And there was the Kiiden, where theatergoers and other, less benign varieties of sensation-seekers populated nighttime streets.

Among its other functions, the Hose & Springbow served as gathering place and refuge for these poor disreputables Tamet had referred to, as they prepared themselves to ply their degrading evening's trade. Except in size and manner of dress, their surmale partners (and partners there must be, for perversions of unnatural number or combination found even less official tolerance than our Service customarily accords to common "decent" . . . oh, for Trine's sake, *say* it—prostitution) were hardly distinguishable in the dispirited manner with which they built up a sort of inebriated indifference to what they must endure this night for the sake of keeping spirit and carapace together.

There were, of course, also my fellow surmale paracauterists, who reacted appropriately as to their individual natures to the spectacle I had thus far created of myself. Poadpo looked toward the timbered wall, pretending not to notice. Zoddu winked and rippled rher pelt conspiratorially; though rhe lacked the courage to initiate these things rherself, rhe nevertheless admired my temerity and, on occasion, had told me so in private.

"Am I to understand," demanded my self-appointed but nonetheless welcome protector, "that you'll willingly serve my surmale companion in the saloon, breaking lifetimes of tradition, rather than have me, a male, take his tickle in the public bar?" There was another quality that I admired in Mav: he was never loath to identify the hearts of a sticky situation forthrightly—in the loudest of syllables, if necessary.

The barlam nodded miserable assent, wringing his apron.

"Then set us up, good lam, and be quick!" He flourished

7

a gleaming newly minted silver crown before the fellow's unhappy eyes as the three of us watched females and surmales, Bucketeers and trollops alike, get up and cross over to the saloon bar. "Or would you have us take our custom elsewhere?"

I sat uncomfortably upon my sand-filled cushion in the booth that Mav had chosen, six walking hands dangling several finger-widths above the floor, the underside of my carapace rocking slightly despite the elbows I had planted firmly on the rough-hewn tabletop. On one account Tamet had been the soul of verity: this part of his establishment had never been intended for the smaller sexes.

"My dear Inquirer," I admonished, our conversation having returned to the subject of Tis, "there are three sides to every argument. . . ."

"Assuredly," he responded, "the right side, the wrong side, and the *surmale* side." He let his furry covering crinkle a bit, indicating a humorous sentiment behind the barb. Then he lifted a hand to signal the proprietor for another.

His third, as I recall it.

His pelt assumed a pensive, almost bitter expression. "Why is it that there are those whose singular duty and delight it is to practice nothing but obstruction for obstruction's sake?"

I replied, "While there are those—in the opinion of my father, principally the young—who embrace novelty for no other reason than that it is novelty." I could quote the old gentlelam nearly word for word, for he had said this often enough, usually about me.

"I thank you, dear Mymy, for the implicit compliment, but I am scarcely any longer young—and bashing shells against the likes of Tis has aged me further than my years alone account for. You know, I'll wager our nominal superior was *never* youthful in the way your father complains of, but fearful and suspicious of change perhaps before he even knew what gender he would be. How it would surprise him that this attitude makes me more often sad than angry with him."

How odd, I thought: it was quite the other way with me. The very fabric of my being burned indignantly when confronted with this seemingly instinctual wariness of progress.

"My principal obstruction," Mav continued, "has never

8

been Tis, but my own uncertainties and incompetence."
This he rendered quite without the lackluster droop that in
any other lamviin would accompany such an admission.
The former of his statements, I knew, was within certain
fuzzily defined limits, assuredly correct. Mav's family connections guaranteed him a place in our Service (or any of
several higher callings) nearly regardless of his behavior
toward authority. This surely must have been a major point
in the contentions between him and our Chief, yet something that elderly civil servant, jealous of his own humble
position in the scheme of things, as any Lord might be,
could never introduce into their discourses, lower classes
being so much more formal about these matters.

At long last Tamet came round to our booth, fingering
his large tavern keeper's key, which he inserted in the side
of a small wooden chest sitting on the table before Mav and
gave several enthusiastic turns, making certain that the
latch upon the top was securely locked into its gear. This
having been accomplished and the reckoning calculated
against Mav's earlier generous advance, he nodded and
went on to serve another patron.

Mav placed a finger from each of his outside hands in
the appropriate pair of apertures in the top of the box and
with his middle hand reached for the latch, pausing for a
moment before he released it.

"Mymy," said he, "have you ever considered this endeavor of mine? I know in all my hearts, as surely as the
sky is gold and sand gardens bloom in springtime, that it is
possible somehow to examine the location of a crime—
provided that no one has disturbed it—and logically determine what transpired there, and how, and who the culprit
must be. Each of us leaves his own distinctive mark in
whatever he undertakes."

He fingered the latch but again refrained from releasing
it. "However, in the year since I 'persuaded' Tis of my
theory to this effect, I have yet wholly to prove it sound. I
confess I understand his impatience. The methods, whatever they must be, continue to elude me."

"Perhaps," I offered, "the natures of the particular
crimes this last year have not been such as lend themselves
to—"

He uttered then a phrase that I had heard before only on
two occasions, once from these same nostrils that repeated it
now, and once from those of a common dock hand I

9

chanced to overhear while on an errand in the Imperial Navy Yards. With this he flipped the latch. The key-wound engine whirled within the box, turning an armature. Mav snapped into a rigid posture for the briefest moment, then, as the infernal mechanism slowed and halted, relaxed with a sigh.

"I'll say this for our landlord, he generates the smoothest current this corner of the Kiiden." He blinked and took up his inhaling tube from the table.

"I wouldn't know," said I, "though it causes me to wonder whether you'll eventually embalm your sensibilities with that pipe of yours, or coagulate them first." I gave the box a little push with my finger.

"You have neglected mentioning the fire hazard that the two, combined, amount to. Mymy, you are a fine, intelligent, attractive surmale and a capital paracauterist. But you are also a nag and the poorest of juicing companions. Nonetheless"—he reached into a pocket of his uniform—"it occurs to me that you might find enjoyable what promises to be a highly stimulating discussion this evening at the Imperial Museum of Natural Philosophy. An old and extremely respected friend is conducting the lecture." He flourished a triad of tickets with the title boldly printed upon them:

"THE ASCENT OF LAMVIIN"
RECENT CONTINENTAL EVIDENCES
Srafen Rotdu Rizmou, Prof.

"And who," I asked with perfect foreknowledge of the answer it would evoke, "will be completing our trine this evening?"

"Why, Vyssu, of course. She has a commendable interest in all subjects pertaining to natural philosophy."

Particularly the most intimately biological ones, I thought. "Honestly, Mav, why can you not fraternize with persons more suitable to your . . . well, more representative of your own estate? This rubbing knees with hooligans of every—"

"Because, my dear Mymy, with the delightful exception of your esteemed self, I find the upper classes of this city—indeed, of this entire Empire—the most excruciating collection of bores and simpletons imaginable. It pains me you will not regard Vyssu more charitably, for she, too, is a

10

valued friend and an astute adviser. Tell me, though, will you come out with us this evening?"

I hesitated. Mav had never before asked to see me socially, and his invitation seemed both flattering and full of promise—I mean to say that perhaps he was at last beginning to seek his own level in life. It passed my mind that I might be a better moral influence upon him than was the case with his accustomed companions.

There was, however, the requirement of making myself publicly visible in company with this awful Vyssu creature—not that it would do my reputation any great damage. On the contrary, I am ashamed to say, she was recently quite the darling of the aristocracy. Perhaps they deceived themselves that her matchmaking among the upper classes did not have some baser equivalent for those of meaner stature and more casual moral persuasion, who were also her clientele. Possibly these noble patrons even *knew* and somehow found her all the more attractive an acquaintance. Perhaps, as was often rumored, they even found some use *themselves* for—But no, there *are* limits, after all, aren't there?

I began to answer my companion, when someone shouted at him from across the tavern and, swaggering or staggering (I am unsure which), approached us. Perhaps a bit of both. I knew him quite as well as Mav—in fact, as well as anyone would wish to, it being one of my more unfortunate official duties to Triarch and Public to deal with those of his sort—and this abrasive rudeness was quite consonant with whatever it was served him as character. The juicing box he held unsteadily before him had a well-used look for which, in justice, he could not be held entirely responsible. Yet to judge from his slurred and sleepy manner, it had seen recent and repeated application.

"Ahoy there, Mav, ol' cactus-hopper! How goesh it with th' Bucketeerses t'day? An' Mymy, too—in th' saloon bar?—how charmin'ly radical of you!" He maneuvered closer despite my pointed appeals to Mav to ignore him.

"Rewu Uomag *Niitood*," responded the detective, "I'd know that intoxicated shuffle anywhere. Why aren't you out making up lies for that journal that so generously supports your vices?"

Niitood collided with the end of our table, braced his hands upon it and used one of his walking hands to seize an unoccupied cushion from the next booth. "M'dear In-

11

veshtigator, I am preparin' myself in th' only 'propriate manner for an ordeal bebove and ayond th' call of duty-hood. The *Mathas Imperial Intelligencer* hash ordained in its editorial wishdom that I musht cover a crackshell conf'rence thish very evening. . . ." He waved the juicing box before our eyes. "I'll charge thish off to reshearch!"

He reached into one of the several apparatus-laden pouches draping his carapace and legs to extract a certificate identical to those that Mav had earlier shown me. " 'Ascensionism—Fraud or Hoax?' Or, how does a senile ol' sailor keep the money flowin' from a gullibubble government?" He wobbled one inebriated eye in my direction: "Wanna go, cutie? I gotta press pass, too!"

Somewhat hastily: "Mav, nothing would give me greater pleasure than to accompany *you* to Professor Srafen's lecture—though I am expected at an informal musicale my family are holding for the Lord, Lady, and Lurry Kassafiin. I'm sure my father will forgive this obligation in the interests of bettering my education; I'll neglect to mention the name of our third companion."

"And Vyssu," said Mav, an odd expression forming in his fur, "who has apologies of her own to tender for a previous engagement, will likely neglect to mention *yours*." He turned his eye again toward Niitood, who had continued mumbling to himself, somewhat incoherently. "What was that you said?"

"I said goddamp philosophical johnnies just can't leave th' world alone. Always pokin', always tinkerin'. Always makin' it a more dangerous an' confusin' place. If I had *my* way—*hic!*"

Before my friend could frame a suitably acidic reply, the reporter gave a sort of bobble of his carapace, his walking legs collapsed from beneath him, and he settled, half upon his cushion and half upon the floor, in something mimicking the state of hann, brought on, no doubt, by the electrical current of which he had so freely imbibed. Mav lifted the juicer from his hands and set it on the table, repeating this undeservedly kind gesture with a box camera, which had fallen from an unfastened pouch into the floorsand.

"Wretched fellow." Mav examined some electrical attachment to the camera, connected where there should have been a trough and caplock for flash powder. "Small wonder the Empire's in such a despicable condition, given the

12

quality of its sources of information. I— Hallo, what have we here?"

I, too, had been alarmed by the familiar racket emanating from across the street. All the bells and trumpets of the Precinct sounded loudly as the giant doors of the station rumbled open upon their massive hinges. I guessed there was a major conflagration somewhere in our district.

"I must fly," I told my companion, "for though I have just come off duty, it appears as if perhaps I shall be needed." Outside, the first straining team hurled themselves into the street, drawing the new steam-driven pumping engine behind them, its steel-rimmed wheels thundering and sparking across the cobbles. Above the rearmost of them the steerslam clung to his tiller, narrowly avoiding catastrophe with every lamheight the vehicle moved down the narrow street.

"Good-bye, then, O Paragon." Mav crinkled his fur at me good-naturedly. "I'll call at your door this evening in a conveyance appropriate to our rank."

"We will meet at the Museum," said I, seizing my bag and hurrying to the door where others of my calling pushed and jostled. Like the six high-strung draft-watun, I found myself exhilarated and anxious to be gone. "My father will have fewer questions to ask that way, and I shall have fewer deceptive answers to give him."

II: The Ascent of Lamviin

The inception of the Bucketeers is shrouded by the dust storms of antiquity. Legend credits Neoned the Aggressor, discoverer of Foddu, with recruiting the first such body for protection of his beachhead encampment on the Gulf of Dybod. But then legend credits Neoned with much, including running the one-minute fymo and setting the moons in their races. More likely some successor, possibly his son Adetpo Zimyin, provided Mathas her first company of "sand-slingers."

They came to be sorely needed. Unlike the Continent, whose primordial stands of cactus our ancestors leveled long before the first bronze tools were cast, Foddu was an untouched desert paradise. Moreover, on the northern and western coasts, windward to the Arms of Pah, whose ramparts defend this blessed island from unwanted and ungodly moisture, there existed (as there exist today) trackless tangles of that peculiar organism whose trunks and limbs have proved even better suited to architectural intentions. Harvesting these wet-weather flora is a dangerously shell-softening occupation, more highly recompensed than common labor, and regarded as unfit employment even for the many convicted miscreants Their Majesties otherwise set to perilous or unsavory tasks.

Thus, until more recently when improved marine conveyance rendered quarried stone a more practicable material, residential Mathas has been built largely of vegetable matter, and subject to terrible and repeated fires, some of weighty historical significance.

Paracautery shares a similarly obscure but equally reasonable origin. How ironic it is that one of the more pronouncedly robust species in the world succumbs so rapidly once the carapace is breached! Although it takes considerable force to do so. Contrariwise an adult of any sex can lose an entire limb, enduring only the humiliating incon-

14

venience of a few months' regeneration, even suffer his jaws to be completely severed (a disgustingly barbaric practice among primitives in certain of the colonies), and, if proper curative measures are taken, little permanent damage will result. Yet once penetrated by an arrow or a bullet, the victim may be saved only by the most modern and heroic exercises, immediately applied.

For octaries it was assumed that males must dominate here as they continue to in other callings. Yet at the insistence of Rher Imperial Highness Wiidytno, several years ago, a series of experiments determined the unquestionably superior native surgical abilities of surmales, who have subsequently secured the majority of such positions offered by the State. It remains, in my opinion, the shame, not only of the Bucketeers but of the entire government, that compensation in this branch of Service was immediately reduced by half.

At the appointed hour, I was, by circumstance, nowhere remotely near the Imperial Museum. The fire had proved unusually severe, threatening the better part of several streets along the riverfront across from Pauper's Island. As so large an area could not be given to the flames, especially so near the city's principal railway station (in truth, had it not been for the suffering of thousands of working-class innocents, it might have been a benefit to dispose of these last remaining frame buildings this side of the river), an unusual and dangerous measure had been proposed.

Between the roaring of the fire, the shouts and moans of people roundabout—victims, passers-by, and Bucketeers wrestling with equipment and terrified animals—and the noise of the engines lifting bucket after chain-linked bucket full of sand to drop into the blaze, I nearly missed this novel maneuver, attempting to revive a female well gone into perhaps her dozenth wretched pregnancy, my thirtieth or fortieth patient of the evening.

The fur was burned away from two-thirds of her carapace where some errant blast of flame had withered it, blackening the naked chiton and blinding her in one eye. This would heal, and she was lucky not to have lost the sight of another.

She'd be luckier still if I could stem her premature delivery. Her jaws were frozen wide and rigid in prepartum tetany; I was thankful for a series of unblushing lecturers at

Royal College who'd insisted that we learn all the signs of even so delicate and personal a thing as this. I did for her what I could, supplying a relaxant, tincture of fedizeto, administered in atomized form to the nostrils, splinted up a leg where she had fractured it, and rose as she was lifted onto a waggon. Looking over the carapaces of the litter-bearers, I beheld one of the most terrifying spectacles I believe I shall ever have to witness.

Department Chief Lydoraino Hottyn *Niifysiir* had authorized the movement of our sand pumps toward the edge of the river. There, whitepowder charges were dramatically employed to clear away the rotted planks and shoring of the docks (at no great loss to anyone, as the bulk of commercial traffic had long since been removed to the opposite shore across King's Island). A squad of firelaun detached their breathing-hoses—so common an appliance that they have, with the sandbucket, become a symbol of our calling—from their nostrils, in order to discencumber themselves for what they were about to undertake. So thickly swathed in protective clothing they could scarcely stir a limb or see what they were doing, the nine gallant Bucketeers forced their balky teams to back the rearmost corners of the engines into the very water itself!

The chain-driven scoops began to churn the evil-looking surface, lifting mud and vile liquid stories high above us. For once the sightseeing crowds evaporated without the urging of our peacekeepers, unwilling to chance that single random drop that might (in their ignorantly exaggerated belief) dissolve its way through hair and bone into their very brains. It is, in fact, the scientific truth that not only may we survive brief exposures to moisture—complete immersion under certain well-controlled circumstances (else sailing would be far too perilous even for those hardy souls who take it up)—but that some amounts of water are even necessary to sustain life! Fortunately these minuscule traces are present in our victuals and the air. I have tried to imagine taking liquid, say, as one might eat a morsel of food; the thought has never failed to sicken me.

Nonetheless, not a single pelt among the hardened veterans all around wasn't set in the attitude of grim determination overcoming instinctual terror. The river seethed and bubbled hideously, the engines hissed and clanked, dripping from their every seam and truss.

16

Suddenly the first measures of wet filth fell from the uppermost mechanical extremity and into the flames. There was a great, nasty frying noise, and unimaginable volumes of steam began to rise and mingle with the smoke until I felt the heat diminish perceptibly where it had radiated upon my carapace even as far away as this aid station, a street removed.

A mighty cheer resounded through the neighborhood, and bells were rung upon our waggons.

Definitely the fire had been parted in twain. It is a fact that dampened wood and furnishings will not readily burn; our Bucketeers proceeded to divide the fire again and again until conventional methods sufficed to put it out. Fodduan ingenuity once again had triumphed, though there would be considerable cursing tonight among the recruits as they scrubbed the sodden fire equipment with clean dry sand to remove all evil smells and corrosion.

My final charge had been carted off to Charitable Sanctuary, an institution which the Church maintained across the river in Commoner's Bridge. I closed my bag wearily, looking forward to a pleasant sandy scrub myself, when I happened to glance at the railway clock a few blocks away. Why, I'd completely forgotten my evening's engagement with—

"Rather more exciting a spectacle than a museum lecture, I am compelled to agree!" Mav stood suddenly beside me, fur arranged ironically, his uniform exchanged now for dashing evening dress. "I took the liberty," he told me as he lifted my bag into the hired carriage drawn before us, "of sending a messenger to your girl, who will be ready to assist you in dressing. Why in heaven's desiccation will you not have a line put in? This is the twenty-sixth century, after all. Now we'll have to hurry, just to be fashionably late!"

I climbed into the cab to discover, with some pleasure, that we were quite alone. "Is Vyssu given to fashionable lateness as well, or is she stamping an impatient hand for us in front of the Museum?"

"Neither, I'm afraid—*as she was able to explain upon the telephone a while ago*. She had a social obligation which she couldn't break, after all: a musicale for the Lord, Lady, and Lurrie Kassafiin at your fathers's house this evening."

17

By the time we arrived at the Museum, our driver was hard-pressed to convey us through an angry-sounding crowd of demonstrators who had gathered all around the ancient edifice. The streets were overflowing with lamviinity, and Mav, after several vain attempts on the part of our conductor to make a path for us, at last decided we should walk, despite the cablan's earnest protestations of our safety.

Through annoying oversight I had left my bag in the carriage while Mav waited outside my modest lodgings, staring at his watch upon its chain. I might, in perfect propriety, have asked him in, but I knew full well this would be transmitted to my mother immediately upon her weekly visit tomorrow afternoon. My maidservant occupied her position far less for my convenience than for my family's regular edification. That she had a reliable weakness for places like the Bucket & Truncheon and was to be found on such premises more frequently than at her duties suited me perfectly. But it would avail me nothing in the instance of so recent an "indiscretion" as permitting Mav to see my rooms—she had, after all, to have *something* to report every nine days.

Accordingly, rather than entrust my instruments (a cherished present from my surfather) to be returned to my apartments by a driver I did not know, I elected to carry them to the lecture, winning, on this rare occasion, an argument against Mav's archaic insistence that he shoulder the burden. Given the long and arduous day behind me, perhaps I shouldn't have tried to be quite so persuasive.

The crowds made quite as much commotion as the earlier fire had. I found myself astonished that the object of their protest was the very lecture we were looking forward to. Of course, the subject of Ascensionism was controversial; but what was there about this esoteric topic to incite what promised soon (were it not for the doughty Bucketeers who formed an inner barrier around the place) to become a riot?

Many in the throng were carrying torches, while others brandished large sheets of resinboard fastened to sticks after the manner of Continental radicals and labor insurrectionists. I fear that proper conduct precludes me from recording here some of these pronouncements (which in any case were echoed loudly by those who bore the placards), but the import was that they disagreed with Professor Srafen's ideas and desired that rhe refrain from public discussion of them.

Either that, or conduct rher next seminar at the bottom of the River Dybod.

On the bed of a waggon whose shabby watun were tied to a hitching bar before the massive doors of the Museum, a figure pranced in soiled robes that might, a long, long time ago, have originally been white. Atop his jaws he wore a cone of parchment on which was crudely described a lidless eye.

This I recognized from recent newspaper accounts and from history lectures at College, was an ancient religious insignia lately resurrected by an unauthorized sect of fundamentalists in distorted mockery of the Church of the Martyred Trine, which is the official State religion of the Empire of Great Foddu. The ragged form upon the waggon harangued the gathering, and I began to be amused, imagining what my parents' friend the Archsacerdot of Mathas might make of the fellow's rude theology:

"Lamviin was instantaneously and miraculously created at the ordination and in the image of Our Maker, Pah!" Thus far the cant was orthodox, though I am given to understand certain sophisticated scholars high in the Church will entertain without prejudice the notion that this is more a matter of poetic metaphor than philosophical necessity.

"And yet this vile blasphemer is allowed to teach that we 'ascended'—through uncountable and monstrous accidents of birth—from creatures such as eat the bugs off arms of desert cactus! Will we permit this evil and indecent slander against the written word of Pah Himself?"

"NO!" the crowd roared back at him, affrighting me far more than had the volumes of inanimate slime raised from the river earlier this evening. At least that foul substance had *extinguished* a blaze.

"NO!" they shouted once again. I began to be afraid that here was more than some small collection of benighted crackshells. I grasped Mav's arm all the closer, taking comfort in the hard-edged outline of the pistol beneath his cloak. He signed to one of the Bucketeers at the door who recognized us and immediately detached himself from the cordon to escort us the few remaining yards. We passed through many a muffled threat, which discreet cuffs from the officer silenced only momentarily.

"You're the last," announced an elderly lam at the top of

19

the steps as he carefully ticked our admissions off against a roster of invited guests he carried with him. His uniform differed somewhat from those of our protectors in the street and I guessed, correctly as it turned out, that he was with the Museum. "We'll lock the doors now and bar them for good measure. Any more as is late'll hafta read about it in th' mornin' papers!" With this the guard secured the entrance and guided us across the dim, enormous front display hall toward our destination.

Srafen Rotdu Rizmou, Professor and Curator of the Imperial Museum of Natural Philosophy, proved to be a surmale of sufficient age to make the elderly Museum guard who led us to our seats seem sprightly by comparison. Mav advised that I should not be deceived altogether by appearances, that Srafen had been ill in recent months but was now recovering and in fact complained of gaining weight. Here and there a patch of the professor's carapace and limbs showed through rher thinning pelt and rhe moved upon the speaker's platform with a gingerly stiffness that betrayed the ravages of a lifetime spent in moister climates than perhaps our bodies are ideally suited for. This, by interesting coincidence, seemed the very topic that rhe was addressing as we found our places toward the rear of the chamber:

"Everywhere you look in Sodde Lydfe, everywhere I collected specimens during my youthful service to Their Majesties' Navy, everywhere from which today's youths with a similar penchant send me samples, everywhere but in our planet's *deserts*, which I'll be turning to in due course"—rhe leaned upon the lectern and held a finger aloft—"*everywhere*, you will discover a single, common, highly educative circumstance!"

Whether they agreed or not with Srafen, rher illustrious audience seemed captivated by rher unusually persuasive voice and assertive gesticulations. I cannot recall more than a teacher or three from my own school days who displayed this talent for making even dull things interesting, and none of them a third so good at it as rhe.

"Predators! Colossal, frightening, efficacious *monsters*, many of them ninefold and more the size of any lam who ever walked, most of them far faster, more ferocious, and better-endowed by a vindictive nature to live a life of mayhem, murder, and mastication!" Here rhe struck a comically menacing pose as though about to leap upon those seated in the front row and devour them.

In contrast to the public's usual disinterest in the wonders of natural philosophy, the room was filled to bursting with a gratifying variety of individuals—such characters as one might properly expect: academics, students, officials of the Museum and their staff (some of whom assisted the fragile old erudite in manipulating rher often bulky specimens). In addition, naturally, the press—I spied Mav's friend Niitood, recovered from his earlier excess and seated toward the front among his colleagues. Thereafter I assiduously avoided meeting his rearmost eye. Bucketeers were present inside, too, apparently in case some hypothetical infiltrator tried duplicating the chaos out of doors.

"It can be no coincidence, then," continued Srafen, "that our humble ancestors prospered only where no predator of any size could threaten them—where there was no easily obtained supply of, you will pardon my expression, water."

There passed among the listeners a small, uncomfortable shudder.

"It is equally no mere happenstance that every major prehistoric and contemporary carnivore lives in some damp and moldering environment, dependent on that vile fluid for sustenance. Even we—"

Rhe paused, for here there was a whimpering echo of the "No!" outside from some more tender-stomached soul among rher auditors.

"Yes, even we, by which I mean our remotest forebears, were once of similar unsavory persuasion. Yet the fossil record clearly demonstrates that, as we discovered safety in the sand, little by little we eschewed all but the slimmest remnants of our foul ancestral addiction to . . . well, let us pronounce it with scientific dispassion: dihydrogen monoxide. It is only now, through dint of our technological achievements, that we may return—however unwillingly at times—to moister climates for purposes of war and commerce . . . which in the Empire amount at times to much the same thing." There were a few embarrassed chuckles.

Much of the gathering this evening consisted of the Empire's loftier lights, a scattering of nobility, popular intellectuals, and a leavening of the socially elite. I counted several dozen Members of Parliament—all three Houses repre-

21

sented—including a cabinet minister or three. Officials of
the Church were here, which must have sorely galled the
demagogues outside. It may be this which inspired them to
make their protests heard, however faintly, even through
the ancient walls that, with many a stoutly barred and
bolted door, separated us from them. This arrangement
suited me most excellently, were I compelled to tell the
craven truth.

"In the friendly desert, through random alterations to
the medium of inheritance—an unknown process which, I
am afraid, I shall perforce be leaving to another generation
of investigators—and circumscribed, as it were, by the
trials and tribulations of an unkind world, the little creatures that were to become, in countless ages, lamviin,
changed and multiplied in variety." Rhe pointed to a chart
on the lefthand wall. "Common observation demonstrates
those fundamental similarities in structure shared by all advanced species: trilateral symmetry; trinary reproduction
of all vital organs; three major limbs extending from the
body, which trifurcate again before they reach the ground
and terminate in three-fingered paws, or hands.

"Even birds are constructed on this simple, elegant plan,
though Ascension has modified them severely, inverting
their carapaces so that the jaws are carried downward,
transforming legs into wings that they might whirl about"
—here rhe suited action to words, turning several times and
circling the lectern—"in a manner that would confuse the
eye and confound the sensibilities of any lamviin."

Here, someone shouted, "What about the watu, then?"

The professor stopped rher whirling suddenly and crinkled rher thinning fur with satisfaction. "Had not this
kindly inquisitor spontaneously cried out, I should have
had to pay someone to do so, for the watu is often raised as
an objection to my theories, and on that account is the
principal subject I have selected for this evening."

At some sign unnoticed by myself, Mav began shifting
restlessly upon the cushion he had previously occupied in
peace, those well-trained Bucketeer's reflexes of his poorly
suppressed as he glanced, his fur aligned in suspicious expression, about the crowded hall. Perhaps the press of those
outside had affected his nervous disposition as it had done
mine. Then, too, there was a certain tension palpable within
the door of the Museum as well. Presently I ceased chastiz-

22

ing myself for cowardly imagination, and returned my full attention to the lecturer:

". . . their feet. By the time we get around to *mesowatu*," continued Srafen, pointing to the diagram again, "this specialization favoring speed and agility is increasingly manifest."

At this point Niitood stood, inspired in all likelihood by the Professor's dramatic caperings, and fumbled with some accessory to his camera. He signaled up at Srafen as if to beg rher please to hold that photogenic attitude for just a moment, in which the elderly scholar assented with a kindly ripple of rher fur.

"Gone is that flawless symmetry that our own species has preserved. The central branching of the 'frontal' leg has atrophied, leaving but two delicate extremities. Both 'rear' legs have diminished even further, to a single branch apiece. See how much longer all the limbs have become, proportionate to the—"

At last Niitood seemed to have persuaded his apparatus to be as cooperative as the Professor. He held the instrument before his eye, tensed both walking legs, and shouted, "Hold it, Doc!"

And suddenly the entire room exploded!

III: A Natural Philosophy of Murder

Srafen had vanished in a blinding, lurid ball of flame, as if smitten by Him whose wrath the angry fanatics outside invoked. The air was filled with smoky vapor, my ears with screams of fear and anguish, my eyes—how can mere words convey the horrifying spectacle revealed to all as the atmosphere began to clear?

In place of the kindly old Professor stood the fire-blackened framing of rher lectern. Platform, charts, the very walls around them dripped a gory emerald; a mist of greenish hue still hung before our eyes. At such a sight my professional and lamviinitarian instincts took charge. With a strength I was surprised to own, however momentarily, I battered my way through what had dissolved into a frightened mob, oblivious except to those whose suffering called me. It was a startled Mav who followed in my wake, shouting to the crowd for orderly behavior.

Somewhere in the background the shrill peal of bells was to be heard, although it is possible there was some transitory effect upon my hearing. Perhaps I am too imaginative as I began attending the victims, it was clear to me they had fallen before a volley of uniquely grisly trajectiles: in addition to the ghastly splinters of the lectern, many sizable particles of carapace and other tissue had not originated with those whose bodies they now penetrated. Upon the bandages of each victim I wrote instructions that the surgeons might gather and preserve these pitiable fragments, lest Srafen's cruelly violated form be denied decent interment.

I have learned the virtue of setting aside emotion at such times, although I often afterward collapse in quakes and trembling quite as any laylam would. Thus momentarily detached, my hands and two front eyes pursuing their own ends, I observed Mav as he leapt upon the stage, his wicked foreign-looking reciprocator in one extended hand.

"Your attention, Bucketeers!" he shouted, and, failing at first of the desired response, whistled discordantly through all six nostrils. "Comrades, allow *no person* to quit this hall unsupervised! Block the doorways, and— *By the twenty-seven legs of God, stand clear, you cretins, you are destroying Queen's evidence!*" This latter was addressed to a sacerdote, two cabinet ministers, and the Lord Mayor himself, who, like any common curiosity-seekers, had wandered rather nearer the focus of events than suited our Investigator—and narrowly missed upsetting my medical bag in hasty retreat.

The bells at last stopped ringing, resumed at once, and then fell permanently silent.

I could not discern whether Mav's forceful manner stemmed from grief and anger at his old friend's hideous demise, or from realization (which had not been lost upon me) that here, at long last, was the very sort of circumstance he had sought so long for the sake of proving his theories. However it may be, he rapidly organized affairs so that, regardless of dignity or class, no individual might depart before being clearly identified by some Bucketeer or guard who knew him, or vouched for by another known to the authorities. A list was begun, but Mav apparently had reasoned there was small chance the likes of the Minister of Trade, the Sheriff of Randwod, the Associate Curator of this establishment himself, or any other from this august assemblage, would be fleeing guiltily aboard the next Continental steamer. In this, I must confess, I felt him overly confident.

He did take the precaution of ordering the speaker's platform and the first few rows of seats strung off and left as they had now become, a gruesome tableau spattered in rapidly desiccating body fluids.

My final patient was all too familiar. Niitood lay in apparent agony, several articles of mechanical debris lodged firmly, albeit superficially, in his carapace. His principal concern, however, appeared to be whether his employer would provide him a new camera or require him to replace that costly instrument out of a salary which, he went to some pains to impress upon me, was criminally penurious. Whatever the outcome, I informed him, he would not be photographing with *that* eye for many days.

Not more than half a dozen persons proved seriously enough endangered that they required more attention than

I was capable of rendering. These few were appropriately seen to and their names duly inscribed upon Mav's list, as it was not beyond reason that the perpetrator of this terrible deed might inadverently have incurred injury in its commission—or deliberately chanced doing so to divert suspicion. Arrangements were made to transport them by the most efficient means available to various establishments of mercy according to their social class.

Thus I became free to witness Mav's first tentative methodologies—indeed, if I may say so, to offer him another set of eyes and ears and hands toward that effort.

From earliest consciousness, I have sternly disapproved of a lam's life being forfeit to the State, regardless of the provocation. This predisposition, I suppose, I have from my surfather, who would be terribly distressed to learn that I considered that evening making an elaborate and painfully prolonged exception for the sort of craven canaille who deposit anonymous explosives and skulk away to let their killing be done indiscriminately. By comparison, the common, carapace-to-carapace murderer should be set free, perhaps even awarded the Queen's Own Order of the Walking Glove, rather than consigned, willy-nilly, to that ignoble fate that, in justice, might be singularly reserved to bombers.

Killing, in all decency, ought to be a personal thing.

The setting of the murder—and I do not believe Mav ever doubted it was anything but that—was a large room more than thirty lam-heights along each of its three sides. Its northern corner held the speaker's platform, itself precisely equilateral and perhaps eight or nine lam-heights in width, a simple elevated expanse of treewood planking not more than two or three hand-widths off the polished granite floor. It had obviously been constructed as an afterthought, for the ancient laminated cactus door beside it in the northeast wall (one of two such entrances leading into the next room) terminated at the original floor level, rather than that of the stage, and for that reason had been nailed shut, by all appearances, for nonades.

Near the southeast corner, the second door allowed access to one of the smaller display halls on the ground-floor level, a place where archaic memorabilia of war were exhibited along the walls and in numerous glass cases scattered about. This door had been left ajar for the night's

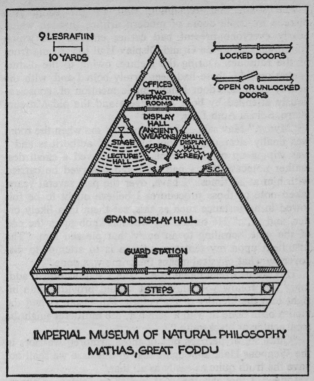

IMPERIAL MUSEUM OF NATURAL PHILOSOPHY
MATHAS, GREAT FODDU

lecture, affording admission to sanitary facilities across the Weapons Hall in another room beyond. Both smaller chambers (the second, I recall, was a place where thousands of insects were pinned horribly to neatly labeled cards) had been partitioned off across their southern ends, leaving only narrow access to three modern restrooms on the east side of the building.

The northwest wall of the lecture auditorium, hung with faded tapestries and battle-weary banners from an earlier age, was architecturally featureless, lacking doors or windows, as it formed a portion of the outermost perimeter of the Museum, one of few relatively ancient structures in the city made of stone (no doubt at hideous expense in those days) that had, at one time, been a garrison upon Mathas's northern edge, and later, for a briefer period, a prison.

The south and remaining wall of the room was pierced by triple doors of modern artifice through which nearly everyone present had earlier entered and which communicated to the Grand Display Hall toward the front of the Museum. During the lecture, owing to the disturbances outside, these had been firmly bolted and, with the nearby open side door I have made mention of, conscientiously attended by both Bucketeers and the old Museum guard, Sdinsu Amh *Leds*.

"Mymy," Mav said as he approached me when the room was finally cleared of all but uniformed authorities and I was wiping up my instuments. He displayed a small desleather notecase that I had long ago observed he carried with him at all times. "I have, over the past several years, taken note of those procedures I believe ought to be followed in an instance such as this, set them in a likely order, and . . ." He turned the wooden knob upon the end of the case, scrolling to an entry that pleased him. "The first item upon my tentative agenda is to attempt to discover by what physical means the crime was done."

This seemed reasonable to me, and I said as much, adding, "If I follow you, this effort should provide some insight into the identity of the culprit. For instance, had the victim been done in with a hammer, the murderer might be a carpenter or blacksmith."

"Quite so, or perhaps one of those armored warriors in the Weapons Hall, although I fear in this case we shall not have the truth quite as easily as all that."

Indeed, I thought, for what sort of profession or avocation predisposes someone to secrete a substantial charge of whitepowder in a philosophy professor's lectern? This, in turn, set me to wondering by what means the bomb had been ignited, and much the same question must have been on Mav's mind, for he questioned me at considerable length concerning what I had seen before the explosion and what I had done afterward. Not even surgical details were insignificant to him, and he had me repeat many an observation more than once. Finally:

"I thank you, Mymy, for your perspicacity and diligent memory. And now, is it not considerably past the time by which respectable lurries ought to have been home?" Here he made to tuck his notecase away. "I fear, in all this confusion, I've been sorely remiss in my duties as a—"

"I am more than capable, my dear Inquirer, of seeing to

my own well-being. Furthermore, it seems to me, since I have had to patch and mop up a deal of this 'confusion' myself, that I may lay legitimate claim to an interest in its resolution."

He paused, perplexity racing against amusement in conflicting waves through his fur. "Indeed you may, and well spoken, my dear. I warn you, however, that I do not know what hours looking into this will keep me up to."

"When you are quite ready to depart, so shall I be, and not until then. In the meantime, tell me how I may be of further assistance—it strikes me that we might call for some refreshment, since you are fatigued enough to have uncharacteristically left a preposition dangling in your last utterance."

He failed to reply, but signed to the Museum guard. "Good Leds, will you be kind enough to bring my friend and myself some kood or whatever else suits your convenience? Rhe has complained of a spell of fatigue, and—"

"*Mav!*"

"—and I suspect that we lamn could all profit from a respite, as well." He retrieved his case and looked again at his notes. "You know, I rather fancy old Srafen would be amused by what has happened here tonight."

"Amused? I scarcely—"

"Well, perhaps 'relieved' would be a more appropriate term. Rhe hated being aged and feeble, you know, especially after such an energetic and productive youth. And to finish in so spectacular a manner! I take it back—'amused' is the only suitable word, after all. Rhe always appreciated a well-delivered punchline."

"I had wondered that you weren't more aggrieved than you appeared. And what, precisely, *was* the manner in which rhe departed, would you say?"

"Do not mistake me, Mymy." He once again surveyed the platform, hopped up upon it, and began looking closely at the floorboards. "Someday the world will learn how much it owes to Srafen, and the scoundrel who did this will be made to pay if I have to make the collection my life's work. Nonetheless— Oh, Dapod, there's a good fellow, bring your lantern over, will you?"

I knew from my own occupation that, whenever work is close, there's never enough light. Although the place seemed adequately illuminated with electric candles, spots here and there, particularly the corner behind the lectern, were in partial shadow. Mav seemed interested in the sealed door to the right. I thought a moment, then plunged a hand into my bag:

"I say, Mav, might this be of some use to you?" I held the object up where he could see it.

"Capital, Mymy! You've justified your presence here already! Do hand me Mymy's glass if you will be so kind, Dapod." This uniformed worthy, having a longer reach than I, stretched out and gave over the magnifier, a large and powerful one I use for removing splinters and finding cinders and the like in patients' eyes. He also handed the detective his Bucketeer's carbide-acetylene lamp, taking care, at my companion's admonition, not to venture on the platform himself.

"Odd," mused the detective, and a little later, "Hmm?" He crawled about quite comically, his carapace tipped up nearly vertical, suspended but a finger-width from the floor by his middle hand. "Extraordinary!" he exclaimed, and, "I'll be drowned!" At last he seized upon some loose object lying on the boards, stood abruptly, marking the position with a bit of chalk, and tucked both in a pocket, leaping lightly off the stage.

Both Dapod and I met him, questions written blatantly in our pelts. I asked how he imagined the lectern bomb might have been set off, but he signed negatively and marched across the room to where Leds had laid out the makings of our kood.

Indeed, I reflected, quieting my annoyance, there are only twenty-seven hours in a day, and we were all long overdue by now for that brief hour of oblivion which revitalizes mind and body. It suddenly occurred to me that, with the fire this afternoon, I had missed *two* periods of hann. Physiologically speaking, kood was no adequate substitute, but it does provide relief and satisfaction and is perhaps the most civilizing custom that the Empire has spread abroad—the cease of all meaningful activity in favor of a pleasant, empty social grace. I rather suspect that deprivation of some equivalent custom is what makes Foddu's rival, the Hegemony of Podfet, so barbaric and distempered at times.

At the back of the hall, Leds had rearranged chairs into a cozy circle about the little wheeled serving table he'd brought with him, and we gathered round as he struck a match to the wick. It sputtered, and in a moment or two delicious invigorating vapors issued from the silver service as he placed its perforated lid atop the kood holder and took a chair of his own.

I inhaled deeply, relaxing. "Tell me, Mav, what is it you discovered up there on the plat— Mav?" My companion had quite disappeared while all of us had been preoccupied with the kood. "Mav?"

"Just coming now, Mymy," an unseen voice replied, then he stepped out of the shadows through the door that had been open to the Weapons Hall. "Is that the kood I smell?" He rubbed his hands together. "How delightful!"

As he took a seat beside me and inhaled the vapors, I could tell that he was far more pleased than mere refreshments or a trip to the s.c. alone might account for. However, social decorum demands that nothing of moment be discussed while still the wick burns, so I would have to be content with the rough sort of small talk that serves not only males, but, worse luck, Bucketeers, for polite kood-time conversation.

Or so I had believed.

"I say, tell me, Leds old fellow, that's a splendid kood service you have there. Does it belong to you?" Perhaps the strain had been too much for Mav, for he uttered these words in the same tones employed by the kind of person who sells my mother draperies.

The old lam puckered up his fur. "To me? Oh, no, sir, it's the Museum's. Seventy-five years old, it is, an' once th' property of Lord Admiral Roytoyt hisself. His heirs donated it, but Professor Srafen had an older one, an' nicer, so he lets us—that is, he *let* us fellows use this one." His voice betrayed the strain and grief of losing such a kindly and respected employer, and his fur was all adroop.

"I see," answered Mav, seemingly unaware of the old lam's feelings. "And where is it that you keep it when it isn't in use? The Curator's office at the north end of the Weapons Hall?"

"Sir? Oh, no, sir, in the atrium guard station, out front. You passed through it tonight when you came in."

"Capital! Well then, what do you think of Ednotem this year? I hear the odds-makers give them three-to-two to take the City Medal."

When the kood was nearly done with, Mav held up a finger and spoke quietly: "Now, Mymy, I'm aware you

31

have a question for me. Do be good enough to come with me into the other room, for I believe I have this mystery more than two-thirds solved already."

My amazement must have shown, but he was silent as I gathered up my bag and followed him through the door into the Weapons Hall. Here, instead of going straight across to the sanitary closets as I'd assumed he'd done before, he turned to the left, pushing aside the portable screen that blocked off the rest of the room. When we were on the other side, he reached into his pocket. "I trust you'll forgive me that idiotic piece of conversation earlier, about the kood service. I had to be assured that no one had come through this screen and disturbed the contents of this room. Tell me, Mymy, what do you make of this?"

The article he'd handed me, an iron implement of some kind, was obviously ancient, for it showed that brownish-blue patina to which such metals are subject after prolonged exposure to the atmosphere. About twice as long as my hand, it appeared to be a solid rod about the circumference of my finger, and of unremarkable features save one end, which, through some cataclysmic force, had blossomed into a scorched and jagged deadly looking flower, the unmistakable stink of whitepowder smoke plain to discern. The other end was slightly worn and battered, little specks of bright, untarnished metal showed through the corrosion, but nothing so spectacular as the end, which had been . . . well . . .

"Exploded! You found this on the stage? What is it? Is it—"

He silenced me again with a gesture and led me down to the extreme end of the room, where there was a door to the left, flanked on either side by suits of iron battle dress, one with a massive sword, the other with a giant war-hammer. In the center of the panel hung an olden shield displaying the arms of one of good Queen Viigoot's ancestors.

"This door," said Mav, "is that which, on the other side, adjoins the speaker's platform. As you can see"—he pointed to the frame all round—"it has been nailed shut for rather a long time." In fact I had already noted that on the other side. We were now just opposite the place where Professor Srafen had been murdered, and I said as much.

"You are correct. Observe what else we are near." He gestured broadly at the room behind us, and my eye fell upon a display case, not more than a lam-height away, which had been—

"Broken into! How did this happen, Mav? Surely the explosion couldn't have—"

"You're quite right again, Mymy. This doubtless occurred sometime beforehand, when the villain removed . . . the murder weapon!" He pointed into the case, and suddenly I knew the identity of the iron implement that he had shown me. Lying on the velvet amidst a shameful mess of shattered glass was an old Podfettian springbow, much as the one Tamet's tavern is named after. Octaries ago, before the invention of whitepowder and firearms, the device had been a potent weapon well thought of, at least by those who think of such things.

"Yet innovations," Mav observed, "are never wholly taken up at once, nor reliable devices rapidly abandoned. Note those quarrels in the case." He pointed toward a number of short, heavy arrows, some with ugly barbed warheads, others plain, as if made for target practice. But the one he indicated in particular must, at one time, have been a mate to the damaged bolt he'd picked up off the stage. Instead of barbs or blades, it had a bulbous, hollow end. "You see how it unscrews? It is empty now, of course, but if you were to fill it with whitepowder and place a percussion cap on the end, so . . ."

From somewhere on his person, he'd obtained the sort of little brass cup one finds with old-fashioned pistols such as were used before self-contained metallic cartridges came into general fashion. My father had equipped himself with such a gun in his youth, and it was hanging now, if I recalled, over the mantelpiece at home.

BANG! He'd let the springbow bolt plummet, point-first upon the granite floor. Without a charge of powder, only the cap had exploded, but I began to understand what must have become of Srafen. "You mean to say that someone shot him with this antique weapon?"

"One can hardly avoid the conclusion. Mymy, I have been right about the art of detection. The inherent logic of the evidence is such that it directed me immediately to this place. I *knew* no bomb could have been placed in the lectern—"

"What?"

"Precisely so, for in the first place, the only possible

means of ignition would have been a lighted fuze—which surely Srafen, if no one else, would have noticed—or a clockwork timer, and the explosion would have strewn its gears and springs all over the stage. I found no such mechanical remnants.

"Also, what you told me of the injuries among the audience made it clear: one might reasonably have expected splinters from the podium, but *never* fragments of Srafen's carapace—may rhe rest in peace—which a lectern-bomb would have propelled upstage, and *not* into the audience!

"These caps, and this whitepowder flask in my pocket, were tossed into the display case afterward where I found them. And come, look at this!"

We stepped back to the door and Mav made to pry up the shield, which I had assumed was nailed upon it. Instead, the thing was only hung there, and behind it was a large and ragged hole smashed brutally through the wood!

"Why, Mav, you're brilliant! Obviously the culprit fired through the door! Now it only remains to question the guards to ascertain who passed through the *other* door during the lecture, and—"

"Slowly, Mymy. It's possible the villain lurked in here for some time before the lecture, and thus did not have to pass through the door when it was supervised. Also, some practical questions still remain: how did he aim so accurately through solid wood. Well, perhaps he paced it off beforehand. In any event, I'm satisfied that we will soon find out— Hallo, what in the eternal dampness is this?"

I shifted my attention to the display case again as Mav began to trace a fabric-covered metal filament that dropped down from the glassed-in top and ran along the grooves between the blocks of granite flooring, out through the screens at the front of the room. This we followed around into the lecture hall and beyond, into the Grand Display Hall. Along the way, we met old Leds, who accompanied us to the atrium guard station, where the wire joined dozens of others at a complicated and very modern-looking device attached to the underside of the cloakroom counter.

Disgust began to affect the texture of my companion's fur as Leds explained how the Museum's new electrical alarm-system operated.

Or sometimes didn't.

"Musta been the explosion, sir. For some reason, right

afterward, th' clammy thing began t'ring its bloody jaws off. Soon's I was able, I shut it down, but every time I try t'turn it on again, it rings." This he demonstrated with a quick throw of the knife-switch. "Loosened wires somewheres, no doubt. Now I'll have t'go over every one of these goddamp cases . . ." He waved an arm out across several acres of displays inside the Grand Hall.

"I think not, Leds. We've found your broken case and, I suspect, broken some rather fervent hopes of my own in the process. You see the difficulty, don't you, Mymy?"

"I believe that I do. If the case containing the springbow was breached to permit the murder, then why did not the alarm go off until *after* the explosion?" My mind began to reel from exhaustion, confusion, and disappointment for Mav's sake.

"And furthermore," he said, again examining the damaged springbow bolt, "if this accursed thing passed violently through the door, why did it *not* explode upon that initial impact?" He held my glass very close to his eye and thrust the ancient weapon before it.

"And why, pray tell, if it did *not* explode until it struck our poor Professor, is the bottom of the powder cavity packed with fragments of cactuswood?"

IV: A Dubious Incarceration

It is a curious fact that no one uses more than two-thirds of his brain at any given time. Following the brief hour of hann, recommended some three or four times daily for healthsake, an active lobe retires, its functions assumed by that one previously dormant, until the next hann, when the third lobe falls insensible. This phenomenon, though yet little understood by natural philosophy, was written of even in ancient times, for often soldiers, otherwise mortally wounded, commonly displayed no sign of it until some hours later, when the state of hann slipped over them, whereupon they instantly expired.

Whatever the underlying mechanism, had it been possible to employ all three lobes at once, my friend Mav would have been doing precisely that as he conveyed me home. Whether his occasional mutterings and inarticulate stirrings of pelt were at some unacknowledged grief, the destruction of his premature hypothesis, or the generation of a new one, I could not discern. With scarcely an intelligible word, he saw me to the door, where awaited an anxious maidservant. So concerned was I for Mav's sake, and so fatigued myself, I didn't particularly mind whether, on the morrow, the treacherous girl informed my mother I had arrived by prisoner's van, there being so few cabs available at the hour.

Next morning, I came as usual to North Hedgerow Precinct, having walked the few blocks from my lodgings. The early accounts at the newsagent's were full of the murder of Srafen, treated variously according to the style and bias of the publication, and illustrated both with cuts and photographs that pushed aside the usual news of Podfet's latest evil doings in the world and of the Empire's valiant, civilizing resistance. Conspicuously missing was such a picture in the *Intelligencer*; I'd surgically removed the reasons for the omittance from Niitood's carapace, article by article, the evening before. I rolled the papers back upon their rods, tucked them between two arms, and, shouldering my bag, proceeded on to work.

At the Precinct, I was surprised to see a handsome and richly appointed coach-and-three in the process of departing. It wasn't necessary that I strain to make out the arms emblazoned upon its doors, as I had witnessed this very carriage many times drawing up before my father's house, bearing his old friend the Archsacerdot of North Hedgerow.

I thought this circumstance a bit peculiar, but put it out of my mind, as there was much work to be done, and I could trust the usual informal flow of news within the Precinct to bring me up to date eventually. As I entered, then, imagine my amazement when another, equally luxurious conveyance drew up on the cobbles to the curb behind me. Its driver clambered down to assist some personage of obvious dignity; as I would be conspicuous in the entryway, I was unable to remain there watching, but in any event, I had recognized the distinguished Lord Ennramo, principal adviser to Their Majesties and a prominent member of the Lezynsiin, or Upper House, of Parliament.

Exactly what to make of all this, I had no idea, so for the moment abandoning further surmise, I climbed to the first-floor infirmary where I belonged.

North Hedgerow Precinct, like many another public building (much like the Imperial Museum, in fact), occupies a city block, in this case bounded upon the south by Rihnat Road, the northeast by Kevod Lane, which wanders into the Kiiden, and northwest by Gesnat Street, an artery of The City. It is a massively imposing edifice in the style of architecture perhaps three generations old, whose ground floor is occupied by the watu barn, the pump and ladder companies, and a small, depressing chamber where criminals are brought to book before being taken to the basement, where the gaol is kept.

Above, the first floor is partitioned into working spaces for the paracauterists and shift-quarters for the Bucketeers, as well as permanent lodgings for those unmarried individuals who think it good to reside within the territory of their duties. This custom, octaries old, dates from a time when Fodduan soldiers, returning from the Continent after nonades of war and finding themselves unemployed, threatened, in the King's view, the peace and civil order of the city. Thus the peace-keeping Bucketeers were commissioned and tranquility immediately restored—due in no small measure to the fact that it was the soldiers themselves who were hired to do the job.

Upon the second floor, Tis and his lieutenants maintain their offices. Inasmuch as North Hedgerow is not only the neighborhood Bucketeer station but also Battalion Headquarters for a third of the City, facilities are made available for administration of Sound Point Precinct, upon the upstream tip of King's Island, and for Riverside, at the northernmost extremity of the town. Although it is not officially a part of our Battalion, we also associate quite closely with King's Hall Precinct, possibly because our own Sound Point is little more than a formality as Precinct stations go, nominally protecting the Palace and Royal Grounds and, more important, providing brilliant-emerald dress uniforms and showily trapped watun for Their Majesties' frequent parades.

Walking along the drab corridors of government-pink and red, at last I found my fellows busily at work sterilizing bandages in an essence not unlike those Mav inhales in his silver pipe, and rolling them for their kits. My own supplies in this regard had dwindled severely, having been twice called upon the evening before, so I cast the scrolled-up papers aside and joined my half-dozen comrades at the worktable. A pleasant wick of kood was smoldering as I offered a modest contribution to the morning's gossip.

"The Lord Ennramo?" shrieked Poadpo, "Surely you must be mistaken, Mymy! Here, at old North Hedgie? What would a _Lord_ be wanting here?" There followed numerous unlikely guesses, a few of them unrepeatable in mixed company. Poadpo always pretended neither to understand nor to believe whatever tidbits were presented by others. I suspect this disagreeable tendency of rhers arose at puberty when rhe was disappointed at not becoming male. In any case, rher own stock of rumors were invariably of the most personally ruinous variety, and I shudder to imagine what rhe said of me whenever I was absent.

"Perhaps," offered Zoddu, "it's something to do with Chief Niifysiir, who visited our Chief this morning shortly after sunrise." Indeed it seemed unusual for the Chief of Chiefs to call, particularly at such an hour as to require our own superior to arrive early. I added that I had seen the Archsacerdot—or some deputy, I conceded—which

38

only generated more inane remarks from Poadpo, but was confirmed by Zoddu and others who lived here at the Precinct. "We're attracting all sorts of celebrities today."

"Aye," agreed Nrydmou, leaning in the doorway. "An' maybe it's our prisoner that we booked last night. Plenty hot, he was, goin' on about th' rights of th' Fourth Estate, whatever that might be." Nrydmou and Zihu, the other male paracauterist, preferred avoiding our "little surrie koodklatsches"; his sudden appearance now was nearly as unusual as the rest of the morning's events. "In any case, I bear a message from our Glorious Leader upstairs, Mymysiir, m'love. I'm to inform you he desires an interview, whenever you find it convenient."

Another precedent demolished, I thought, as with some trepidation I climbed the stony steps around the spiral slide of brass down which our gallant Bucketeers ride swiftly to their waggons when the fire trumpet calls. Before I could give much thought to what else Nrydmou had disclosed, I heard raised voices at the far end of the office-lined hallway.

"Great Blessed Anhydrosity, lam, what do you take me for? You said yourself how the soggy bastard stood and primed his deadly mechanism, whereupon your Professor simply—"

"Sir, I have also shown you this springbow bolt, which—"

"Which, in your own words, it is dampening *impossible* to've employed in the manner you originally . . . 'deedooced,' did you say?" Tis's blustering was unmistakable, as were Mav's somewhat more restrained replies.

"Yet it's sturdier evidence than that upon which you have— Hallo?"

I knocked upon the frosted glass somewhat timidly.

The door swung open, its knob in Mav's leftmost hand. "Come right in, Mymy, and guess, if you can, who has been detained in the unfortunate matter of Professor Srafen!" He stood before the old Battalion Chief, irritated certainly, but crisp and undisheveled, as if he, too, had not skipped one or two periods of hann. For my part, when I miss my rest, my lobes cannot decide which pair of them should properly be on duty, and take a day or two to get things sorted out again.

Waad Hifk *Tis* squatted behind his battered treewood desk, thinning fur erect in indignation, as was ever the case when the two of them were in the same room. I was sorry indeed to witness, let alone be expected to contribute to, this altercation. The elderly civil servant looked rumpled, but there was nothing novel in this; he was the permanently rumpled sort, likely the despair of both his wives.

The ruins of Niitood's camera lay scattered upon the desk in pieces large and small, and Tis poked at them occasionally as he spoke, as if they were some small, dead, venomous inhabitant of the damper regions east of the city. I'm sure that being summoned at an early hour to his post had done his disposition no great good. The cornerstone of Tis's character was regularity of habit. Indeed, I have heard (from an Extraordinary Inquirer who shall otherwise be nameless) that upon the stroke of second hour every morning, as he has done unfailingly for thirty years, Tis removes his service revolver from a drawer in which he keeps it at home, carries it upon his person to the Precinct, and promptly discards it in an identical drawer. He has discharged it neither for practice nor in line of duty during all those years, except upon the Queen's Birthday, when his family takes holiday in Tesret. Then he fires it three times in the air, emptying the cylinder, and reloads from a packet of cartridges purchased twenty years ago. On the first day of each month (and this I have observed myself), he disjoints and scrubs the poor machine with a ferocity that has caused it to become quite as worn as if he fired it every day.

Small wonder Bucketeers set both clock and calendar by him.

Some hardy spirit once inquired why he takes his enormous brood each year to Tesret, since he invariably complains for weeks afterward of the food, weather, prices, and accommodations. Why not Feviikdyho, or even East Gymnat for a change? He replied that he always holidays in Tesret and saw no reason now to alter the practice—which makes me wonder how he *acquired* his habits in the first place. They must have been new to him at one time or another, and hence unthinkable.

Returning my attention to lesser mysteries, I replied to Mav's rhetorical question: "I gather Rewu Uomag *Niitood* of the *Mathas Intelligencer* had been blamed."

"Too right," muttered Tis with belligerent satisfaction, "And there's an end to it!" He deferred to a corner of the room where sat an individual I hadn't noticed until now and did not recognize, a smallish, professionally anonymous lam in the drab pink civilian "uniform" of a career bureaucrat. This socially invisible creature nodded confirmation, causing Tis to relax visibly.

"Of course, there's *proving* it," Mav offered mildly.

Tis began to splutter once again. *"Technicalities,* I say! By desiccation, we'll demonstrate he had some sort of fiendish weapon secreted in this picture box of his! That is why I've called you here this morning, Mymy." He pushed and poked the shattered remains around his desk top. Some portions had survived the violence surprisingly intact. "Would you say this is all of it, or has anything been removed or left behind?"

I leant over his desk to examine what was there. "It's difficult to say, sir." (The poor old fellow grimaced, as he always does. It confuses him that well-born individuals such as Mav and myself desire the work we do and, accordingly, address him by the honorific.) "It has certainly been severely damaged, although not quite as much as I recall under the strain of last evening's events. The coincidence of Niitood's standing at the very moment does bear consideration. Nonetheless—"

"Yes?" growled Tis, echoed by Mav with kindly encouragement. The plainly dressed stranger sat silently, as before, puffing on a little brass inhaler.

Summoning courage: "Nonetheless, these fragments bear no mark of having had a greater part in the catastrophe than simply being in the way when it transpired. They're unscorched, nor do they have that odor of gunpowder, which Mav's springbow—"

"Ehrumph . . . *thank* you, Mymy, that will be all."

"Sir, if I may—"

"Yes, Mymysiir, you may *go* now. Ahum!"

"Sir, that isn't what . . . I mean, I don't particularly *like* Niitood, but should he be convicted, would they not—"

"Premeditated murder? The Blocks, of course, as he jolly well deserves!"

"I'd much prefer the ancient honored custom of *drowning,*" Mav remarked.

"Mind your language, Bucketeer, there's a lurrie present!"

"Oh. Sorry, Mymy." On the side of his carapace neither Tis nor his mysterious guest could see, Mav let his fur ripple humorously. "In any event, sir, I'm afraid you'll have to let your prisoner go. You see, by peculiar circumstance,

41

I examined this very camera not long before the murder, and I assure you—"

"You *what?*" Tis stood straight up, and even the stranger seemed suddenly to pay more attention to the conversation. Briefly, and with many a kindly emendment, the detective related how we had met Niitood in the Hose & Springbow. However, all that this anecdote accomplished, at least for the moment, was that Tis seized eagerly upon the reporter's somewhat threatening intoxicated remark's against the Professor.

Mav did protest that this, too, was insufficient evidence.

"Never mind," insisted Tis. "The fellow's clearly a dangerous radical and has condemned himself. Here's the way of it, then." He glanced once again toward the stranger for approval. "What I want— Aren't you gone *yet,* Mymy? There's surries' work below, I'm sure, and lamtalk yet to be accomplished here. Now *off* with you!"

The remainder of the negotiations between them I shall, in the manner of ancient historians, be compelled to relate from inference, as if I had stood eavesdropping outside the office door. Naturally, I did no such thing, but returned, instead, to my comrades in the infirmary.

"Look here, Mav— Oh, do sit down, Inquirer, and get your pipe out, if you wish. I've a stimulating new mixture from the Continent you might enjoy to try." Here there was a pause as the gentlelamn attended to the mechanics of their vices. "Now, as I was saying, you needn't take this situation as irretrievably wet and without hope. In your belief, we haven't enough to put this Niitood between granite slabs where he belongs. Well, here's your chance, then. *Prove* his guilt completely, beyond any question; we'll see if we can't do a bit more in future about this detectiving business of yours, eh?"

There followed some few words, which were indistinctly rendered and didn't seem to originate from Mav's or Tis's corner of the room.

"Quite right," Tis replied. "We only ask that you do it quickly."

"I was not aware there was a need for haste," Mav said with an ironic tone.

"Erruhm! Well, the sooner we are shut of this nasty business, the better. And incidentally, with the firm understanding that we are not establishing a precedent, I have decided that we'll try your other idea as well."

42

"Which idea, sir? I have many."

"So you do, Mav, ahum! I refer to this notion of pursuing your duties unencumbered by your uniform—although why you should not be perfectly proud to wear it . . . well, er, never mind that now. It is settled: you shall go about your duties in this matter in civilian attire."

"Anything you say, sir, and thank you. I do have one additional request which—"

"Oh, for Pah's sake, Mav, what is it now?"

"Well, sir, could you spare me a Bucketeer or two as assistants?"

"Absolutely not! We're overworked as it is, and I'll not take firefighters from where they're needed and waste them on—"

Here, again, there was that mumbling as before.

"Oh, I say, *indeed*, good Inquirer, take Mymy! Rhe'll be of little use until this nonsense is done with; possibly rhe'll prove so adept at it, they'll make *detectiving* a surmale occupation, too! Haw, haw—how'd you like that?"

I confess that my hearts gave a discoordinated flutter when I—er, *inferred* this development later. I was busy, quite busy at my ordinary work when Mav arrived, somewhat reluctantly, I believe, to inform me of it.

I'm not sure how I personally felt about conducting my new duties in civilian dress. I was rather fond of my uniform, having been put to somewhat greater pains to earn it than any male. It was, indeed, adapted from male clothing and appropriately spare and utilitarian—quite unlike the clumsy antiquated fettering of "proper" surmalehood. The insignia were sewn into the cap and sleeves, but it was now Mav's idea (among many, many others recorded in that notecase of his) that one of the embroidered patches might be removed and carried in a billfold so that we might, upon appropriate occasion, officially display our credentials.

"What was it, do you suppose, that changed our Chief's mind?" I asked as we descended the stairs from the first floor to ground level. I'd had time to replenish my bag, but wondered now whether, in civilian attire, I ought to carry it, since it, too, was emblazoned with Bucketeer insignia.

"Nothing ever *changes* Tis's mind, Mymy, he is the scion of countless generations of civil servants, father and grandfather of legions more who are destined to follow in his well-worn footsteps: as Srafen was often wont to express it, the stolid, unprogressive backbone of our Empire—and an increasingly crippling drain upon its resources."

At the ground floor we made our way back to the shabby office where Mav obtained permission to visit with the prisoner. We were also given a carbide lamp and admonished to mind the stairs. I ventured reserved agreement with Mav and his Professor when we were once again alone, for it seemed to me that every year there were more and more of us who wore the livery of Parliament, and fewer businesslamn and workers to support us.

"However, you have not answered my question: why, at this particular moment, does Tis decide that—" I began.

"It should be obvious, Mymy. There are some few who would prefer the Bucketeers not put up too publicly enthusiastic an inquiry into the death—which many regard as well-deserved and possibly a social benefit—of one they looked upon as a dangerous heretic." He warned me further of a tricky twist upon the ancient stone-cut stairway.

"Surely you don't mean to name the Archsacerdot? I had been under the impression that—"

He held up a hand. "Of course not, nor the Lord Ennramo, who was here this morning. Theirs is simply a concern for whatever interests in the matter Crown and Church may have, principally that justice be pursued despite a considerable political pressure to the contrary—have a care here, I'm afraid the steps are actually *damp*—we have *them* to thank that any action is being taken at all."

Finally, we reached the floor at the foot of the stairs, only to discover that it exuded the unmistakable odor, in concentrated essence, of the watu stalls above. Mav struck a bronze bell attached to the wall, removed and hung his pistol upon a peg beside it.

"Then who is left," I asked, "powerful enough to exert such an influence?" I shifted uneasily from foot to foot, distressed in the presence of so much chilly moisture.

An unhappy-looking Bucketeer, no doubt assigned this post as punishment, arrived to challenge us from behind a heavy grillework of rusted interwoven iron strapping. Mollified by Mav's assurances that we were here officially, he threw a switch. Electric candles blazed into the gloom, and Mav extinguished his lamp. The officer turned a key, admitting us among squeaks and groans from the corroded door. The illumination was a questionable blessing, for the nitre and dampness of the floor and walls were rendered by it even more disgustingly perceptible.

"I refer, of course," Mav whispered as the gaoler shuffled off to find our prisoner, "to the gentlelam you saw in Tis's office. You know, if I were Battalion Chief, these dungeons would be closed forever—they do our Service no credit."

"That undistinguished little fellow? I took him for a busybody from the Exchequer—he had the look of an accounting clerk."

"Which, in a manner of speaking, he is—of voting in the Nazemynsiin, the Middle House of Parliament. He represents our masters, Mymy, the Ministry of Public Safety. And, one would infer from his presence this morning, those worthies now find themselves caught between two stones."

"Scarcely a pleasant figure of speech, considering the—especially Niitood's—circumstances." I looked around distastefully at the moldering drippy walls, imagining, despite myself, small slithery things crawling about in the pools of shadow.

"Nonetheless, it is appropriate. Surely you recall last night's demonstration outside the Museum?" He led me to a crude and crumbling table apparently used by Bucketeers at mealtimes—although how the lamn could bring themselves to eat down here . . . Judging by the facilities afforded those on duty, I shuddered to think of the conditions endured by their unfortunate charges.

"I hardly thought that rabble represented *anything* significant."

"They are the veriest tip of the cactus sprout, or so Professor Srafen feared. You see, while this octary's progress has brought inestimable benefits to all, most particularly the masses—public sanitation, mass production of launderable clothing, cheap, abundant foodstuffs, and the like—while it promises yet to bring forth many more, there has been slowly gathering among the lower classes an irrational reaction as the memory of what came before begins to fade. The brutish existence led by common people generations ago has begun to acquire a perversely romantic appeal, while the genuine improvements in their lot today are dismissed as trifling and commonplace. Those miseries that still persist, though far less severe than those of nonades before, are nonetheless more vivid to the lower classes than those that no living individual remembers."

45

"I'd no idea that Srafen's interests extended beyond natural philosophy, Mav. Further, I myself confess to a view that the wholesome country life the people led before all this dirty, citified, industrialization—"

Here, Mav arranged his fur in scornful negativity. "Srafen's interests *were* in natural philosophy, and rhe believed there was a natural philosophy of lamviin behavior and political economy waiting somewhere to be discovered. In a sense, this concern of rhers was essentially defensive, being, as rhe was, the center of so much popular controversy.

"Moreover, there has arisen lately a newer fear that machinery, which has already doubled life expectancies and tripled Foddu's population—so much for the wholesome country life—will somehow deprive the common laborer of his work. Never mind that ten times as many are profitably employed today than was the case in our great-grandfathers' time, when most individuals struggled for mean subsistence upon some baron's lands. And worse, the makers of machinery continue stupidly to emphasize that it will do the work of many, rather than how many it will make new work for. It is the former, not the latter, that the workers hear, believe, and act upon!"

"And what has all this to do with Niitood's incarceration?"

He drew out his pipe and inhaling fluid, employing the ritual to gather his thoughts. "Consider the position of the Middle House. Until recently, they embraced all modern innovation for a variety of reasons that seemed good to them: it distinguished them from the Upper House, appointed by Their Majesties and thus inclined to a certain conservatism; the tendency of all new discoveries and inventions is to increasingly secularize society and weaken the hold of the Church; and, perhaps most importantly, industrialization is a source of power. There are some radicals, and I'm inclined to think they have Nazemynsiin connections, who speak openly in the streets of seizing factories and turning them over to 'the people'—which can only mean, of course, the politicians."

"How horrible!" I replied. "And why are these radicals not down here in gaol?"

"For the same reason the Church is hurrying to understand and accept the fruits of modern natural philosophy—prudence—it is prudent not to make martyrs of a small but potentially deadly enemy. Besides, the Lower House, the Mykodsedyetiin, whose chief concern is civil liberties, protects them, as I trust it would protect *my* right to speak, and yours as well.

"However, Srafen's death has put the Nazemynsiin in a quandary—or rather punctuated a conflict that already existed. Its members are elected on a district basis by the masses, and the masses, as I have explained, apparently do not share their delight with all that is modern. Thus you and I, dear Mymy, represent an unsatisfactory but necessary compromise between the proper investigation favored by some and whatever substitute would quiet the crowds. Out of uniform, we'll be less conspicuous, and I fear we shall have to depend on whatever other resources we can muster for ourselves. I suspect even our time will be severely limited. We must— Hallo, here's Niitood, at last."

The journalist, appearing battered far beyond whatever the explosion had done to him, limped from a filth-encrusted corridor. The guard was gentle and solicitous with him, which made me proud to be a Bucketeer.

"Mav, old fellow, and Mymy . . . What in the name of everything wet and slimy are you doing here?" He took a chair and rested weary arms upon the rough table. His bandages were soiled and ragged, his trousers unspeakable. I opened my bag and made to change his dressings.

"I have good news, Niitood, for I have persuaded my superiors that you must be released under bond. Five hundred silver crowns, I'm afraid—I didn't name the figure. Is there a chance that you can make it?"

The reporter was thoughtful. "More than eight golden triarchs! You know that I cannot. Yet, however flinty-souled they are, *my* superiors may feel the story of a journalist, falsely imprisoned in a sensational murder, might be worth that amount in improved circulation. Can you get me to a telephone?"

I cut his bandages as he spoke, examining the wounds beneath, which, as I had thought last night, were minor and rapidly healing, despite the cold and damp of the gaol. Giving assurances that the prisoner would be adequately supervised, Mav dispatched the guard to find a messenger, as the only telephone within the station was another unwelcome intrusion in Tis's office. Then he spelt out the complexity of our situation for Niitood, as he had done so patiently for me.

"Ha! I suppose," snorted the reporter, "that you expect me to be grateful. Why, you're nearly as naïve as Mymy, here, and with less excuse! Things are *far* more twisted than you believe, and far more ugly! Of *course* Ennramo wants 'justice' done—to the embarrassment of his rivals in the House below! The Uppers, too, have problems: they love the booty that their factories bring, yet their servants and retainers are flocking to the cities—better to work like an animal for yourself than polish the gloves of some toff for room and board! Mark me, Bucketeer, the staunchest foes of industry someday will be the propertied class themselves!"

"Such cynicism is scarcely worthy, even of you, Niitood."

"Is that so? Then take the Middle House, torn between the egalitarian sermons of Ascensionism—for how can class difference be justified if we are all ascended from the same cactus-hoppers—and the popular appeal of *anti*-Ascensionism! Pah forbid the 'House of the People' oppose their own beloved rabble!"

So much, in far more genteel words, my friend had said already, which I pointed out to Niitood. Thanking me for my support, the detective added that, in fact, the industrialists of Foddu were not the upper classes but a new breed of self-made individuals who found political comfort, not with the Lezynsiin or Nazemynsiin, but with the Mykodse-dyetiin.

"Ha again! Even your much-vaunted Lower House is hoping this case'll be bungled—that they might wrest control of the judiciary from the Uppers, and the Bucketeers from the Middle, as they have so long wished to do. But do you want to know the *real* culprits in this matter? None other than the Royal—"

"For shame!" I cried. "Have you no decency or loyalty?"

"Loyalty to what? To a brood that reigns because its ancestors bashed in more carapaces than others? To the liars and thieves they appoint and approve to govern us?"

"Why, Niitood," I asked dizzily, "are you an Unarchist, then?"

"Beautiful, *all* good journalists are Unarchists, deep inside."

Mav chuckled, unaffected by the reporter's seditious rantings. "And nihilists in practice. That's as may be, Niitood, but we'll need your assistance if we're to free you and track down the real murderer. Are you willing?"

"Rain upon them all! I'll help find your goddamp Professor's killer—though I must warn you, Mav old sandshrimp, that my sympathies are with the anti-Ascensionists. It's just that I find little to admire in those who'd countenance an innocent party being falsely imprisoned and squashed."

"Oh, you'd have been most *genuinely* squashed, my friend, believe me. There is one small thing you can do." Mav held up a portion of the broken camera, which he must have taken from Tis's desk. Someone once said that a good Bucketeer must be as larcenous as those he would capture, and, in this, my companion was certainly well-qualified. "I believe this contains the photographic emulsion. Is it likely that the image is still intact?"

The journalist seized the object and examined it as closely as the light here would permit. "You know, I had this custom-made—a model maker I met through the Inventors' Club—very, very expensive. I wouldn't say for sure until the plate's developed, but it's possible. Imagine—taken just at the moment the old crackshell let go! My editors will—"

There was a groan and clatter at the iron door.

"Your editors will stand your bail—reluctantly," said Mav, reading from the note our guardslam had just handed him. Apparently the enterprising gaoler had simply stepped across the street and used the new telephone in the Bucket & Truncheon, for there was about him that mildly unsteady aspect that I associate with electrical current liberally administered.

V: Out the Door and
Innuendo

How I could ever have perceived the police court on the ground floor as shabby or unpleasant, I shall never understand. After the dungeon, it was practically as warm and familiar as my own tidy apartments. Alas, however, I wasn't destined to witness Niitood's scientific miracle of photography at first hand, for, as he made arrangements for his bond, Mav produced that accursed notecase of his.

"Mymy, I have failed to learn much from consideration of the *means* of Srafen's murder. Although I do not mean entirely to abandon that line of inquiry, I think it behooves us now to take up the *second* of three legs upon which any such investigation must stand."

"And what might that be, consultation with a medium? I doubt that even Srafen knew——"

"Flippancy ill becomes a lurry of your class, my dear . . . although in one or two circumstances, such a notion might be of some use. . . . Hmm." Then he scribbled off a rapid series of notes, temporarily lost to the world of reality. After a while, his eyes brightened and his fur stood crisply once again: "Now, what was it you were saying, Mymy?"

I glanced around the guardroom for someone who might share my exasperation—vainly, for all were busy helping Niitood fill out the blanks on numerous forms. "*You* were telling *me* about the next line of inquiry we shall——"

"Ah! Forgive me, Mymy, but you gave me an idea for future use—spiritualism might be just the thing for rooting out the superstitious criminal. But I have digressed once again. What I meant is that we might profitably begin with Srafen's personal and professional associations in hopes of finding someone with reason to wreak violence upon rher."

"I see—merely half the ignorant population of the city, it would appear." I shifted my bag uneasily, liking less and less this business of civilian dress. Perhaps I simply didn't

want to return home to change clothing, knowing that my
mother would be there, full of awkward questions.

"Hardly. More and more it appears to me that Srafen's
death was at the hands of some singularly clever and determined being. Perhaps the anti-Ascensionists possess the
means of such a diabolically complicated act as was required, but . . ." Again he spent some moments lost in
thought, then brightened:

"But look here, Mymy, I was not entirely idle after my
humiliation of last night." He led me to a chalkboard,
which, as might be expected in this place, was unwashed.
With a swipe, Mav smeared the chalk around, then proceeded to outline his plans:

WHO KILLED SRAFEN?

SRAFEN'S PRESENT:

POLITICS
    enemies & allies

BUSINESS
    rivals & partners
    employees & employers

ACADEMIA
    superiors & subordinates
    students & colleagues

FAMILY
    Parents
    Spouses & children
    other relations

SOCIETY
    friends & acquaintances
    enemies

SRAFEN'S PAST:

SCHOOL
    fellow pupils
    teachers

THE NAVY
    superiors & subordinates
    fellow officers

MISCELLANEOUS:
    random violence or insanity
    someone intending another victim—or another crime
    accident or act of Pah
    someone, past or present, unintentionally offended
    suicide

Some indication of despair must have betrayed me, although I put up as brave and enthusiastic a front as I was

51

capable of, for he hastened to add, "Not every one of these, of course, are real possibilities, and by no means is there need to look into every one of them."

"For example," I suggested, "'Accidents or acts of Pah'—if no deliberate lamviin agency was involved in that explosion, I shall take my own suggestion about spiritualism and give up paracautery."

"Quite so, and we shall strike it out. Equally, we may eliminate all business connections. Srafen had an income, but its technicalities were administered each month by rher solicitors—"

"Who ought, on that account, to be added to the list. In fact, I'd advocate a separate category for solicitors, barristers, every other creature of that ilk, simply on general principles!"

Mav got out his pipe and dripped inhaling fluid into it. "You're beginning to sound like Niitood. Let us strike out parents, as Srafen was very old and all three of rher parents undoubtedly dead. Likewise, although rhe felt that all young persons interested in natural philosophy were rher progeny, I know that rhe had no children. Rhe also had few political interests that rhe *acted* upon, but I shall leave that category for the anti-Ascensionists—theirs seems a sort of political effort, wouldn't you agree?"

"Why have you a category for political *allies*, then?"

He took several puffs on his pipe before answering, in the quietest of tones: "Because, my dear paracauterist, one's friends can be as dangerous as one's enemies. There are always those who feel a martyr will do some good for the Cause—whatever it might be."

"*Now* who is it sounds like Niitood?"

He crinkled his fur. "You're absolutely right, of course. Cynicism is contagious, it would appear."

Between us we eliminated academic superiors, subordinates, and students, for, since taking charge of the Museum, Srafen had none of these in any formal sense. However, we appended Museum employees and, at my continued insistence, family solicitors. Likewise we struck out teachers on the same logic as parents, and Naval superiors, who were likely to be dead by now. Mav had doubts about most of the Miscellaneous column, particularly suicide. "Which leaves us once again with politics, of a peculiar sort: academic colleagues—many, and on both sides of Ascensionism."

"How so?" I asked. "Do professors desire martyrs to their Cause, as well?"

"I can think of some who wish they'd thought of Ascensionism themselves and might not resist becoming the foremost *living* authority on the subject."

"I see. Well, to continue, we have Srafen's social ties to examine—"

"Precisely, and there, I believe, you can be of enormous assistance. I suggest you go home, change, and spend the rest of the day chatting with your friends."

"*What?*"

"Just so, for Srafen's death is bound to be the topic of much conversation, and if you are clever—and not too obvious—I'm sure that you can find out much about rher social life that I cannot, and a little about rher family, who, I suspect, travel in the same circles as your own."

That much was possible. In the meantime, Mav would take up the remainder of the list; we would arrange some place to meet in the evening. I bade farewell to him and to Niitood, who was still completing paperwork and expressed the heartfelt wish that we had left him in his cell belowstairs.

The sky was a beautiful golden yellow—indeed, the day had reached the very pinnacle of loveliness as I walked back to my flat in Gamlo Road upon the lower edge of North Hedgerow. To my surprise and delight, it was not my mother but another of my parents who greeted me with a positively wonderful-smelling clutch of cactus pears simmering in oil, which, over the objections of my hired girl, rhe had personally prepared for our luncheon.

"How very splendid, Sasa. As you well know, they're my very favorite! But tell me, why is Mama not here, and what is it brings you in her place?"

My surfather crinkled rher fur fondly at me as rhe lit the kood and placed the cover on its holder. "Your dear mother, I'm afraid, has taken ill again—no, there is nothing you should worry about; indeed, if she had not reacted so dramatically to the news we had this morning, I should have been far more alarmed." Rhe swept a finger along the tabletop, examining some crumbs of something-or-other that had found refuge among the weavings of its cover. "That girl of yours is an indolent watun; I shall have to speak to your father about her."

53

"Speak to Mother, then—these pears are delicious, did you use my oil or bring your own?—she's Mother's eyes and ears in my affairs, and perhaps inclined on that account to regard any housekeeping she does as an additional imposition. But don't keep me in suspense. What is ailing Mother?"

"In general, your choice of vocation—as always. Bad enough a child of hers should seek some productive activity rather than marry the son and daughter of some useless, idle families, but the Bucketeers? And now, according to a crudely lettered message we received unsigned, you're abandoning paracautery to involve yourself with criminals. I confess that even I felt a trifle disappointed in that, if it is true, but before we speak further on the matter, be reassured in one respect at least: it is your life you are leading, my very dear; you must allow no one, not your mother or your father, no, nor even myself, to determine how it is to be led."

There are several dozen parents I know of, including two of mine, from whom this speech would have had precisely the opposite meaning than its words conveyed. Not so from *Mymysiir* Viimede (*née* Kedsat) Woom, one of the Empire's greatest surgeons—its first and only surmale one— and, I am extremely proud and happy to say, my own surfather.

"I can't imagine who might have sent such a message, Sasa. An anonymous tattler, really! But I have not abandoned paracautery or my ambitions to follow in your profession. On the contrary, they are precisely what has gotten me into the investigation of Professor Srafen's murder, of which I am certain you have heard or read by now. Permit me to explain. . . ." Thus for the next two hours, rhe and I discussed the events of the last twenty-seven. I found myself (as I have always done) telling rher everything, including the reasons I was home now and about to change out of the uniform I love.

"I see," rhe said at length, "and I approve entirely. This fellow Mav seems quite the most dashing you have ever—"

"Oh, Sasa, that has nothing at all to do with it!" With no small effort, I regained control of the texture of my fur. "Well, very little, anyway."

Rhe crinkled rher fur again. "As you say. Whatever the case, I do believe that I may save you some steps today. But wait— Oh, Zoobon, there's a good girl, do be a mefiik and pop over to the Cactus Rose." Rhe handed her a few coins. "We'll want the afternoon papers and a twist of that new Femean kood Mymy likes so much."

No sooner had the door shut behind the maidservant than my surfather rippled rher fur conspiratorially. "Now if I read your girl correctly, the extra change I gave her should afford us privacy for another hour. I was about to say that much of what young Mav has asked for in the way of information about Srafen's family I believe I can provide. He's quite right, of course; his Professor's death has stimulated every sort of tale imaginable. Also, I'd be pleased to have you carry *my* bag this evening when you go to meet him, so that people will take you for a civilian physician."

"What will you do for a bag, then, Sasa?"

"Why, I'll simply trade the contents of mine into yours—I have another at my offices—and send yours back by messenger tomorrow."

"Oh, Sasa, you are too kind, really, and you think of everything!"

"Not at all, my dear. I simply find all of this intrigue quite fascinating, and I'm very pleased to be of some help. Now let me tell you what I know—within the bounds of medical ethics, naturally—and you may compare it later with what you learn from others."

I do not believe I've ever had quite as much kood in one day as I was compelled to take that afternoon. At the time, I thought I'd be quite happy if I never smelt another burning wick again. My surfather bade farewell only after a lengthy conversation ending with rher assurances that my mother would eventually recover from the shock of having offspring who wished to live rher own life. Afterward I paid a number of not terribly exciting calls upon what seemed an endless parade of uncles, aunts, and eits, cousins of every variety, nieces, nephews, and nerries, all of whom my mother would have heartily approved in their useless idleness. These were distributed broadly from the palatially wealthy Upper (Most) Hedgerow—the parenthetical being added only as a gibe by those not living there—to the genteelly improverished neighborhoods of Brassie, populated mostly by Navy pensioners and pantsleeve relatives of the rich.

I also thought it wise to visit the Royal Mail office in

Empire Point, where I was informed it would require some three months to have a telephone installed in my apartments—until I gave my family name, whereupon this estimate, like Pah's alleged creation of Iamviin, was instantly and miraculously reduced to "tomorrow afternoon."

While at the counter, I amused myself watching the telephonic operators shouting numbers out and dancing back and forth before the huge display of switches and connections. There might have been a thousand filaments woven in some arcane pattern across the great board at any given time, and I recall thinking that, were it not for proper Fodduan ethics, this might be an excellent place to overhear the sort of conversation that might be of use to a detective. The operators had to listen, at least part of the time, so that they might introduce speakers to one another, disconnect the wires at conversation's end, and plug them in again where they were next wanted. I made a mental note to speak of this to Mav.

That thought, in turn, led me to another, so that, before I paid the clerk his usurious deposit, I insisted upon a demonstration with the instrument reserved for convincing balky potential subscribers. It took me quite two-thirds of an hour to locate Mav, by which time the several operators were hopelessly entangled in a weaving of arms and legs and electrical connections, the sales clerk's impatience held in check only by frequent mention of my father's patronymic.

"Ahoy, Mav! Is it really you?"

"Ahoy, yourself, good paracauterist. There isn't really any need to shout. I can hear you as plainly as if you were in the next room."

It was awkward manipulating the instrument so that its receiver was next to the ear on my shoulder and the speaking tube properly before a nostril. My bag kept slipping off onto the floor, which made the clerk suppress a snigger. Additionally, I found I was embarrassed even *speaking* to the place of Mav's whereabouts, for it seemed that he was at Vyssu's . . . establishment, and who *knows* what went on there at this hour of the afternoon?

"Now that you have found me, Mymy, what was it you wished to tell me?"

"Well, I . . . that is, I have some information, which I can't imagine passing along in this manner, since I am standing in the post office with at least a dozen persons listening. Where was it you wished to meet me later?" I twined my arms in a childish wishing gesture, but his next words disappointed me:

"Why, here at Vyssu's, if you do not find it inconvenient. I've been discussing matters with her, and I believe you'll find she has some fascinating notions to share with us."

"With *us*?" Merciful Pah, a male like Mav, a surmale like myself, and that *person*, Vyssu, alone together in the Kiiden? This career of mine was beginning to demand too much. However, we are strongly constituted in my family, so I continued, "Very well, I believe I'll take a cab, as it is getting dark, and—"

"And the Kiiden isn't any place to be alone on hand? I quite agree, my dear, but . . . what's that? A capital idea! Mymy, Vyssu will send her carriage. Did you say you were at the post office? What on Sodde Lydfe are you doing there?"

"Speaking to you by telephone. The Royal Mail office in Empire Point. Shall we say good-bye, then?"

"Say good-bye. We'll see you in a third of an hour, not more."

I handed the instrument back to the clerk, paid the deposit, and went out to stand at the curbing. Shortly a stylish rig drew up and an imposing, darkly furred fellow with a scar cut deeply in his carapace and a patch over one eye asked if I were not Missur Mymysiir, to which I replied (not without some thought of denying it) in the affirmative. He assisted me aboard the machine, and it was, if you'll believe it, only then that I noticed there were no watun fastened to the front!

"Wull jiss bee a meenut, Missur," he said in a sinister and unknown accent; I began to think about the many warnings my mother had taken pains to convey before I knew what sex I'd be. "Gotta drann th' rotor houseeng." He reached beneath the chassis of the contraption, manipulated something, and stepped back abruptly. There was a *hissss*, and as I watched, confused and frightened, a considerable volume of abominable aqueous fluid fell, splattering obscenely in the street. When he was satisfied with whatever measure this accomplished, the mysterious and ugly creature reached beneath the machine once again, made another adjustment, then hopped lightly onto the driver's bench, and we were off!

The pace was something unbelievable, perhaps as much as twelve or fifteen fymon per hour, and I was surprised that I was not crushed by the velocity. Then I realized that we were doing nothing, actually, compared to the magnificent Tesret Hurrier by which my surfather used to take me on holidays to North Wyohfats. I relaxed and looked about me in the carriage (which was much preferable to watching streets and citizens and frightened watun stream past in an incoherent blur).

As one might expect, the vehicle was well done up in perfumed satins, silks, and velvets of the most expensive and . . . well . . . lascivious cut. Upon the glass were painted and engraved no small number of elegant flowers and birds. Pulling a tassel that bobbed up and down suggestively, I unfolded a cunningly contrived table in which nestled a kood holder and, beside it, both a gold-framed lacquered treewood juicing box and matching receptacle for several inhaling tubes. There were many such tassels flouncing up and down upon the other two walls within the carriage, but my imagination shuddered to think of what they might conceal, so I refrained from pulling on them, and devoted the remaining minutes of the ride to vainly attempting to fold the little kood table back into place.

Vyssu kept herself (in a manner of speaking) in Fadet Road near the corner of Fadyedsu Street, as sinister and gaudy a neighborhood as the city offers this side of the river. Nonetheless, the little lave was nearly as quiet and undisturbed as that in which my parents made their home—if one could disregard the uncouth music blaring up over the housetops from the theatrical district.

I alighted from the amazing watuless carriage, and Vyssu's driver led me to the door, took my cloak and hat, and tried to carry off my bag, which I would not permit. Afterward I was conducted into a sitting room where Mav was puffing on his pipe, the very picture of domestic tranquility, and a female, rather more handsome than pretty, and younger than I had imagined, was, of all things, sitting opposite him doing needlepoint.

"Good evening, Mymy," said Mav, rising as I entered through the archway. "I don't believe you've met Vyssu before, except by reputation."

That person turned upon her settee, crinkled her fur in an unreservedly friendly expression that left me no alternative but to reply, "Good evening, Mav. I'm pleased to meet you, Miss, er . . ."

"Vyssu will do nicely, if I'm permitted to call you Mymysiir. Will you have some kood? We've just finished a wick, but I can call for—"

"Please, I have had kood and more kood all afternoon. Nothing will suit me quite nicely, at least for a while. Mav, I've so much to tell you, I scarcely know where to begin."

"Then begin by sitting down, dear Mymy, for I have much to tell you, also, after which we'll hear from Vyssu on the same subject. Here, you can put your bag beside the door."

Vyssu patted the settee beside her so that, in courtesy, I could not refuse to join her.

"Thank you. Vyssu, I must thank you, also, for inviting me and for sending your driver round. I have never ridden in a watuless vehicle before; it's rather exciting, isn't it? And *speedy*."

"You must forgive Fatpa, my dear. He used to be a highwaylam of sorts in Old Niimebye before the Podfetiin moved in. Sometimes he lets a little of it seep into his driving."

"A highwaylam? How, er, fascinating. In any event, Mav, I've learned from several sources that, were motive alone sufficient for conviction, we'd now have solved the mystery. I know of two, at least, who might wish Srafen ill health."

He nodded. "Rher wife and husband? Oh, I'm sorry to have spoiled your surprise, for it appears your news has been purchased through a lot of effort. Do not forget I knew Srafen well—but tell us what you have learned in any event."

I hope that I did not betray my disappointment. As bravely as I could, I began: "I hesitate to pass on news as personal as this. It is only because the principal is deceased, and rher mates such transparent villains, that I do so now. That, and the fact that everyone from Brassie to Riverside seems to know anyway.

"Srafen has been twice widowed, mates of rher own age and a marriage of long standing. In recent years rhe unaccountably wed two of rher students, upper class, and considerably younger than rhe. The first—"

"Tobymme Toodhagomm *Law*, a foppish spendthrift and

scientifical dabbler," supplied Mav, Vyssu twitching a hair or two in recognition of the name. "Indeed, he might well make a good suspect, given the understanding he no doubt possesses of things mechanical. And his possible motive?"

"Another chance, perhaps, to marry well—or at least the liberty to carry on the many indiscreet relationships with which gossip credits him."

"And his considerable gambling debts," offered Vyssu. "I shouldn't speak of a client in so freely a manner, either, except that he is no longer welcome here."

"Indeed?" inquired Mav, the motions of his fur exactly imitiating those of Vyssu's upon first hearing Law's name mentioned. "For any other reasons besides the reckoning he owed?"

"None," acknowledged Vyssu. "The romantic side of his life he seemed quite capable of providing for himself. He was unskilled as a gambler, the reckless type, inclined to play even when the odds were obviously too steep to justify it. And likely to accuse the winner of cheating."

"I see," said Mav. "And what of Srafen's other mate, Mymy?"

"Liimevi *Myssmo* (*née* Kysz) Law. Given to séances, palmistry, lunology—and lunologists. One in particular, and his surmale assistant. It's really quite the talk of Hedgerow, all that holding hands around a table and so forth. But you know, there isn't any séance planned for Srafen: perhaps Myssmo is afraid of what the Professor's spirit might reveal."

"Indeed. Know anything about Miss Myssmo, Vyssu, my dear?"

"Nothing more than common gossip. This lunologist, Mymy, he wouldn't, by any chance, be a Doctor Ensda, would he? He has come up in the world—I have it that he used to operate a carnival around Kodpiimeth until the local Bucketeers asked him politely if he wouldn't prefer to leave."

"Good heavens! You two, just sitting here, have discovered quite as much as I have, running my hands off all over town. I feel quite futile and redundant, and I believe I'd like that kood now, if it isn't too much trouble."

"Not at all," answered Vyssu with a surprising kindness. "Nor should you feel your effort has been wasted."

"Indeed not," echoed Mav, "for you have confirmed much that I have heard—and from an elevated viewpoint I have neglected to cultivate for some years. Great desiccation, if this information is spread roundabout, as you say, Law and Myssmo would be idiots to do old Srafen in. Then again, people are often idiots."

"Moreover," I suggested, "it seems to me their separate romantic interests militate against their guilt. I mean, if they were still enamored of one another and seeking a new surmale for their trine, that would be different."

"Unless they conspired from the beginning to do in Srafen for rher money," suggested Vyssu, accepting the kood from the servant. "Thank you, Fatpa, that will be all for now."

"If that's the case"—Mav chuckled and crinkled his fur—"they will be sorely disappointed, for Srafen left rher fortune—that amount rhe had not depleted in scientific ventures—to the Museum for the furtherance of Ascensionism."

"Oh, dear. All that trouble for nothing. I do hope Law and Myssmo weren't the culprits, Mav. It would be so sad, in a horrible sort of way."

"You're a larcenous one, Vyssu. I'm glad that you're the one with money around here."

They both rippled their fur and laughed with a politely restrained fondness that made me both heartssick and furious at the same time. Oh, I could see why this Vyssu might attract a fellow like Mav. She was pretty in a sort of older, sophisticated way that even I found interesting at moments. But it was only a veneer, disguising her lower-class origins. Despite her luxurious surroundings, which even my parents might have found tasteful, we were at this moment (a fact I could scarcely forget) deep in the notorious Kiiden, and it was not safe for a respectable person to so much as step into the street without a capable and intimidating escort.

I did find voice to tell Mav of the mysterious unsigned message that my parents had received this morning. I could well imagine Tis informing them of this temporary change in my occupation, for he had at times a fatherly attitude toward me. But he certainly would never do so anonymously, and, reluctant as I was to believe the communication was germane to the case we were investigating, I was even more loath to neglect telling Mav, in case it meant something.

"Oho! How very interesting! You will not believe this,

Mymy dear, but yours was not the first call on the telephone I received today. No, for I was at my house acquiring the civilian trappings you see before you, when someone rang—a coarse, artificially assumed voice it was—to suggest that this was not the field of endeavor I wished to spend the rest of my life pursuing."

"That's odd," I said, "do you really think it will take us that long to—"

"The implication, Mymy, was that the rest of my life would not be very long. Let me ask you—in all fairness, given that we are being watched, and now threatened—whether you think it wise to continue with the case."

"Do you intend to do so?" I looked at Vyssu and looked away. "Then so shall I, Inquirer, unto the very end—whatever that may be. And now, pray tell me, what is the next unnecessary thing that I can do for you?"

The next thing, as it happened, was to accompany Mav back to the Museum. "You see, Mymy, this examining-of-evidence business has turned out to be far more complicated than I had imagined. A broken wire, a piece of thread, a tiny blob of wax—anything may have significance, and yet none. How does one catalog every separate item in a room, up to and including age stains upon the woodwork and shadows on the wall?"

I was disinclined, after spending the evening as I had so far, to commiserate much with him, but the evidence gathered thus far was a fascinating and frustrating logical puzzle. "Quite so—I suppose even a splinter out of place might be significant, mightn't it? After all—"

"By Pah's sandy plains, I believe you have something there! We must hurry. I am sorry now I insisted upon walking—you were right, we should have taken a cab. There's work to be done at the Museum!"

I looked around me, having forgotten for a while to be afraid of my surroundings, and now, reminded of them once again, felt my fur falling flat with nervous anxiety. "You're the one who said it would be 'broadening' for me to walk with you through the Kiiden. Well, you're—"

"*Stand where you are!*" hissed a voice from an alleyway. "*Compose yourselves, for you're about to meet your Maker!*"

VI: Lam of the Eastern Plains

With vision-blurring alacrity, Mav leapt between me and the vicious brace of eye-blades that slithered around the corner. We retreated, step by step, as a daunting figure emerged from the alleyway, a darkly pelted lam of giant stature in the rough attire of a seafarer, his furry covering shirred in many places with a multitude of ancient and badly healed scars. Fully a hand-width taller than my companion and of incomparably greater bulk, his glittering sword points made tiny, menacing circles in the air before us.

"Remsi vy' by onsen, nrdeikaz!" He gestured with his empty middle hand. *"By reban yat ot me avima!"* We'd backed ourselves nearly to the curb, Mav reaching beneath his cloak, when a Fodduan voice behind the sailor warned:

"My friend says stand where you are—there is nothing you can do to save yourselves!" I let my kitbag slide a little from my shoulder, ready to swing it with all the energy at my command, for I was determined, despite the trembling in my legs, that neither of our accosters should buy our lives as cheaply as they apparently expected.

Mav drew his pistol, and the sealam *lunged!* One sword thrust through the eye—the only certain way to reach the brain—would leave its victim lying dead upon the paving stones.

BANG! The sailor lurched, one of his weapons ringing where he dropped it, yet Mav's bullet whined without further damage off the fellow's carapace, gouging a brick wall across the alley. Dust and splinters showered down upon the second footpad, distracting him as he, too, made to reach beneath his cape. Mav held the sailor at bay a frozen fraction of the same instant, reciprocator muzzle to sword point.

Marveling that I could even stir a limb, I crouched to scoop up the fallen sword as the Fodduan whisked out a smaller pistol of his own. Scarcely thinking, I slashed downward; his rightmost hand, the weapon locked between its fingers, leapt off his arm, thudding to the ground. He *screamed*—there was the briefest gout of blood before his reflexes fully took over—then, without turning, he ran and vanished down the street.

Mav's reciprocator never waivered. The bullet-stunned foreigner, deserted by his wounded comrade, cast an eye about desperately. *"Katbami to hamodypen, vezis-ldesa! Fy tid ledyn wad fatat . . . Vyom hyden—!"* He threw his sword point-first at Mav, who batted it away with relative aplomb. Yet before either of us could recover, the sailor ducked into the shadows and, like his companion, was gone.

"Damp!" Mav reholstered his pistol, retrieving the other fellow's gun where the slowly dying hand had released it. "Ah, well, I suppose it would have done us little good to shoot him, though there are a number of questions I should like to have—" He stepped back to fix me with a quizzical expression. "That lizard-sticker's definitely *you,* dear Mymy. With ragged breeks and, perhaps, an eyepatch, you'd make *quite* the pirate!"

I stared at the deadly thing in my hand, suddenly aware what I had done. The discarapaced hand squirming ever more slowly on the flagging at our feet seemed to point an accusing finger at me.

I dropped the sword in revulsion. "Please be kind enough not to joke! For the love of Pah, Mav, I have just commited mayhem upon a fellow lamviin!" In the deepest recesses of my being, I felt ill and actually made to sit down upon the dirty paving.

"Get up from there, Bucketeer! Do you hear me? That fellow was preparing to *shoot* one of us, and his accomplice seemed more than willing to put my lights out forever!" He turned the little pistol over in his hand, examining it.

"But I'm a paracauterist," I mumbled, a queer paralysis beginning to settle over my limbs, "sworn to *saving* lives, not taking them!"

"Which is precisely what you have done. Get up, I say! The miscreant will grow a brand-new complement of digits before the year is out, and we are still breathing—an altogether ethical and satisfactory transaction, in my opinion." He picked up the sword I'd let drop, turned, then plucked out, from where it still quivered in a telegraph pole, that which the sailor had thrown at him. "Great Desiccation, they're Podfettian Navy issue!"

This prompted further scrutiny of the pistol—a double-barreled contrivance designed chiefly for concealability—which, according to Mav, was of expensive private manufacture, the handiwork of Rammeth & Rammeth, a local firm that even I had heard of. He began searching round for other evidence, complaining bitterly at the lack of a lantern.

I regained my composure, comforted—at least intellectually—by Mav's earlier words, yet still inclined to tremble rather more than I cared showing. "Podfettian? I thought I recognized the fellow's lingo. I wonder what—"

"He asked us not to hurt him, and vouchsafed that he had only done what he was doing for the money. *That* is when he threw the sword!" He tucked the small, lightweight weapon with its mate under an arm, then did something with the little gun.

"Well, do you suppose—"

"Mymy, if I have learned anything at all from this adventure so far, it is not to *suppose* too much on little evidence. You're still quite shaken, aren't you? Take my arm, then, if you will, and when you feel equal to it, we will walk back to that cabstand, as we should have done in the beginning."

Which is precisely what we did. Despite Mav's dissertation on the ethics of self-defense, I couldn't rid my memory of the wounded fellow's screaming. It was little help, indeed, that Mav had insisted upon wrapping the amputated hand in a kerchief and bringing it along with us. "One never knows the sort of thing that will eventually constitute evidence, my dear." He assisted me in boarding the cab, advising the driver—who was taken aback somewhat by the many weapon-shaped lumps beneath my companion's cloak (yet this was, after all, the Kiiden)—of our destination. This surprised me; however, it was unlike Mav to be deterred by even such an occurrence as being attacked in the street. My own self-esteem required that I agree cheerfully to accompany him to the Museum as we had originally planned.

The taxi rocked and jostled us about, further troubling my uneasy stomachs. "I do apologize, Mav, for being such a child, but surely you must understand how deliberately hurting someone flies directly in the eyes of everything I've believed since long before I knew what gender I would be."

His fur rippled kindly assent. "Indeed, my dear, and I

sympathize. I myself owe *you* an apology, not only for my unfeeling words back there, but for failing to remember how I took my own first exsanguinary experience."

"Your first? You mean to say—"

"Yes, I am ashamed that, in my checkered career, I have had rather more than one. But there was a time, when I was considerably younger than you are, when all of that was still before me. . . ."

You will recall (he told me) that my father was an Army colonel with our Imperial garrison in the Dominion of Dezer, whose ancient and mysterious culture he came to love and respect and whose subjects he attempted to govern with kindness and enlightenment. My mother was—or rather, is—a fine lady of the native nobility who shared her husband's dream of blending the best from two civilizations and, for all that she deplored the violence of conquest, was grateful that the Empire of Great Foddu had come to end the ignorance and poverty of her people.

I should likely have grown up to be a colonial officer as well, except that my surfather, a newspaper correspondent—and yes, a Podfettian national—taught me to dream of adventure in faraway places vastly stranger and more wonderful (as is always the case with faraway places) than even Dezer itself. It is the simple truth that rhe had been dispatched by rher government to spy upon our garrisons, if possible to foment rebellion, but rhe fell in love, both with my father's visions and my mother's great beauty. Thus the trine was married and I came into the world.

In consequence of my unorthodox upbringing, I sometime later lied about my age and joined the Imperial Air Navy. Although he uttered not a word about it to his dying day, I'm certain Father never overcame his disappointment with my choice of Service. But admirable as they were, his dreams and ambitions were not mine, and my own, however nebulous and unformed they may have been, cried out for satisfaction. Eventually I was billeted to a post two whole continents away, deep in the interior of Einnyo, a rough-and-ready, totally uncivilized, and sparsely inhabited place of unparalleled promise—and instant death for those even momentarily unwary.

I'd dreamt of flying giant airships, but instead—there being so few of the expensive craft available, I suppose, for the amusement of half-caste subalterns still adjusting to a newly entered masculinity—found myself appointed the number-three lam at a two-officer hydrogen station from which irregular patrols were launched across the flat and endless prairie that composes most of the continent. Occasionally savages, fierce peculiar fellows of smoky-gray color and short, bristly fur, would come to barter with us in their stoic manner. They hadn't very much of worldly goods—scrubby little half-tamed watun, woven tents that folded up quite cunningly, and now and again they killed a game animal or two they couldn't use, which was welcomed by us as a supplement to dreary Imperial rations. They were happy to receive in return what trinkets we could scrape together—chiefly mirrors and, if you will believe it, magnifying lenses much like yours with which they found it more convenient to light campfires than by rubbing dried-out cactus stems together. They were fond, too, of our inhaling fluid, but we were officially proscribed from trading amber to them, which they ardently desired, because the Admiralty feared that, employing furs or other fabrics in the ancient manner of *our* ancestors, they might become intoxicated, arousing some baser passions within them for rapine and murder.

Service on the frontier is chiefly characterized by unendurable periods of stifling inactivity. Yet I discovered ways to ameliorate this condition. I found that I could persuade the airshiplamn into giving me occasional rides—my skill at games of chance had rather a lot to do with this, and, for their part, they were delighted I was willing to accept such excursions in lieu of the money they owed me. A thousand lam-heights above the rolling plains . . . I can't recall being happier in my life, then or now. The steam engines—also driven by hydrogen, which we supplied— were exceedingly quiet—far quieter, indeed, than the soul-stirring sound of wind whistling through the airship's wire bracings and the creaking spars of rher gondola. After a few such outings, even the captain grew to trust me with certain homely little chores of airlamnship, and I was highly gratified.

Upon the fatal day, we had driven deeply into the empty plains, farther, perhaps, than these patrols were accustomed to flying ordinarily, certainly well beyond sight of the semaphore towers by means of which the Navy communicates with its ships at sea or in the air. Below us, yellow algaesand and low-lying orange cactus forests seemed to stretch into infinity; the shadow of our little craft raced and rippled like a living creature across the gently undulating countryside.

Suddenly we spied a waggon convoy of colonists, and I knew why this exceptionally long mission had been posted. Their teams of great, slow-moving ajotiin lumbered toward whatever far-off settlement earlier brave and hardy souls had established in the interior. We drifted lower, giving them a cheery wave, and, as we did so, from a declivity ahead some several hundred savages arose, thundered toward the waggons as rapidly as watun can be driven, and filled the air below our keel with arrows.

The bows these fellows used were something to write home about—provided that you lived through the encounter. Over two lam-heights in length, they cast an arrow half that long nearly a third of a fymo to bury its shaft in seasoned treewood (if such should happen to obstruct its path) so deeply it would take a squad of Bucketeers and a brace of watun to extract.

The pioneer company did what pioneer companies always do: formed their waggons into a triangle, watun yoke to rear wheel, and prepared themselves to receive the hostiles. The glint and flash of Fodduan gun barrels was plain to see even five hundred lam-heights above.

The savages were master watunslamn, having, for all that they were primitive in other respects, invented something we of Foddu have failed even to conceive: instead of battle chariots or waggons, they strap a circular device of leather, not unlike the tyre of a carriage, atop the beast to force its jaws shut and provide a comfortable seat for a rider. This harnessing they duplicate above, as well, fastening themselves so that they may dash about with frightening agility and use *all three sets of arms* to deliver arrows, eye spears, or stunning blows from massive war hammers. Fighting one of them is like engaging any three ordinary soldiers, so brave and intelligent are they.

Nor were they without a sense of tactics. They formed a rapidly moving ring around the company, nearly out of rifle range, drawing Fodduan fire and showering their deadly arrows down into the triangle of waggons. A dozen people fell before even the first Fodduan volley was fired.

The captain of our airship was inclined to swoop down to the colonists' aid. We had aboard a newly issued rotary machine gun, but it had been intended for use against other aircraft and, on that account, could not be depressed far enough in its mounting for targets on the ground—a typically stupid Imperial oversight. He gave an order for descent and I drew my sidearm—a Navy revolver in those days—which I was accustomed to carrying in hostile territory. We wafted lower and lower, delayed considerably by a mild headwind, which made the ship bob up and down and forced us all to cling to stanchions and guy wires to keep our footing.

Forward in the gondola, the gun crew, readying their weapon, cried out that we were nearly low enough to suit them, when abruptly, the lookout sitting at the top of his tunnel tube through the gasbag shouted down for us to observe the savages, some number of whom had dismounted and were employing the same breeze we fought to their own advantage. Through a telescope mounted on the rail near me, I coould see that they were wrapping some material around their arrows and setting it afire—most likely with the very glasses and inhaling fluid we had traded them. These flaming projectiles they were raining down upon the colonists, who doused them frantically with the abundant sand around them. The captain's fur stood straight upon his carapace at the sight, and he cursed and screamed at the crew to get us aloft again. Should even one of these fiery missiles penetrate the skin of our aircraft, rhe—and we with rher—would perish in a trice.

However, it was clear that the waggoners below were dreadfully outnumbered, and if we could not assist them, they would die in our stead. This, I maintained somewhat forcefully to the captain, was not the proper order of things for the Imperial Air Navy, but he continued giving orders that would take us safely out of range of the flaming arrows.

On their little railed porch at the front of the gondola, the gun crew were frantic, having had their prey snatched from them and being forced to watch the slow but certain attrition beneath us. One glance into their fur and I was sure of them. I leveled my pistol straight at the captain's eye and ordered him to halt his unlamly retreat. You see, I had remembered a chemistry demonstration from my school days: our ship was surely doomed if we aided the colonists, yet if our altitude were such to permit the gun

69

crew to operate, then the rest of us might jump clear toward the end of the run—because hydrogen burns *upward*, leaving cool air below.

I stood my ground, confronting the captain across his steering wheel. His minions were stunned into silence by my mutinous behavior, but behind me I could see the gun crew ripping off the tops of crates of loaded magazines and twisting their elevation screw nearly off its threads to get the muzzle down.

At the click of my revolver hammer locking in the sear, the captain's fur drooped resignedly and he shouted out the orders I had given him. Our bow fell once again and we headed toward the waggon train. The rotary machine gun began to chatter and spew empty brass cases long before we were properly in range, but the puffs of dust near the savages' position had two immediate effects: they ceased firing at the colonists—we could hear hearty cheering from the waggons even at this great height—and the savages began firing upon us!

Nearer and nearer we drew, our trim adjusted at a steep bow-angle, until the savages must retreat or be churned to sausage beneath the hammering of our gun. I forgot the captain now and slid a window back to add my minimal firepower to that of the machine gun. To his credit, the captain maintained course, and I was joined in my efforts by others who had taken long, very accurate rifles from the ship's locker.

Lower and lower we sank until the updrafts from the fires started by the savage arrows made it necessary to cast off hydrogen and we dropped with a heartsstopping rush. The savages, to give them their due, refused to be routed, but continued firing as we passed over the waggons and approached them. Yet they were being inexorably nonimated—we afterward counted upward of a hundred bodies, riddled with large-caliber bullets from the rotary gun, lying heaped among the carcasses of their faithful and equally valorous watun. They no longer had time now to get their fearsome arrows lit—which was a blessing and a comfort—and, consequently, those that penetrated our thin hull only lost us gas and added further to the headlong speed with which we fell upon them.

Finally, our enemy nearly vanquished and our supply of hydrogen exhausted, we came to a gentle crash several hundred lam-heights from the colonists' position. Our gun crew gave up steady firing for lack of targets, though occasionally an arrow sang past our carapaces, to be answered with a futile hail of bullets. We leapt from the gondola as the fuselage above it began slowly collapsing for lack of internal pressure to support it, and hastily formed a column for a quick-march toward the waggons, those in the center of the formation struggling under the weight of the machine gun, which the gun crew had unbolted and insisted on taking with them.

We were halfway to our goal when a small group of hostiles, no doubt cut off from the main body as we'd passed overhead, rose from the prairie cactus in front of us and began discharging their wicked arrows at us point-blank. They grasped their bows with their outside hands and drew them with the middle, assuring tremendous striking force, and we soon learned another deadly secret of primitive technology: a tiny ball of wax impaled upon each arrow point gives even a glancing missile enough momentary adherence—and possibly lubrication—to assure its evil purpose. A lam's carapace that might, in certain circumstances, deflect a bullet would invariably be pierced clean through. And should the arrow strike an eye, most likely the lam standing behind the victim would be killed as well.

When the colonists observed our plight, they set up a crossfire that, regrettably, did us more harm than good: the savages charged us, realizing that the waggoners would cease fire for fear of shooting their allies. Thus it was hand-to-hand until the last person standing—be he Fodduan or savage—claimed ironic victory. I fought as best I could. Whoever ordained that there should be but three chambers in a military revolver must surely have done all his combat from behind a desk. I used my pistol as a club until an arrow struck me in my upraised limb. I switched, standing upon the damaged leg and employing another set of hands for fighting, but the long arrow, sticking out four hand-widths on either side of the penetrated joint, hindered me sorely, and at last I fell beneath a native war hammer.

When I regained my sensibilities, our tormenters were departed, driven off with the blessed rotary gun and a sortie from the waggons. In the camp I was the hero of the day.

And I was also under close arrest.

None of this had any meaning for me. Just hours ago I'd been a young, untested ensign, eager for adventure. Now I was personally the killer of at least a dozen of my fellow beings—I had watched them spill their blood upon the sand and die—and, indirectly, of perhaps hundreds more. There is no way of being certain; the savages recover their dead when they can, and those lying upon the field were merely those few we had denied them. If I may claim any virtue at all in the matter, it was that I mourned their slaughter fully as deeply as the slaughter of my comrades.

"I believe I see what you are getting at," I answered after a rather long silence. Outside the windows of our cab, I could see we were approaching the neighborhood of the Imperial Museum. "It is little consolation, whenever someone is injured or killed on your account, that you have acted aright."

"Quite so," my friend replied, puffing at his silver pipe. "Or thus I found it then. They gave me a medal for saving the waggon train: some admiral's daughter and her family had been among the settlers. I mention this not from immodesty, but because these questionable honors failed to dispel my feelings of culpability. I was thereupon cashiered—gloved right out of the Navy—for threatening a superior with deadly force, endangering vessel and crew (the ship was recovered intact, else I should have rher on my conscience, as well), and complicating relations with the natives."

"Why, of all the nerve!"

"It was precisely what I deserved, and lucky I wasn't shot for mutiny in the bargain—in fact, that might have been a mercy, considering how I felt. The 'native relations' charge was perhaps unwarranted—they still came atrading to the post and treated me with uncommon kindness while I was there awaiting transport back to Mathas. But, Mymy, I had been *wrong* in my feelings. It was the savages—who were not quite so savage, after all—who taught me differently." He reached beneath his cloak and produced the little pistol. "I believe you should take this. You're entitled, and ours is beginning to look like a perilous undertaking."

"But, Mav, how could I—"

"The same as I, Mymy. You see, those savages weren't the stoics I had taken them to be, but graced with a simple dignity and a wry appreciation for life's inconstant seasons. They no more held me to blame than I held them: circumstance had made me an enemy, of whom they expected courage and tenacity; a different circumstance now permitted me to be a friend, to whom respect and courtesy were due.

"True, there are certain principles of conduct that must never fluctuate. One of them is the imperative of self-defense and the right to protect the lives of others; this the natives understood far better than I. Another is the dual importance of sentiment and cerebration in lamviin life; frozen-pelted they may seem at times, yet they wail for a fallen comrade like children over a lost balloon. We Fodduans are scornful of the overly emotional. Yet it's easier still to drown one's feelings until one is only half a lam. What's *difficult* is balancing both thought *and* feelings in harmony. I determined thereafter that I would never permit an unexamined conflict to endure between what I feel and what my reason tells me is correct."

Reluctantly I accepted the gun and sat back for a time in thought. "And have you succeeded?"

A ripple chased itself across his carapace. "My dear, I'll not be altogether certain even when I draw my final breath. But I try, Mymy, every day I try. Now I see we are nearly at our destination. Let us consider, if your stomachs are up to it, this dismembered hand—perhaps a callus or some other characteristic will give us a clue as to its former owner."

VII: Experimental Methods

As upon the evening of Srafen's lecture—which seemed to me by now at least a year ago, but which, of course, had actually occurred fewer than fifty hours before—we were greeted at the entrance of the Museum by a now familiar figure:

"Ah, good Leds!" exclaimed Mav as he draped his weapon-laden cloak over the guardpost counter. "I trust the preparations I requested have been seen to?"

The elderly lam bestowed upon my companion the ghost of a military salute. "Aye, Cap'n, took care of everything myself, I did." He hesitated then, patterns of embarrassment and uncertainty rippling briefly through his thinning fur.

Mav kindly intervened: "Do please speak freely, Leds. Is there some difficulty?"

"Only Acting Curator Liimev, sir. He's that impatient to get the place opened up again, and asked me to ask you . . ."

Mav crinkled his fur with amusement. "You see, Mymy, I have been relying upon my family connections to preserve our evidence intact. However, we must not permit the pursuit of justice to inflict further injustices upon others." To Leds: "Please inform Professor Liimev that he may begin repairs in the morning and open doors to the public as soon thereafter as his own efforts enable him to do."

"Why, thank you, Cap'n." Still the old fellow appeared discomfited. "One more thing, sir, if you please . . ."

"And what is that?"

"Well, sir, the Professor was concerned that every caution be exercised concerning the . . ."

"The springbow? I quite understand, and assure you I'm aware of its high potential for destruction. Also that it is an ancient and fragile implement in its own right. Do not fear, Leds, I shall be careful."

At this, the guard brightened considerably. "Very good,

sir." He dusted his hands together as if having disposed of an unwelcome and unsavory task. "Is there any way I can assist you?"

"Not at the moment. Missur Mymy and I will be in the Weapons Hall; should we require your further help, one of us will call you."

Of these arrangements they discussed, I had not the faintest inkling, though I surmised that they had occupied some of Mav's attentions this afternoon while I had been visiting relatives. In this I was proved correct.

"You see," he told me as we entered the Weapons Hall from the lecture auditorium, there being no direct access from the Grand Display Hall, "we have before us here a very pretty puzzle. I have decided I shall call it a Closed-Chamber Paradox—one door was nailed shut, three more securely bolted, and the only one remaining closely guarded by both Bucketeers and the Museum guards. Moreover, all outer entrances were securely sealed as well. Some two hundred or more individuals witnessed what transpired, but no one—not myself excluded—can say how the murder was accomplished."

"In this respect," I observed, "it is rather like a feat of theatrical magic, isn't it?" This thought gave rise to speculations concerning Myssmo's lunologist.

"Quite so, Mymy, and consequently I have ordered that nothing be disturbed, in hopes that we may eventually determine the magician's methods. Here, for instance, is the screen, precisely as it was night before last . . . and along here, the broken springbow case and the nailed door with the hole in it. I did permit Leds to eliminate the display case from the circuit of alarms so that we would be annoyed no longer by its incessant ringing, and the alarms for other cases could be rendered operative again."

Somehow this must have been accomplished at the panel in the atrium, as there was no sign of it in this chamber.

"Now, before we properly begin," May said, extracting his notecase from a pocket, "perhaps you'd like to hear what else has been established since this afternoon."

"Indeed, I had believed you'd spent the time rendering my own efforts redundant." And consorting with disreputable females, I added mentally.

"Now, now, Mymy, we are bound, in circumstances such as these, to stumble independently upon the same facts now and again. Actually, such duplication serves our purposes quite handsomely, as I'm inclined to trust twice-proven evidence all the more." He began to rummage through his pockets once again.

"I could wish I shared your aplomb. But tell me, Mav, will you not report the attempt upon our lives this evening?" I thought about the severed hand, lying, at his insistence, within my bag. "After all, there's been a serious injury, and—"

He stopped and looked at me directly. "On no account! Can you imagine Tis's reaction to the news? We have sufficient obstacles before us without adding yet another." He produced the exploded springbow bolt, laying it carefully upon the glass of a nearby display case. "That's as it may be. There is work now, and you have heard me promise Leds that this is the last evening we'll keep his Museum closed. Thus it is our final opportunity to collect and interpret physical data *in situ*. Speaking of which, I find I have neglected to show you something that may prove to be of some importance."

He handed me a paper disk, the photograph of a scene I had excellent reason to recall most vividly. "Why, it's Professor Srafen, virtually at the moment of the explosion. I remember that dramatic gesture quite well, for Niitood had requested rher to 'hold it.' "

"More accurately, a fraction of a second *before* the explosion. It is my belief that this image exonerates Niitood completely, for it is, of course, from his camera, and had he concealed a weapon in that instrument—"

"Which he had not, for you examined it beforehand, and I its fragments afterward—"

"Quite so. As I was just about to say, I doubt that any such device could function simultaneously as a camera and a weapon. Niitood produced this picture for me once he was released. It was a highly disagreeable process involving several odorous liquids, which I nonetheless watched closely to avoid his being accused in future of practicing a deception. You really ought to see his flat, Mymy. It's like some mad philosopher's laboratory."

"Pah forbid," said I with indignant propriety, "nor do I necessarily concur that this releases him altogether from suspicion. It seems to me that there was room aplenty in that so-called illuminatory attachment of his for field artillery and a company of cavalry, chariots and all."

He rippled his fur with gratified amusement but delayed

comment until he'd prepared his little silver pipe. "Yours parallel my own thought processes admirably. I went to some pains establishing the operating principle of Niitood's illuminator; in function it is not unlike a juicing box."

"Somehow," I replied, "this does not surprise me. By what means is such a foul habit turned to constructive purpose?"

Mav puffed upon his pipe. "Elementary, my dear Mymy; although in present application the instrument is large and somewhat heavy, it shows some advantages over the use of flash powder, and Niitood has hopes that future progress will render the device lighter and more compact.

"The juicing-box portion boasts three magnetos instead of the usual one, and a singularly powerful spring escapement, which generate sufficient current to stun a watu or an ajot."

"Or perhaps even such an habitual imbiber as our Niitood?" I inquired.

"You are the very model of tolerance, my dear. For my part, I had rather be infested by carapace lice than afflicted with a well-intentioned friend motivated 'only by my best interests." Had you ever thought of going into Church work? Never mind: the electrical potential is communicated to a simple pair of copper clamps in which there have been placed a pair of rods exactly like these."

He handed me two chalky black cylinders perhaps half a finger-width in diameter. "Carbon?"

"Nothing else. When the distance between their ends is properly adjusted and the spring motor released, there is produced a momentary brilliance in which it is possible to make pictures such as that in your hand."

"I see. Ergo: no weapon in the camera; none in the illuminatory—"

"Arc candle, Niitood calls it. I could wish he put as much effort into journalistic excellence as he does in his inventions."

"Arc candle, then. As you yourself have commented, this is the Age of Invention, Mav, when everyone fancies himself the harbinger of progress. Very well, at the moment of the photograph, Srafen was still alive. I am compelled to agree with you at last: Niitood is not our murderer. But you did not have this evidence when you argued for his release. . . ."

Now it was my friend's turn to betray embarrassment:

77

"My reasons were the polar opposite of scientific, Mymy; they were psychological in character. I simply never believed Niitood was the sort to do murder, particularly a complicated premeditated one. As you now comprehend, I pay great attention to such feelings, and if I require any further defense in the matter, it is my experience that journalists as a class are inherently passive creatures—spectators, not participators in life. Why, I have witnessed correspondents taking notes and pictures while watching soldiers bleed to death in the field, instead of taking the lamviinitarian measures any sane or decent person would."

I found that difficult to credit. "Perhaps you exaggerate somewhat. But tell me of these preparations Leds discussed with you."

"They are various. To begin with, you may recall my hypothesis that someone might have hidden in this room before the lecture, thus evading notice by the lamn who guarded the only open door."

"Yes, although I am surprised that I do, considering the many events that have demanded my concern in the interim."

"You've been a paragon, Mymy, there's the straight of it. In any case, my guesses have been shattered once again by Leds: there was considerable movement of furniture in here, preparatory to the lecture; he and his assistants weren't quite finished with it before guests began arriving. Thus, by inadvertence, this chamber was well supervised the entire time, and, as you can see for yourself, there isn't any place to hide, even were that not the case."

I looked around the room. "Unless one donned one of those suits of armor over there beside the damaged door, perhaps the one with the enormous hammer."

"That would require our quarry to be surmale—our ancestors, Mymy, were appreciably smaller than we are, and very few males or even females could fit comfortably into that iron apparel. Now, do you notice anything different about this place?"

Again I scrutinized the room, finally seizing on a sizable object back toward the entrance. "Why, yes, what is that contraption over there?" I referred to a series of large triangular panels I had not noticed before because they were on this side of the screen and set close by the southeast wall. Closer examination proved them to be a trine of unmounted doors, one behind the next, perhaps three hand-widths separating them, and attached to one another by long planks nailed at the edges. Behind this contrivance, all decoration had been stripped from the stone wall and the floor cleared for a lam-height or two all round.

Bemused, I rapped upon each triangular panel and walked around them, attempting to discern their purpose, In all significant respects they were identical to the pair—one on the other side of the screen and the other nailed shut—that communicated with the lecture hall.

"Leds found them for me in an attic," Mav explained, watching my investigations closely, "left over from some past reconstruction of this place—there are many fewer walls within the building now than was the case at one time and hence, fewer doors. Employing these, and the springbow he and Professor Liimev are so solicitious about, I hope to solve some of the infernal contradictions of this case."

At my companion's words, I shrank back from the doors. "Oh, Mav! Surely you do not intend—"

Laughter was written plainly in his fur. "Not unless it is absolutely necessary, I assure you. I remember, quite as well as you do, the force of that explosion and the damage that it visited upon so many innocents in its vicinity." He reached into yet another pocket, and I began to wonder whether there was any limit to what they contained. "Also, my dear associate, although I'm told by the manufacturer there seems a small revival of the sport recently, *these* were expensive. . . ."

He drew out and displayed a pair of springbow bolts that differed from the others I had seen in that they were bright and untarnished, striations of the lathe-worker's tools plain upon them. One was a featureless rodlike target missile, the other of the hollow, bulbous variety with a nipple screwed into its tip for a percussion cap.

"I believe," Mav said, "that we will try the less-spectacular projectile first. Will you assist me?"

We had returned to the violated display case at the opposite corner of the room. Mav reached down and grasped the springbow, removing several fragments of glass from atop the weapon and shaking smaller particles out of the mechanism.

In design, a springbow is an elegantly simple device—although this specimen was considerably embellished with wood carving and engraving on the metal parts—essentially a hollow cylinder of iron with a deep groove pressed into the top for placement of the arrow, and slotted along the sides where a heavy coil spring is visible.

Mave tucked away the hollow quarrel and we walked back to the other corner of the room. "As you can see, this rear portion is made to fit one's upper limb like the stock of a rifle." Indeed, extending from the receiver was a stout rod that terminated in a large two-thirds cylinder of leather-padded sheet metal. Mav placed this around his upper limb just above the point where it branched and, with his middle hand, grasped the handle, being careful not to place his finger in the trigger guard.

With his leftmost hand he pressed hard upon a stirrup underneath the weapon, swinging it down and forward. A pair of longish levers thus were pivoted upward so that the internal spring was compressed until it locked in place. Mav returned the stirrup to its original position.

"An archer used to wear a pair of quivers," he explained, "one on either walking leg. Cocking and loading with the outside hands, he might achieve a rate of fire superior to any breech-loading cartridge rifle short of our very latest magazine repeaters of today." He fitted the target bolt into its groove.

I said, "In that event, I am surprised that firearms ever came to replace this weapon." The tensed and powerful spring behind the quarrel, I discovered, was making me quite nervous.

"I've often wondered about that very thing myself," said he. "The powder guns of the time were crude and inefficient in the extreme—although, in justice, they were lighter and required considerably less muscular effort to charge and fire them. Now, here we go!"

He swung the springbow upward, pointing it at the doors, and pulled the trigger. There was a dull twang, and the bolt flew foward—with a disappointing *thud*. The arrow bounced off the first door, rang and clattered on the flagging at our feet.

"Peculiar," said Mav. "There's scarcely a mark to show where it struck." Indeed, except for a small fingertip-sized dent, the door was quite undamaged.

"Do you suppose you operated the weapon incorrectly?"

"I doubt it greatly. The mechanism is simplicity made manifest, as you are at liberty to ascertain for yourself." This time, he allowed me to arm the device, in which enterprise I failed miserably, being unable to swing the stirrup more than a few degrees from its resting place. This prompted two ideas on my part.

"Now I appreciate the popularity of firearms. But look here, Mav, your notion of a *surmale* murderer hiding in a suit of armor is all wrong." I glanced once more at the imposing, albeit hollow, figures by the door, one grasping a mighty chariot sword, the other a war hammer of massive proportions.

"Please be reassured," said he, "I never seriously entertained it." He replaced the bolt and fired again.

With precisely the result as before.

Mav placed the weapon butt-first on the floor, leaning against the foremost of the three doors, and prepared his pipe again. I could see him trying to do his *Resre* breathing without calling my attention to it, but he was not to succeed on this occasion. *"This vile contrivance!"* he exclaimed. "It embodies more annoying paradoxes than a herd of metaphysical philosophers!"

Despite my disappointment for his sake, I had a difficulty of my own—suppressing laughter—for Mav is ordinarily so calm and unruffable. And besides, he is quite appealing, somehow, when he is angry. To preserve his pride and my composure, I wandered back to the other corner of the room and lifted the old shield to examine the large ragged hole that *something* had to have made in the door—a hole that Mav's experiments had so far failed to reproduce. "Do you suppose, if you had used the hollow, explosive arrow . . . ?"

Even at this remove, the negative pattern in his fur was easily discernible. "No, in the first place, it is heavier, and thus capable of even less velocity and penetration. Nor do I believe—as I anticipate you are about to conjecture—that the arrow blasted its way through the door. How, then, could it have killed Srafen? Now if we had found *two* arrows . . . No, I suspect that the spring in this bow has simply fatigued with age. I felt it was a little too easily cocked. And once again we are left with a myriad of irritating questions."

My fur rippled despite my best efforts. "Have you not frequently quoted the late Professor Srafen to the effect that new questions are the result of the best experiments?" Idly, I fingered the shredded edge of the hole in the panel.

"Your memory is altogether too good tonight, Mymy. Perhaps you ought to take over this investigation!"

"Perhaps I— Mav, come here! Does this mean anything?" The edges of the hole had crumbled like stale algae cakes under my fingers.

"Heaven's sweet evaporation, Mymy! I congratulate you! This door is positively eaten through with damprot, unlike those that were preserved, high and dry, in the Museum's attic. Why, I could practically—"

Thump! He slammed the springbow bolt in his hand against the panel. It made an ugly wound, yet did not quite penetrate. "Well, there's more integrity there than I suspected, but even our worn-out springbow might drive a quarrel through and some distance beyond."

I gave that a great deal of consideration, and an answer to another problem flashed upon my mind. "How much effort is required to detonate a percussion cap?"

He paused. "Oh, I see what you are getting at. But no, I am afraid the impact, even against so insubstantial a barrier, would still be sufficient to set the explosion off. An admirable effort, however; you are beginning to think like a detective. . . . I could wish the same thing for myself." He moved to reexamine the exploded bolt. "In any case, we still have these considerable traces of wood fiber *within* the whitepowder cavity to account for. Had not Professor Srafen died so horribly, one might reason that— Hallo?"

Abruptly there was movement at the edge of the screen. "Cap'n?"

Mav sighed. "Yes, Leds, what is it?"

"Will there not be any explodin' after all? I been sitting, braced for it, this past hour."

"I'm truly sorry, old fellow, to have imposed upon your nerves in such a manner. No, there will be no explosions— unless you count those of frustration, which even now are going off inside my brains. And you may definitely tell your superior tomorrow that he may restore this place. We'll be learning nothing more of value from it, I'm afraid."

The old lam said, "I'm sorry, Cap'n. Well, I'll just be getting back— Oh, I near forgot: here's the paper you asked for. That's why I disturbed you in the first place, beggin' your pardon."

"Excellent. Thank you, Leds. Mymy, here is another of the preparations I mentioned. You'll recall that, on the night of the murder, I caused a roster to be collected of everybody present, along with certain details such as precisely where, as well as could be remembered, each individual was seated. For example, here is the Archsacerdot, and you will notice half a dozen of Srafen's old Navy chums sitting in the southeast corner to our right. Now this new list of Leds's is of the original holders of tickets to the lecture, which, primarily owing to the anti-Ascensionists, was conducted by invitation only. See, here am I, duly accredited with three admissions—comparing that to the later Bucketeer account, you'll notice that you and I are listed, and that one of our tickets remained unused."

Indeed, I thought, although that hadn't prevented me from having to personally associate with Vyssu in the end. "And what is it that you hope to learn from these accountings?"

He pored over the scrolls: "Well, I have just learned something already—that Srafen's husband, Law, was among those individuals invited, yet he did not attend. Instead, their wife, Myssmo, was here that night, along with a guest."

"A Dr. Ensda, by any chance?"

"Not particularly discreet or subtle is our Myssmo, is she? It must have galled Srafen particularly sorely, as rhe believed such pseudophilosophies as lunology and the reading of jaw striations were soon to be rendered extinct by science. Do you notice anything else about this charlatan?"

The Bucketeers had him down as "Professor Doctor Zanyw N'botpemy *Ensda,* Lunologist and Celestial Counselor."

"The springbow," I replied immediately, "the eye swords, and the sailor. And, unless I am mistaken, Mav, is this Zanyw N'botpemy *Ensda* not a Podfettian *name,* as well? Could it be a pattern is emer—"

At that very instant there occurred yet another commotion behind the screen, around which appeared—despite Leds's best efforts to the contrary—a ragged and disheveled-looking Niitood, his bandages trailing behind him like a train.

"Mav! Mymy! You've got to come at once! *Someone's broken into my apartments and smashed every piece of equipment to bits!"*

83

VIII: The Shrine of Fundamental Truth

BANG!!!

"Now you see, Mymy? The trigger must be squeezed, not jerked." Mav took the little weapon from my hand, pressed the spring-loaded button upon its side just forward of the *T*-shaped handle, gave the barrels a quarter-turn, and ejected both spent cartridges.

As relatively small-bored as the pistol was—precisely a standard Fodduan finger-width, or thirty-three to the pound by old-fashioned reckoning—still, my middle hand was tingling after half a dozen rounds; I was desirous of leaving off and getting back to our picnic.

This much credit I will give to Vyssu: she had laid a splendid feast before us—smoked sandshrimp, obrega taproot sliced thin and highly spiced, and my favorite, cactus pears in an unusual sauce prepared from a steeping of crushed nopal scales. She'd spread a layer of clean white sand from one of our panniers upon the ground to make a table, and even where I stood, a dozen lam-heights away, the aroma of the pears pricked tantalizingly at my nostrils.

Mav gave the barrels a twist. "Try it again, Mymy!"

"Must I?" I grasped the handle as Vyssu rippled encouragement. I'd been told she'd been through this before and was a creditable shot herself. Sighing, I aligned the rear sight blade so that it stood between the paired horns of the front, centered this arrangement upon a pad of spiny leptocaul toward which Mav was directing me, and carefully, despite a nervous trembling in my hand, squeezed the trigger.

Click!

I'd started violently as the striker fell, then turned to Mav in confusion. "It didn't explode; is something wrong?"

His fur gave signs of alarm until he pushed the muzzle of the pistol away from his eye; then it turned to exasperated amusement. "Nothing that cannot be instantly corrected—provided you do not shoot your instructor. *Please* be mindful of the direction you point that thing, Mymy, and forgive me, for I did not load the chambers that time, in order to determine whether or not you were developing what is called a flinch. I fear that you have."

I felt annoyance ripple across me. "I could have told you as much, myself. How can you *bear* discharging that reciprocator of yours, much less a service revolver, at twenty-two and twelve to the pound apiece, as you have said?"

"There is a difference," he replied patiently, "between feeling the weapon *moving* in your hand, and feeling it *hurt* your hand. It is common, with the noise and everything, to confuse the two. The object is to endeavor to 'follow through,' to finish up after the gun discharges with sights and target in the same relative positions as before you pulled the trigger. Now have another go—this time I'll really load it—and then we'll have our luncheon."

This was a day of novel experiences, as were many which I spent with Mav. I'd often picnicked here in Lovely Sands, a few fymon above Hedgerow, with my family. Never before, however, had such an occasion included shooting lessons.

Nor had I come by watuback.

Yesterday, the morning after our second trip to the Museum, I had received my telephone several hours earlier than anticipated. (I suspect this was some subtle means of evening accounts on the part of the sales clerk, for the early morning visit put both Zoobon and me to some inconvenience, yet how could I complain of such zealous service?) Not thirty minutes later, I accepted, as well, my very first telephone message.

"*Mymy?*"

"Is it you, Mav?"

"*None other. I trust I haven't interrupted your breakfast. We have a busy schedule today; I must first see Niitood, whose jaws are out of joint because I sent a uniformed Bucketeer with him last night instead of attending to the matter myself. I ordered the place left untouched, which perturbed him even further until I made amends by billeting him at Vyssu's . . . er . . . establishment.*"

"I see, and did he find the prospect entertaining?"

There was a considerable pause, then: "*Mymy, Vyssu also operates a perfectly conventional rooming house upon her premises—well, conventional enough for the Kiiden, anyway. But, since you mention it, it did occur to me that some company might cheer him, after being blown up, jailed, and burglarized within the space of two days. Did you know they broke another camera for him, as well?"*

"I began to understand that such was the case the twenty-seventh time he mentioned it last night. Did Vyssu supply his companions, or did she herself—"

"Mymy! I'm ashamed at your attitude. It may edify you to learn that she is an entrepreneur rather than an assembly worker, so to speak, and in any event—"

"What does your schedule include for me today? Nothing so redundant as my errands yesterday, one would fondly hope."

A disadvantage to the telephone is that it will not convey physical expressions. However, I knew Mav well enough to see, in my mind's eye, the chuckle in his fur. *"Indeed not, my dear, puritanical assistant. You will undertake a highly important task while I attempt to complete a wholly different one. Do you recall the fellow in front of the Museum the evening of the lecture?"*

"Why, there were *hundreds*," I replied with irritation. It occurred to me that this sort of blind conversation had its positive side as well, for Mav could not see my angry fur at the moment. "Oh, you mean the ragged, dirty person on the waggon, the one haranguing the mob?"

"One Kymmi Kiidit Adem, according to the report, proprietor of something called the Shrine of Fundamental Truth located upon Pauper's Island."

"And what is it you wish me to ask him?"

Another pause, and I could hear him first prepare, then inhale from his pipe. *"Simple facts as to his whereabouts during the murder we already have from our lamn outside the Museum, watching him at the very instant they heard the explosion. From you, some assessment of his character—had he sufficient animosity toward Srafen to delegate an act of violence? I appreciate the subjectivity of such a task, and its consequent difficulty, but frankly, I can't think where else to begin. In some ways, it is worse than the tangle of physical evidence that confounds us."*

It was my turn to chuckle invisibly, but more at the situation than at my friend's expense. "I'll do the best I can, my dear Inquirer. May I ask where you can be reached while I am negotiating with religious fanatics?"

"I plan spending the day in the Imperial Navy yards, locating those old friends of Srafen who were present at the lecture. I suggest, when you have had enough of Pauper's Island, that you inquire at the Precinct for messages. Unless some emergency arises, you can bring me up to date tomorrow morning in Lovely Sands."

"And who are we interviewing there, suspicious birds and cacti?"

"We shall interview ourselves. I need a rest to think about what I have learned—and failed to learn. And I believe that I shall teach you to shoot and ride upon the back of watun just like an Einnyo pioneer!"

Pauper's Island is the uppermost of three large obstructions—King's Island and Shield being the others—in the winding mouth of the River Dybod where it passes through Mathas and into the gulf that also bears that name.

Now that I have mentioned names, I'll add that Pauper's Island's is entirely misleading. Straight across the Dybod from Riverside is a truly impoverished working-class district called Pauper's Bridge. The island between them, being within the sight of water all round and thus originally an undesirable locale, once housed the poor and indigent, factory employees and mill hands such as one still finds upon the eastern bank—and, indeed, all over that side of the river.

However, some generations ago, a high wall blocking out the watery view was constructed, and the place became a sort of haven for university students, poets, and musicians of a particularly disreputable variety. Thus it remained until perhaps a dozen years ago when others, less unconventional but admiring the peculiar atmosphere, began displacing both workers and loafers. It is now quite the rage for single persons in search of adventure and young triplets as yet unwilling to settle into staid conventionality to lease or purchase a refurbished flat and pretend that they are daring freethinkers, radical friends of the workers, and *artistes*. Their one and only real accomplishment, it seems to me, is to have bidden the rent up tenfold in as many years.

Thus I was somewhat surprised when Mav informed me of the location of the Shrine of Fundamental Truth—one would likelier have expected it to be in Fasmou Common or the Cuff, where one supposes such rabble as we saw at the Museum keep themselves on ordinary days.

I walked south to King's Gate High Road, where I hailed a cab—this time with watun decently attached to it—intending to charge the fare off to the Precinct, and rode into Riverside, across the railroad bridge, which pierces the island wall, and from there to the Shrine itself. This proved to be an unprepossessing brick building, formerly a lodging house by all appearences, with that ugly symbol I had seen at the Museum painted on the windows. It was another splendid yellow-skyed day, and the front entrance lay wide open upon a lobby. I do not know what I'd expected, but the comely surmale receptionist sitting at a little gilt table with a telephone upon it and a mechanical typewriting machine besides, was well dressed, well spoken, and well mannered beyond belief.

"Good morning, Missur, may I be of some assistance to you?"

"I hope so; I should like to see Mr. Adem if it's convenient."

"The Reverend Mr. Adem is here, I am happy to say. Do you have an appointment? Oh—would you by any chance be Missur *Mymysiir* Offe Woom? I see that Mr. Agot Edmoot *Mav* telephoned to reserve an hour for you earlier this morning."

Trust such forethought to the systematic Mav. I wondered what the nature of my business was supposed to be. The receptionist rose and conducted me through the handsomely appointed lobby into an office anteroom, where rhe handed me over to a male secretary who also had a typewriter and a telephone.

And a suit of clothing worth a year's salary as a Bucketeer.

The secretary lifted the instrument from his desk. "Reverend? Missur *Mymysiir* Offe Woom is here by appointment. . . . Very good, sir, I shall." He placed the telephone back on his desk. Imagine, a telephone, just to speak into the next room! "Reverend Adem will see you now, Missur."

Before me he opened a pair of expensively carved doors equipped with silver-plated handles and hinges. That is, I *assumed* that they were plated. As they swung aside, I revised my estimation, for, judging from the sand upon the floor, a delicate aquamarine that could only have been hand-sifted and imported from that farthest of our colonies, Mav's father's beloved Dezer, and the many fine relief pictures upon the elegantly leathered walls, I then had reason to doubt my assessment of the door handles.

A lam whose attire might have traded straight across for ten of the secretary's suits stood in the middle of this opulent expanse of floodsand, all three hands extended in greeting.

"Missur Mymysiir—I believe that I shall call you Mymy, my child. Do come forward, and welcome to the Shrine of Fundamental Truth! I am the Reverend Kymmi Kiidit *Adem!*"

This was the ragged, dirty figure on the waggon? My consternation must have been visible, for he crinkled his fur as he directed me to a comfortable seat and stepped behind a laminated peresk desk that may have required the cutting of a hundred of the little trees—and the risk, perhaps, of dozens of lives.

"I see that you're surprised by the appearance of our humble Shrine," he said. "Or it may be that you have seen me in my more public aspect—perhaps at the Imperial Museum a few nights ago? Well, this is Pah's house, far more certainly than any cathedral upon the western shore; and I am Pah's servant. I greatly doubt whether He would want His work done shabbily! May I offer you some kood? I am afraid that we have little else, as the taking of petroleum spirits or current contravenes our beliefs." His pelt kinked just a little, as if this were a small rule imposed by a slightly unreasonable employer.

"I myself do not partake of . . . current, Reverend. A wick would be most pleasant."

Again that crinkle, and I wondered what there was about it or its owner that made me wish for some privacy with a tin of scrubbing sand. He telephoned for kood, which appeared almost instantaneously in the hands of yet another underling. Pah had *many* servants in this place, it would appear—even the servants had servants.

I might have known: when the wick was lit, it was a sickly sweet blend largely preferred by elderly unmarried lurries and ladies. Adem made a pyramid of his fingertips. "This Captain Mav who rang says that you wish to learn something of our beliefs, particularly those in opposition to the evil heresy of Ascensionism. Very well, my child, may I inquire, in turn, why it is that you are interested?"

89

I'd had, at one time, an uncle who habitually referred to me as "my child." I believe that he deserted from the Army and was shot. I hoped so, anyway.

"You were correct that I was at the Museum during your, um, demonstration. That *was* you, wasn't it?" It was my hope that I was taking the line Mav would desire. I could not, for example, have pretended interest in this strange, repellent little lam's religious prejudices. "My education has been scientific in character, and—"

"Highly unusual and enterprising for a surrie, my child. We could find many uses for such initiative in *our* work— certainly more so than in . . . what did you say it was?"

My mind whirled. What should I say? Then I realized that my bag—Sasa's bag—was lying on the floor at my hands. "I'm a student of medicine, reading for it under my surfather and obtaining such practical experience as I am able. Naturally, my philosophical curiosity has extended to—"

"To the Fundamental Truth, at last! I rejoice with you, my child! You'll not find our beliefs too very different from those of the established Church. . . ." Did I detect a microscopic bitter flattening of the fur at these words? "In fact, if I may say so, our object is to serve as something of a conscience, attempting to stem the theological drift that has been occurring lately toward various materialistic heresies."

"One of them being Ascensionism?"

He returned now to crinkling, this time more in sorrow than in anger. I am morally certain that he'd practiced this one in a mirror every day for years. "My child, this non-sense goes directly against the written word of Pah Himself, and the foundation of our belief is that the Book of Pah is literally true in every line and every verse. Else it would not be worthy of Him, would it, my child?"

I began wondering what he'd say if he knew that "his child" was contemplating taking out rher little gun and shooting off his sanctimonious nostils if he called me by that name again. Patience, Mymy: "I'd find that easier to believe were there not hundreds of obvious internal contradictions in your Book of Pah." This latter was a quote direct from my mentor in such matters, Mav.

Adem allowed himself a ripple of tolerant humor. "The logic of Pah is not the logic of lam. Such seeming contradictions may be nothing more than a test of our faith—just as Pah invented buried bones as a pitfall for the intellectually arrogant, those who place the Mind ahead of the Soul. The ossiferous collection's far from complete, as surely you must know, and this, too, should be taken as a sign by those who consider themselves wise."

"Perhaps," I offered mildly, "the process of fossilization is so rare an event—something like the creation of diamonds, for example—that we may interpret the relative abundance of fossils as a sign that Professor Srafen is absolutely correct about the Ascent of Lamviin."

The Reverend Dr. Adem was well practiced in the simulation of broad-minded joviality. He simply riposted: "My child, you're far too young to be so certain about a world to which you've scarcely been introduced. Your judgment will mature in time, but you must be aware, even now, that Ascensionism, like *all* of so-called natural philosophy, is simply another religion—a pagan one, at that—supported by a faith in certain fundamental assumptions that are no more subject to demonstration than those of Trinism. Scientists themselves admit that Ascensionism is only a *theory*, even as they squabble endlessly concerning its validity."

I was grateful that I'd spoken to Mav about this, and grateful also for my surfather's insistence that I be permitted to attend the university. "Your pardon, Reverend, but you misunderstand at least *one* science, that of epistemology. I agree that the distinguishing characteristic of religion is faith—the blind, unquestioning belief in the unproven, the unprovable, and, if I may say so, the *dis*proven. Those assumptions of natural philosophy of which you speak are subject constantly to revision any moment there is tangible reason for so doing. Or simply, as with antilinear geometry, so that alternative assumptions may be tried and knowledge thereby increased."

"My child—"

"Ascensionism is a theory, which, in the language of philosophy, means an orderly collection of physically demonstrable relationships. You speak of it as if it were an hypothesis, an idea yet to be proven good, which it emphatically is not. No serious philosopher any longer doubts it; it is only the details of its operation that they debate."

"My child, you talk of science and foolishly criticize the illusory contradictions in the Book of Pah. Yet I know something of science, myself. Enough to appreciate that order—meaning life, particularly *lamviin* life—cannot have

91

arisen spontaneously out of chaos; this violates your own precious Laws of Thermodynamics, with which you ought to be familiar; such is possible only by the special intervention of Pah Himself."

Oh, dear, what had I started here? "It seems to me, Reverend, that if I were Pah, I'd place some value upon *not* granting dispensations. A deity ought to have enough integrity to observe the very laws which He Himself has ordained. Has it never occurred to you—it has, I believe, to the Church—that Ascensionism is an ideal means to this end? Perhaps Pah—"

"You're forgetting thermodynamics again, my child. The inevitable direction is from order to chaos. If you were to find an elegant watch and chain upon the sand, would it be more reasonable to assume—and here we stumble upon *another* of your scientific 'laws,' that of the Simplest Explanation—that it appeared there spontaneously, having arisen out of random combinations and permutations of atoms, or that some Great Watchmaker—"

"*Made* it appear there, equally spontaneously? Good Reverend, your explanation fails by far to be the simplest, and the process of Ascension is not remotely random—such mutations as occur are harshly culled and edited by the exigencies of *survival*, a set of very narrow parameters, indeed. Your 'watch' began existence as the tiniest, least-complicated jewel or shaft imaginable. Millions of years were required for each subtle change, each minuscule addition, until the shaft became a gear and gears combined to form a movement—each alteration tested by the cruel world. Why, I sometimes believe that the failure to understand and accept the *fact* of Ascensionism arises—spontaneously, if you will—from nothing more than failure (or fear) to comprehend the enormous gulf of time that separates us from our beginnings."

The Reverend wasn't yet ready to concede: "This 'mutation'—if it exists at all—is far too rare an event to account for our existence. One speaks glibly about so much time, and yet, if we are to believe your fossils, lam himself arose from baser stock in a matter of perhaps a few tens of thousands of years—far too brief for Ascension to have had anything to do with it!"

At this point I began realizing that I had wandered far from Mav's intentions. But what, for pity's sake, could I do? "Reverend, please forgive me an extremely personal question, but when was the last time that some individual hair upon your pelt decided to grow twice as long and quickly as any other? I wager that you'll find just such a 'sport' or mutation even now if you were to look closely. So much for their rarity. I admit that geological evidence confirms your view that we are a very recent species, however, my friend Mav informs me that Professor Srafen was about to publish a monograph to the effect that, once language began to develop, lamkind controlled its *own* Ascension, adding even *more* parameters than those that nature had—"

"*My child!* This is blasphemy far damper than any with which that foul demon heretic corrupted our society when rhe was alive! Unspeakable evil—yet you have spoken it! Is it possible that you are possessed by rher malignant spirit? You were present at rher blessed destruction, my poor child, and—"

"Reverend Adem, you will forgive my mentioning the fact that I am *no* child of yours or anybody else, but an adult, fully capable of uttering my *own* blasphemies." With resignation, I reached into my bag and found the billfold with my Bucketeer's insignia, which I displayed to the Reverend. "I am here upon Their Majesties' business, sir, and I have some final questions to ask—perhaps not quite as stimulating as our discussion so far, but considerably more germane."

His fur drooped suddenly, although I believe that I detected an undercurrent of cunning stirring in its depths. "My . . . rather, Missur Mymysiir, that was a cruel and unprincipled deception you practiced upon me. I've a good mind to write a letter to the—"

"Your opinions are attuned with those of my superior, who has, nonetheless, decided that such deception is outweighed by matters such as murder. If nothing else, I've learned how thoroughly you despised Professor Srafen. Can you now tell me why I should believe you did not feel justified in having rher killed?"

"Young lurrie, you presume too much! Remember to whom you are speaking."

"Quite right: to the leader of a technically illegal sect of religious deviationists."

"It is the *established Church* that deviates in its *increasing tolerance* of this and other *heresies!* Do they not comprehend the *consequences*? Why, should this *fantasy* become

93

generally accepted, it will surely form the basis for a new and *savage* ethic: bloody jaw-and-claw survival above all! Already there is talk of Societal Ascensionism, which will—"

"Your pardon, Reverend, but you have not answered my question."

"The general tendency is toward chaos! Only the blessed mercy of Pah—"

"Reverend?"

"Lamviin is unique in so many aspects; he could *never* have risen from— Do you realize that if survival of the fittest were true, *there would only be one species on Sodde Lydfe? Hahahahahahahaha!*"

"Reverend Adem! Control yourself!"

He breathed heavily for many moments and at last his fur began to settle from the spiky, tangled mess it had become. For a while he looked around in weary confusion, as if wondering how he came to be in this place. Then: "Your forgiveness, my child; I have been guilty of intemperance. Excessive zeal, even in the service of Pah, does little to further His ends. I believe that I should like to rest now, if you'll excuse me. No, don't get up—take these pamphlets if you will. They explain our position in more moderate terms than I have used."

I could not think quite what to reply to this performance—it was certainly a novel way to terminate an argument (or avoid answering questions)—but accepted the little booklets from him as he made to leave the room. He staggered a little, reminding me of Niitood.

At the door, he paused. "Whatever else you think about us, my child, remember that all we desire, in the end, is that, in Foddu's schools and in her children's schoolbooks, alongside this accursed heresy, there be a lecture or a chapter on the truth that Pah instantaneously and miraculously created the world."

The door shut softly behind him, and not many seconds later, I heard the instantaneous and miraculous whirring of a juicing box. I wondered, as I collected my bag and quitted the Shrine of Fundamental Truth, how Reverend Dr. Adem would react if science demanded, in return, a sermon from his pulpit on Ascensionism and a new chapter by Srafen in the Book of Pah.

IX: Voyage of the Dessmontevo

"Thus I fear," I told Mav on the following day in Lovely Sands, "that I did not obtain the information you desired—unless it's possible that Adem's slipped far enough around the dune to have ordered murder done."

"A distinct likelihood, from the sound of it," said Vyssu.

The detective sat with us upon the edge of Vyssu's sand carpet, munched a smoked shrimp, and thought. "My dears, from what I have observed so far from Srafen's killing, it speaks rather more articulately of cunning, perhaps even of genius, than of madness—and before either of you repeats the old canard, I was never one who reckoned that brilliance and insanity are anything alike."

Vyssu and I exchanged guilty glances, both of us having been caught in precisely the mental act Mav described.

Several lam-heights from our picnic, Mav's trine of watun, ordinarily quartered upon his mother's Upper (Most) Hedgerow estate, were idly clawing up clumps of lichen-sand and depositing them in their mouths, evidently enjoying a picnic of their own. Mav had insisted upon removing the circular tyrelike affairs from their carapaces. "Saddles," I believe, was the word he employed. In normal use, these prevented the lamviin rider from a potentially injurious proximity to the animals' strictly herbivorous but nonetheless formidable jaws, and (at least theoretically) gave one a comfortable place to perch. As I was to discover, some hours later, theory and practice suffer no little divergence when it comes to riding watuback; the unconventional postures required by the sport leave every joint in every limb screaming in agony.

Be that as it may, it was singularly bracing, at the time, to travel along atop the beast instead of behind and it was thought-provoking—I suppose that is the best expression—once the rider's straps were snugged up, to be able to employ all three sets of hands at once for something besides perambulation. How a mere two-thirds of a brain can direct three eyes and nine arms without braiding them together in a tangle dissoluble only by radical surgery is something that natural philosophy will have to look into someday.

An equally challenging question, this time for historians, is why no so-called civilized nation has ever thought of riding directly upon watun. Naturally, the practice is now widely known, if not universally exercised, thanks to the many newsscrolls, magazines, and cheap sensational novels about the colonies—we had, in fact, collected a gratifying minimum of fuzzy-pelted stares as we made our way through the northern margin of the city—yet it is peculiar in this age of electricity and steam that we owe a brilliant innovation to the savages of Einnyo.

Which musings brought me back to the present and to our conversation.

Mav was cranking up a juicing box, which Vyssu had brought with her. "Perhaps you'd both like to hear how I spent yesterday," he offered as he paused in his winding to select a slice of pickled taproot. "I began, of course, with Niitood's flat, which looked quite as though a desert whirlwind had passed through it in the night, smashing everything, including the new camera of which he had only just taken delivery, and scattering photographs, negatives, and foul picture-making fluids from kitchen to hannbox."

"Poor Niitood," Vyssu said. "Where was he at the time this tragedy took place?"

"Permit me to venture a guess," said I. "Imbibing at the Hose & Springbow? This clearly demonstrates the sort of misfortune that juicing invariably—"

"Close, but no inhaling tube," Mav interrupted. "He was at the Globe & Anchor, a little place of the sort you'd expect from its name, down in Brassie. And specifically at my request, he had been interviewing some of his acquaintances among the Navy."

You will appreciate (Mav explained) that I was hesitant about confronting Navylamn directly, at least to begin with. The story of my misspent youth still circulates among them now and then, and, although I seem to have my partisans, there are those who look askance upon a very junior officer committing mutiny, even in the noblest of causes.

The purpose of Niitood's mission was to brace certain of

96

those individuals who had attended Srafen's lecture on the fatal night, a task he undertook with an ardor that is a credit to him—unless Mymy interrupts to explain that all of them were long retired, contemporaries of the Professor, and given to frequenting such places as the Globe & Anchor, where electricity flows quite as readily as it does in Tamet's place of business.

Now Niitood's burglary, or vandalism, or whatever it may have been—and I would be foolish indeed to dismiss the virtual certainty that it was vitally connected with this case in some as yet unexplained manner—disrupted the schedule I'd intended. However, as Vyssu will recall, he and I spent several hours in conversation the next morning. I asked him to determine for me which of the officers I might address with lamly directness, and which it would be necessary to impress with my present authority—in contravention to my youthful indiscretions.

Thus, after telephoning Mymy, interviewing Niitood to obtain, as it were, my social bearings, and examining his apartments on the way, I hired a cab that took me to the Navy yards. My insignia were sufficient to gain me grudging entrance (after a brief exchange of formalities with the Navy Bucketeers) and a young rating was detached to escort me to the dockside berth of the T.M.S. *Dobotpo*.

Standing at such a place along the harbor gives one a certain perspective. Such elderly vessels as the one I was about to board rested fender to fender with their sleek modern steam-propelled daughters. There are those who maintain that, in the days of sail, the sealamn were of a different mettle. I cannot testify to that, but there is romance in the ancient, tall-masted ships, their sails rotating lazily in the breeze like the wings of some colossal bird, awaiting only the hand of an engineer who will engage the gears, permitting the screw to turn the ship out of the gulf of Dybod and into the world of danger and adventure.

Dobotpo was such a vessel, double-masted (though with her long, narrow sails furled at this moment and her radial spars naked in the sun), a trimaran of an old and distinguished class. Her guns, of course, were capped, and no one save a crew of scrubbers and broomers remained aboard.

I climbed the gangway and crossed to her high-railed central hull, pausing for a moment between a pair of masts taller even now than the loftiest building in Mathas. The channel was a clear, smooth strip of green where engineering barges had cut a swath and, even considering the vile substance that it was, somehow beautiful and evocative of a thousand exciting far-off places. In the remainder of the harbor and out into the gulf, the ever-present seagrass stood a lam-height above the surface, turning the horizon and all the ocean between it and myself scarlet. This thick growth had once plagued both Navy and commerce, slowing passage and occasionally tangling the most thoughtfully designed propellers. Too, it concealed within its reedy folds the many large and dangerous beasts that the old, less-swift vessels had no means of avoiding.

Perhaps that, alone, is why I had chosen the Air Navy. Sheer cowardice—or at least the chance of a quick, clean death in the sky.

Now, of course, our Navy finds the ubiquitous weed a blessing, and in more than one way. Our coal-fired vessels travel far too rapidly to be bothered by mere sea-monsters, and the scythes upon their downswept bows, the drying racks above, assure a goodly supply of fuel should the coal run low. So swift is their passage that freshly cut vegetation is tinder-dry in a matter of hours.

Since the invention of the air screw, those great caged fans that sit atop the sterns of modern warships and freighters, no one need fear propeller-clogging weeds, yet the profiles of our modern vessels are so low that, providing the fuel is running dry enough to minimize the smoke, a warship may lie in the deep-sea grasses many lam-heights tall, hidden from enemy observation and gunfire until the last strategic moment.

You know, I saw the T.M.S. *Homdou* herself steam by while I was there, a mighty battleship larger than North Hedgerow Station, with three magnificent and powerful propellers, one upon the stern of each iron hull, and cannon big as railroad engines? Did I say the sailing ships had romance? None to match the march of progress! But I digress.

As I say, I made my way to the central hull of the venerable *Dobotpo* and thence belowdecks to the sickbay, where I understood one Commander Zedmon Dakods *Hedgyt* dwelt in preference to Bachelor Officer's Quarters ashore. It was this Hedgyt, according to Niitood, who was particularly responsible for the Navy delegation at Srafen's lecture, for he was an old, old friend of rhers (in fact, if you will look, the first edition of *The Ascent of Lamviin* is dedicated to him) from his midshiplam-cauterist days aboard the fabled T.M.S. *Dessmontevo.*

Dessmontevo, you'll recall, was a light cruiser not unlike this *Dobotpo* ship; today, schoolchildren recognize her name from yet another volume of Srafen's writings, for it was aboard her that rhe made those first discoveries that lead to the Theory of Ascension.

I tried not to let the tubby little *Dobotpo* distort my judgment, for her sister ship and the Professor were both young together, fast and sleek by standards of the day, and well-capable of winning a world (or at least that part of it not won already) for the Empire.

Commander Hedgyt I discovered sitting in a sort of cubicular office the sickbay operating theater. "Good day, sir, I am Agot Edmoot *Mav*, of Their Majesties' Bucketeers."

The fellow gave a little start, and I realized at once I had awakened him from hann—or something like it, for an obviously well-used juicing box lay near one of his elbows.

"Bucketeers? Oh, yes, about my poor old Srafen, is it? I answered all those questions on the night rhe . . . it *happened.*"

"I realize and appreciate that, sir," said I, "but I have been placed in charge of bringing Srafen's murderer to justice, and for that I need more information than was obtained then."

The old fellow seemed at first to have some difficulty following me, but as our interview progressed, his senses made their presence steadily more manifest. I realized, when he began to tell me about himself and Srafen, how deeply stricken he was with all that had transpired.

"I was with rher, you know, aboard the old *Dessmontevo*—ah, we were wild lammies then, the living terror of TM's own Navy! Whenever we hit port, be the locals gray or red, or yellow like ourselves, first thing we'd do is find ourselves a willing shemale—professional or enthusiastic amateur—an' hit th' sand!" There followed many bawdy, yet somehow innocent and touching, reminiscences of their service together, interspersed with violent adventures and the scientific history with which we are all familiar.

"Ah, but *that* educational experience in the Kood Islands never made it into any of old Srafen's picture books, th' sanctimonious surry—*no*, I don't mean that. I don't mean it at all, for rhe was never afterward ashamed about those halcyon days, nor ever failed to hash 'em over with me when I was in port."

I asked, "So you saw Srafen now and then?"

He blinked and rippled affirmation. "Not that I had all that much time once I became a full-pelted ship's cauterist, mind you. Too many endless voyages, too many bloody wars—and undeclared unpleasantnesses, some of which the citizenry know but little of. Showin' th' flag." He mentioned several recent visits, even a minor operation he'd quietly performed upon the philosopher so as to avoid worrying rher family and friends.

"And afterward, when I was slowing down, it was Srafen . . . old Srafen . . ."—he patted the juicing box beside him—"Srafen was just getting wound up, in a manner of speaking. World famous rhe is now—and yes, I use the present tense, because rher work has guaranteed rher a sort of immortality. I'm glad of that, although I'll miss rher sorely."

"You were both student ship's cauterists together, I understand?"

"Midshiplammies—indeed we were, indeed we were. Comrades in arms—and often in th' box, as well. And what slim time I'd left to spend aboning upon medicine (for I was just that bit slower than rhe was, you understand, but who in salty dampness *wasn't* in those days—or in these?) rhe was out at every stopover, collecting rher goddamp specimens. I myself helped preserve an' catalog 'em. Great Pah in heaven, if I'd only been able to see what *rhe* saw, *I'd* be the famous philosopher now, instead of a tired old carapace-cutter. But I don't mind, really, not at all. Rhe deserved everything rhe got, and I still have a chance or two in my inventions."

"Your inventions?" Everybody fancies himself an inventor these days, but my interest was sincere, for, as I think I said, I do delight in progress.

"Indeed." He rose stiffly, shook his limbs out, and walked with steadily decreasing difficulty toward a little storage room between two massive rafters overhead and the after bulkhead of the sickbay. Inside was a veritable jungle of wires and mechanical parts. "This is my Improved Revolving Cannon—not much originality in it, but an idea that I believe is basically sound."

And so it proved, for he'd replaced the cranking lever of a common rotary machine gun with a sizable pulley and run a rubber belt from there to a small electric engine. "What rate of fire can you attain?"

He peered at me, expecting disbelief. "Around six thousand per minute, theoretically. Allowing time to replace magazines—and the occasional sheared firing pin or bollixed casing—perhaps half that."

I was indeed impressed, and told him so, adding something of my own adventures regarding such a gun. He told me his Inventors' Club—which he invited me to join—had given him encouragement.

"You know the problem, though," he said, reshrouding the weapon with canvas. He pointed toward the rafters where, to my astonishment, there hung several oil lanterns on gimbals. "The goddamp Navy hasn't even heard of electricity yet! Why, on one of those new steamers, with a dynamo driven by the engines, we could mount a dozen of these guns for the kind of close protection artillery won't provide and rifle fire can't. But here am I, a rattling hulk of a lam, stuck aboard a rattling hulk of a ship. Nor will the Admiralty answer my letters!"

I commiserated with him, understanding all too well the deliberately backward nature of Imperial institutions, whereupon he revealed to me another of his contrivances. Like the flash gun Niitood had invented, it was based upon a juicing box; only this one was connected, through an incomprehensible apparatus, to a copper coil of some kind and terminated, at the other end, in a railroad telegrapher's key and the earpiece of a telephone.

"Wireless telegraphy!" he exclaimed, and began to describe to me the operating principles, which I still do not fully understand. I did comprehend that this was his intended means of replacing the semaphore towers still employed by the Navy and of greatly increasing the range of communications in general. Someday he hoped to produce a device to transmit the lamviin voice, and he spoke dreamily of a distant future in which photographs—moving photographs such as they are experimenting with on the Continent—might be conveyed through the air as well.

Truly, my dears, this is an age of lamn-made miracles, and we are fortunate to be living at such a time when humble reporters, elderly sea doctors and, if modesty permits, even Bucketeers such as myself, may dabble about and possibly improve the conditions under which our fellow lamviin exist.

Regrettably, as with the rotary electric gun, our Admiralty disdained to show the slightest interest whatever in Hedgyt's wireless telegraphy, and between contending with such recalcitrance and Srafen's sudden death, he was himself rapidly losing interest in life.

I asked the old fellow whether he had ever married, particularly Srafen. In answer, he wound up his unmodified juicing box, for we had since returned to his small office. He offered me a jolt; I thanked him, but deferred first in his favor.

When he had taken it and once again relaxed, he said, "Rhe wouldn't have me—rather, rher family wouldn't, and, radical as rhe may have been in other things, rhe would not disobey in this—I think because a professorship awaited at the end of rher enlistment." He mused and wound the box again, forgetting that he'd offered me a turn. When the magneto stopped, he said, "Not that I blamed rher much—it's a hard row for a surrie, and was harder by a damp sight, then. Rhe got what rhe needed, and I wished rher well. We were always fast friends after an' I was glad t' help when I could."

He wound the box again and took a jolt. "Anyway, I had my career too, what thersh—*there* was of it. Goddamp Admiralty, goddamp ol' worm-eaten sandbucket *Dobotpo*, an' pretty soon—watch it, son, it sneaks up on y'—goddamp ol' *me!*" Again he took the current. "Well, here'sh to ya, Srafen, m'lost love. Y'did good, an' I did ash good ash I could, too. No regretsh, no . . . no re . . . ."

Hedgyt slid sideways off his stool in electrically induced hann. I straightened his limbs as best I could and left him there with his memories. Before I departed, though, I cranked up his juicing box and had one to the shade of the Professor, too, Pah bless rher. Rhe was a second surfather to me, the parent of my intellect, and it made me fond of Hedgyt that he had loved rher, too.

Mav assisted Vyssu and me in clearing away the remnants of our meal, and he stirred the sand blanket into the soil, but he was silent and thoughtful. Perhaps it was the setting or the conversation, but I watched Vyssu and found myself admiring little inconsequential things about her—

the graceful curve of her wrists as she collected the cactus blossoms she'd set out as a centerpiece, her deep and luminous eyes, the humorous, intelligent set of her fur.

I recall thinking that, in this modern world, which Mav loved so deeply, perhaps there was less room for class distinctions than in our fathers' time, and perhaps even our fathers had been wrong. Why, just because my ancestors had conquered her ancestors—

Then I remembered what Vyssu's occupation was, and my hearts shied like a startled watu, my mind amazed at how corruptible even a well-born Fodduan can be, distracted by a pretty carapace and glossy pelt.

Mymysiir Offe Woom, scolded a voice within me—not unlike my mother's—what *could* you have been thinking of!

X: The Field Narrows

I was surprised to learn that Srafen had kept rher home along the northern margin of South Hedgerow, a neighborhood quite comely and fashionable enough, yet hardly what one would expect, given her comparative wealth and renown. Nonetheless, it was entirely consistent with rher naval background, lying as it did just above the military suburb of Brassie, and with what Mav had told me of rher unpretentious attitude toward life.

What surprised me even more, I suppose, was that rher husband and wife, both of the scoundrels, could be found there even still. The many scandalous rumors of their separate . . . well . . . adventures, made it seem, at least to me, somehow indecent that they should not by now have made more suitable arrangements. As I was discovering rapidly in this affair, decency is rather more elastic a conception than my parents had brought me up to believe.

Upon our return from the picnic, Mav telephoned from his mother's carriage house. There was some sort of celebration in her cactus garden; music drifted slowly down the curried lawns in our direction, and he was loath to interrupt the festivities, although I should like to have met the fabled lady of Dezer. In any case, a cab arrived that carried us first to Vyssu's home, where she debarked in pursuit of whatever it was that occupied her afternoons. I must confess my estimate of her, for good or worse, was changing, and, most remarkably, by the knitting I had seen her twice now busy at.

Somehow, one never thinks of disreputable females knitting, does one?

From the Kiiden, we crossed the city again to South Hedgerow, a pleasant drive through varied localities, because, through a second electrical conversation, my friend had arranged an interview for us with Srafen's erstwhile mates.

To my regret, this seemed to be the last of an admittedly lengthy stretch of beautiful weather. The arms of Pah protect us quite well from much of what the Rommish Ocean has to offer, but they cannot defend us from the rare southern storm. Although the sun still shone brightly, there was a narrow band of purple darkness seaward that promised at least a day of the sort of dripping immobility that can paralyze a city like Mathas.

Once or twice yearly, all traffic ceases; lamviin hide themselves behind shuttered windows and sealed doors; fireplaces fill the atmosphere so full of smoke that one can scarcely see the opposite side of the street. I recalled such a storm the year before that had deluged the city with over a finger-width of vile precipitation in the short span of a week. It was a time for confined children to be cross, for elders to complain about their aching joints, for farmers and gardeners to worry that the rot might creep into their cactus or wash their lichen beds away.

However, despite the impending meteorological calamity, it was with considerable high spirits that Mav and I drew up before the residence of the late Professor, for the little penciled tickings upon his list of suspect characters were accumulating with fair rapidity, and it was the detective's fervent conviction that inevitably, sooner or later, we would run across some nervous individual in whom guilt was plainly manifest, and there would be a tidy end to it.

The Srafen holdings, as householders in this neighborhood were wont to express it, consisted of a respectable three-story house with several outbuildings set up upon a knoll several dozen lam-heights from the road. Indeed, in this region of Mathas, we were practically taking another brief countryside holiday. Beyond the ornate wrought-iron-fencing, a high, dense grove of skottii and macrostibs lay wrapped around the place, very nearly concealing the house from casual view, while neatly cultivated notoc bordered the flagging of the drive, and, where no taller growth shut out the light, decorative plots of yellow and orange algaesand lent cheerful color to the somber scarlet of the tall cactus.

Mav assisted me from the cab, paid the driver, and we stepped up onto the verandah, where a male servant bade us enter and took our outer garments. "The *master* will see you directly," he reported without particular enthusiasm, although a subtle sneer in his fur seemed directed toward either us or his employer—I was uncertain which. In any case, sneer and servant disappeared immediately, so I dismissed the question from my mind and tried to remember what I had been told of Srafen's spendthrift husband.

In this I was to be interrupted, although no one's husband *or* master greeted us. Instead, an expensive and voluminous concatenation of crepes and silks and satins in the very latest fashion and the chicest shades of mourning blue swept suddenly around and down a curving flight of marble stairs, which were the centerpiece of the entry hall, and announced itself to be Liimevi *Myssmo* Law, the grieving widow of our late Professor, and wife of that same Law whom we thought we were about to interview.

"You really must forgive dear Lawsy," she gushed, conducting us into a well-appointed parlor off the entryway. Except for narrow paths for walking between the furniture, the colored sand in this room had been set out in occult patterns, and then fixed with resins to preserve the esoteric arrangement. The unmistakable gluey smell was fresh, indicating that this refurbishment had taken place only recently. "He's simply too, too broken up at our loss to be much use to anyone. Perhaps I may be of some assistance?"

This last utterance was accompanied by a curling simper in her pelt, which made the prospect of striking her (an impulse whose intense ferocity took me quite by surprise) most tempting. For Mav's professional sake, however, as well as for the sake of my own dignity, I decided to attempt noble forbearance.

At least until some further provocation might offer itself.

"Indeed, you may, Madame Law, for we had also wished to ask of *you* certain questions concerning the murder of your surhusband. May I introduce my associate, Missur *Mymysiir* Offe Woom, and I see that your butler has placed my card upon your table."

She passed a hand over Mav's card, withdrew it as if it were some small poisonous animal, then made to pick it up again. "Do please be seated, and I'll ring for kood. You are, then, Agot Edmoot *Mav* of Their Majesties' Bucketeers? How very peculiar: I am certain I have heard your name before, sir."

"Then I am flattered." He took a cushion close beside her, while I felt well content with something considerably more distant. "I was a student of Srafen's, as well as rher great admirer. I understand that you, too, were a student of rhers."

The faintest shiver of—what, embarrassment?—crept across her highly decorated carapace before it was drowned savagely in what seemed to be a habitually honeyed expression. "Why, so I was, sir, and a little later on, came to assist poor, dear Srafen in rher laboratory, cataloging every sort of disagreeable and nasty crawly thing in vile, odiferous liquids—and all of them with such long, confusing names. It was there, at the University, we both met Lawsy, who offered to help out with the air pumps and other mechanical contraptions, and a year after that, we were married."

At last she rang for kood, which gratified me, for it promised to dispel the odor of the setting resin rising in almost visible miasma from the carpet. There were upward of half a hundred pointed questions I should like to have followed her last statement with, chiefly why, in the name of everything dry and holy, had Srafen ever even *spoken* to this babbling cretin. But this was Mav's investigation, so with reluctance, I kept my peace.

He said, "I see, madame. Then, all in all, for how long were you acquainted with Professor Srafen?"

"Why, what a peculiar question to ask of a widow." She toyed with the bows and ruffles of her mourning weeds. "Now let me think . . . I suppose, from the first lecture of rhers I attended, some eight or nine years in all. Why ever do you ask such a thing?" Again the revolting curl swept through her fur.

To which Mav rippled polite reassurance. I attempted to compose myself in a similar attitude, despite the strongest of temptations to the contrary. "I apologize, dear lady, if my questioning disturbs you in any way. May I call you Myssmo? Perhaps it won't seem quite so cold and formal then. Very well, my purpose is to attempt to discover whatever person or persons wished to have Professor Srafen out of the way. As that was to be the subject of my next question, would you kindly consider that I have already asked it?"

Errgh! *How* could he be so . . . *civil* with this foul creature? She paused for what seemed to me an unduly long time—in the light of my developing opinion that she did not have that many thoughts to sort through. Perhaps she had simply forgotten Mav's question.

"Why, for the life of me, I cannot think of anyone at all who might wish to injure the poor funny old dear. Srafen was so kindly, absent-minded, and affectionately thought of by, well, just *everyone*. I am quite mystified, to tell the truth."

Yet not precisely wracked with grief, I thought, and, glancing around at her opulent surroundings, I could well understand why. Everywhere, the elegance of what must be presumed to have been Srafen's simple tastes was pasted over with a veneer of cheap—but expensive—artificial gaudiness. From the ceiling hung a cunning furry representation of the Martyred Trine, and everywhere, a thousand little balls of fringe and velvet ropes.

How I positively *itched* to put a few "little surry questions" of my own!

A surmale domestic, rustling in stiff, apparently newly purchased livery, brought the kood in an elaborate service.

"You know," persisted Mav, "of no person, no enemy, who might have desired ill for Srafen?" He asked her, also, whether she might object if he prepared his pipe—a courtesy he had never shown to me. A miniature flurry of calculated indignation and concern skimmed across the surface of her pelt.

"Why, Mav, if I may presume to call you that, I am surprised! Do you not find the unnatural effluvium of such a habit disturbing to your psychic aura? Extrasensory perception is such a delicate, fragile—"

"I humbly beg your pardon, madame," he replied, *and actually put his pipe away!* Perhaps the thousandfold effluvia from the carpet had affected his delicate and fragile sensibilities. "It is my understanding that you were actually present the evening of the murder, is that not so?"

He was answered by a dramatic shudder. "Why, yes. It was such a *terrible* thing, wasn't it? The awful sight, the noise . . ."

Which might have sounded precisely to her, I thought, like the ringing of a merchant's register. I wondered if anyone intended ever to light the kood when it occurred to me that, if someone did, the room positively swimming in fumes, we might witness yet another explosion, this time from its interior.

"Indeed," replied Mav. "And did you not see the religious demonstrators in the street that night? Do you not think it possible that they might hold some deadly animosity toward your surhusband?"

"Oh, dear! I'd quite forgotten them. Such ungentlelamly riffraff they were, at that! If *only* poor, dear Srafen had listened to me. Do you *really* think that they—"

"That is what Missur Mymy and I are endeavoring to ascertain. What do you mean, if only Srafen had listened to you?" Was that an irritated quivering I saw about his nostrils, or merely my increasingly unreliable vision?

She tilted her carapace forward a trifle in what she must have imagined was a dramatically conspiratorial gesture. "Well, you see, I'd had rher trilune cast just the day before—by sheerest of coincidence, you understand—and you simply won't believe the *ghastly* warning revealed in the equations! Why, it cautioned rher plainly to avoid certain business dealings for the rest of the week and that a conflict was in the offing that might lead to personal inconvenience! Isn't that just *too* uncanny? And that *very* evening—"

"Pardon me, did you convey this . . . information to Srafen?"

"Why certainly I did, and do you know what rhe told me?"

There was a long pause. "I can well imagine; Srafen's views on that sort of . . . thing were quite familiar to me. Let me ask you—"

"You know, I've just had the most perfectly *marvelous* idea! Why don't we all ask the estimable Dr. Ensda, a very great lam and my own personal spiritual adviser—I am sure that you have heard of him—to cast a trilune for your investigation? We would need to know the moment it began, of course; I'm sure that he could tell us straightaway whether you will meet with success, and . . ."—here, her carapace tilted even farther, her voice becoming so low that I could scarcely hear it—"and perhaps he might even ferret out the culprit! Well, what do you think of that?"

I concede that it is remotely possible that Mav was taken speechless out of admiration for Myssmo's suggestion. On the other hand, he may have simply been deep in thought, considering it. On the third hand, like myself, he may have been busy framing the reply that it truly merited. At length, he spoke again: "My dear lady, that is certainly an idea. And I will put it, allowing credit where it is due, to

109

the good doctor myself, for this afternoon I intend to call upon him, directly we are finished here.

"As to the precise moment my investigation began, you yourself were there at the instant Srfaen died—I'll not be satisfied until rher murderer lies flattened to a finger-width between a pair of granite blocks!"

At this pronouncement, the tilt of Myssmo's carapace threatened to become an avalanche as she began to swoon.

"Your pardon, madame," Mav interjected quickly. "I see I have upset you. Perhaps it would be better now if we were to take our leave. May I use your telephone to call a cab?"

Somehow, she recovered. "But you have not yet enjoyed your kood, good Investigator. Why not allow me to light the wick now, and I will have your telephoning done. Will that be agreeable?"

Once again, I wished that I had been consulted. She set a match to the wick and then traipsed off toward the hall, mincing between the garish and barbaric patterns in the carpet. The door swung partly shut behind her, and Mav placed a finger before a nostril to silence me (as if, all afternoon, it had really been necessary!), caution written large upon his pelt. Then, signing me to follow, he tip-fingered across the room in the direction Myssmo had gone. The door, as I have said, was still ajar, and we both peeked into the hall, where Myssmo herself held the telephone in her hand.

It was impossible, of course, to make out what she was saying, for the hall was large and properly carpeted. Moreover, she was not precisely shouting into the instrument. She held the speaking orifice close upon her nostril, her pelt aroused in what I believe was sincere anxiety, and glanced wildly about the place as if pursued by some gigantic predator.

She momentarily returned the telephone to its little table, attempting to compose herself, then picked it up again, addressing someone on the line in relatively normal tones. When she set the instrument once more upon its stand, both Mav and I hastily returned to our original positions, my companion remaining standing, which I took as a cue to collect my bag.

"Your transportation's on its way, good Bucketeers," she warbled cheerily as she entered the room again. "I really wish you would be seated until it arrives; perhaps you

110

would be interested to hear about that most *amazing* incident that happened at a séance I attended just the other evening."

Mav's pelt was courteously arranged. "I do beg your pardon, Myssmo, and thank you sincerely for the hospitality you have shown us. But I must have some words with my associate, and we are both in need of fresh air"—here, he rippled his pelt at me on a side Myssmo could not see, a talent I must someday attempt to cultivate for myself—"having been cooped up in our offices all this morning." He indicated the gathering gloom outside her windows. "I am afraid our time for fresh air is growing short, for there are, as you see, definite indications of rain upon the horizon."

To the polite prevarication on Mav's part concerning our morning's activities, I manifested sober affirmation, desiring nothing more dearly at the moment than to quit this polluted chamber. Mav thanked her once again for the kood and conversation and suggested, once our belongings had been returned to us, that we might see our own way out.

In all, this final separation took rather longer than I might have wished, it being necessary to excuse ourselves from several invitations to various séances, entrail-readings, and the casting of our own trilunes. By the time we managed to reach the porch, our cab could be seen beginning its ascent around the long, circular drive.

For the moment, we were alone.

"Mymy," Mav inquired, a cast of puzzlement in his fur, "may I ask why you did not assist me more in interrogating Myssmo? Merciful Pah, I could certainly have used your—"

I had taken sufficient breath for an appropriately indignant reply, when—

BAMM! There was the sound of a pistol shot to our left. The cabman's watu shied and reared, threatening to overturn the vehicle. Mav swiftly drew his reciprocator. I felt about my person for bullet holes. Discovering none. I extended the search into my bag for my little pistol and, feeling quite foolish and melodramatic, followed Mav around the corner of the building.

There, toward the back along a gravel pathway, lay a line of watu stalls not dissimilar to those in which Mav quartered his own riding animals, but evincing relatively recent disuse. Before the nearest of them, a tallish, thin,

aristocratic fellow incongruously attired in soiled work clothing was heaping sand in desperate haste into some complicated wheeled mechanism from which there issued a
considerable volume of black smoke.

Mav holstered his pistol. "Mymy, do be good enough to
go and ask the cab to wait for us. Here's a nickel
crown, which ought to hold him."

Indeed, and it would hold me, too, had it not been for
the clouds gathering overhead. I followed his instructions,
however, hoping that the fellow would not blame us for the
explosion, and returned to my companion's side in time to
hear introductions being made.

"Oh, I say, so *you* are Captain Mav!" The card in the
stranger's hand now bore a greasy fingerprint. "Srafen
spoke quite often and affectionately of you, sir. I am Tobymme Toodhagomm *Law*. Splendid making your acquaintance at last, old lam!" He extended a blackened
hand, took it back and wiped it with an equally unsightly
cloth, and offered it again.

"How do you do, sir," said Mav, "and this is my associate,
Missur Mymy. Mymy, this is Srafen's husband. Is that
some sort of new steam carriage there that you are working
on?"

I'd seen a thousand of Law's sort while growing up,
usually where the idle rich gathered to pop about in little
chariots pursuing a leather ball with mallets. It was one of
my principal motivations for desiring a useful occupation.

"Not precisely," young Law replied, "although it is what
I began with. This is an invention of mine, an idea I had
one afternoon while shooting shrimp out in the Neth upon
a friend's estate. You see, he had this splendid new Continental reciprocating shotgun—about three-bore if I recall
aright—and it occurred to me that one might alter an engine to the same principle that operates the action of such a
gun, employing the same combustible substance both as
fuel *and* the expansion medium that turns the rotor, instead
of burning something to heat water to produce steam."

For the second time that day, I believe I witnessed Mav
rendered quite speechless. "A *capital* idea, Law, a capital
idea!" He drew his weapon again, displaying it to the
young inventor—although I noticed that he stopped short
of offering to let the fellow handle it. "But tell me, has it
not occurred to you that modifying a conventional three-

lobed rotary steam engine is less efficient than following the natural design of the gun?"

Law manifested perplexity.

Mav scraped away the sand that had been thrown into the motor. "Look here, instead of this trochoidal rotor, imagine, if you will, a sort of captive bullet, unable to escape the barrel and attached to a cranking shaft that would drive the wheels. A reciprocating engine, now wouldn't that be something? Whatever would one use for fuel, I wonder."

Law pointed toward a clump of abandoned apparatus leaning against the shed. "I started off with gunpowder, right enough. See, there are the hoppers and metering devices that proved both hopelessly complex and rather dangerous. Fellows at the Club—you ought to join, don't you know?—talked me out of it, eventually. Soon afterward, I hit upon ordinary inhaling fluid, such as you're using in your pipe, there."

I *thought* I'd recognize the noisome scent, and tapped several walking fingers upon the pathway. "It seems to me a rather unhealthy sort of invention. Can you imagine a cityful of these devices filling everybody's air with smoke and unburned vapors? I believe that I prefer Vyssu's steam carriage!"

Mav's rear eye brightened. "Oh, *there* you are, Mymy! Where have you been all this time?" He made considerable show of walking around Law's mechanical contrivance and poking into the discarded powder mechanism. "Ingenious! I have been asking Law, here, a number of questions about his—what do you call it, sir?"

"An internal conflagration engine," he replied, fuzzy with pride.

"And a splendid turn of phrase it is, at that! I will follow its development with great interest, and it pains me that we must now depart. I shall give due consideration to joining your Inventors' Club. Our cabman will be desirous of his due, and it appears that we are in for it, weatherwise. I shall return, old fellow, rely upon it. I'm absolutely *dying* to see your engine running!"

He took my arm and hastened toward the cab.

"My dear Inquirer, have you lost your senses? Humoring that terrible female, tinkering with that disgusting piece of machinery, and apparently forgetting that our cab is already—"

He crinkled with wry amusement. "Mymy, I quite agree with you, any civilization that would adopt such a device in preference to—shall we call it *ex*ternal conflagration?—would have to be quite insane. Nor have I altogether taken leave of my wits. I simply believe that something most important has just transpired, and I'm uncertain what to do about it."

"If one may ask?"

"Indeed one may, my dear. When I was in the Air Navy, I knew an elderly rating who chanced to place his hand between a pair of guy wires as the envelope was being inflated. They tightened, and I'm afraid the appendage was sheared away completely."

I stopped a dozen paces from the cab. "Agot Edmoot *Mav*, what *does* this have to do with . . . with anything under Pah's increasingly forboding heavens?"

"Well you see, the old fellow's enlistment was nearly up, and under some peculiarly cruel quirk of naval law, his disfigurement—and he was of an age that precluded vigorous regeneration—would get him cashiered early and render him a helpless mendicant for the remainder of his life. He begged me not to report the accident, and I did more than that: I helped him to conceal his wound. He bore it with admirable courage for another six months, retiring with a modest but entirely honorable income."

"Pray answer my question directly, Mav, before I find a use for this little pistol in my bag!"

"Mymy, perhaps the wisest thing is to return to the Precinct and draw up a warrant for an arrest. You'll recall the discarapaced hand that you also carry in your bag?"

"Not so! It is now in my surfather's office, packed in ice!"

He assisted me into the cab. "As may be. In any event, had you been more observant—and less impatient to be home before your fireplace, I wager—you'd have seen that our new friend Law wears an empty walking glove upon his *presently* hindmost right walking hand, precisely as my old sailor was forced to do. And, in a manner of speaking, I believe that you're the one who put it there!"

As we left the late Professor's gate, there was a flash and growl of thunder and the rain began to fall.

XI: On Commoner's Bridge

Naturally enough, it was the rain that decided our next steps. It proved a heavy fall, indeed; an actually discernible sheen of moisture glistened upon the roadway as our driver, suddenly unheeding of his commission, turned the vehicle and raced for one of those shelters Their Majesties are pleased to provide at intervals across the city, wishing for his watu and himself that warmth and dryness that we, in his presumption, would desire no less dearly than he. Thus we slowed somewhere upon the northern edge of the central business district to roll beneath the broad and lofty eaves of a vaguely barnlike structure that, in ordinary moments, housed a daily penny market of stalls and handcarts.

Characteristically, however, my companion had very different ideas. As our conveyance nudged its way into a narrow space among a dozen others, hired and private, amidst the clutter of perhaps a hundred highly disgruntled pushwaggon entrepreneurs, Mav drew his reciprocator, rapping with its pereskine handle upon the ceiling of the carriage. In the dampness, it made a dull, disheartened sort of noise.

"I say there, good fellow!" Mav rapped again, more vigorously. "Driver, can you hear me?"

A small three-cornered trap slid sideways, one furrimmed and unhappy eye manifesting itself in the resulting aperture. "Here now, yer Excellency, kindly do not distract me, for, as you can see, I've got me an Emergency Condition I'm contendin' with, here." The reek of inexpensive inhaling fluid demonstrated the extent of his contentions, yet the capitals in his expression were most carefully placed and well advised, a small official placard being attached in plain sight to the inner wall of the carriage stating regulations that, in times of such Emergency Conditions, allowed cabdrivers to delay or discharge passengers in such manner as "safety and convenience" (the driver's) dictated.

And without the unpleasant formality of remuneration.

Mav extracted his own inhaling pipe and saw to its preparation, all the while holding fast the gaze of our driver, yet never uttering a word.

"Something else I can do fer you?" the brazen fellow finally inquired.

"Quite so, my good fellow, though you may wish to debate it upon first hearing." He took a lengthy draught upon his pipe with a certain air of indifferent amusement at the driver's insolence.

"Meanin' what, if one may ask?" Greed and intransigence began to struggle in the fellow's pelt.

"Meaning that, should you agree to waive the privilege of this regulation"—here Mav indicated the placard—"and return once more to the street—*hear me out, I say!*—I will personally see that you are quickly warm and dry again, your animal rubbed down, both of you given a hot meal . . . and sufficient wherewithal to let the pair of you make holiday of the rest of the week." Here, at last, Mav permitted the gleam of silver to escape from between his fingers; it seemed, judging by the cablam's expression, considerably to lighten the gloom of that worthy's day.

Mav gave the street address of his mother's estate.

Abruptly the little door slid shut, and in a moment, the shelter appeared to wheel about, nearly spilling us both between the seats. The scent of rain entered our consciousness afresh and the watu ran as swift and straight a course as is possible anywhere in the city, directly to Upper (Most) Hedgerow.

My companion's mother's home was similar to that of Srafen, a large house with an indeterminate number of outbuildings, immaculate and orderly, surrounded by spacious, well-kept grounds; some foreign touch or accent, difficult to point to in any one particular, lent a sense of unity and style the place might otherwise have lacked. Mav's mother met us in the watu barn, alerted via telephone by a retainer at the gatehouse, and, at her son's urgings, ordered that the cablam and his beast be seen to. She requested, as well, a meal for us, and stood before her son and me quite resolutely until she was satisfied that we both had the most earnest of intentions of putting a proper finish to what she had provided.

In that respect, I think, all mothers are alike.

But a word or two about this gentle and intelligent creature, Ynyn *Sathemoa* Mav, mother of my friend, wife to both a soldier and, well, perhaps a poet, exile from her homeland by loving choice: Sathe, as she insisted that I call her (and, indeed, that is precisely how her servants addressed her as well), must surely in her youth have been a beauty of rare and exotic quality. Rather smaller than any Fodduan female, she was neither precious in her bearing, as many tiny females are, nor coy; her pelt was full despite her age and of a toasted-auburn color, darker than that of our race, though lighter by far than those bigotry-inspired caricatures of her countrylamn that frequently appear in Mathas's meaner publications. Her aristocratic carriage might have made the noblest Fodduan seem a clumsy peasant by comparison.

This comeliness had gracefully transformed itself over the years into a sort of cordial dignity, causing everyone with whom she came in contact, be he humble cabdriver or surdaughter of good family, to feel somehow elevated. Even here, amidst the muck and dampness of the animal shed, she seemed to illuminate the room in a strange and wondrous manner. Each of us felt warmer and more secure for her mere (if that word is appropriate) presence.

When we had eaten our rough meal, Mav disappeared for some moments into a remote corner of the building, returning shortly with a huge bundle of an odd fabric in his arms. "Well, here we have it, Mymy, the reason I insisted upon coming here, rain and all: *my* latest invention, and never one more dearly wanted!"

"Whatever are you speaking of, my dear Inquirer, I see nothing here but lam-heights of most uncomfortable-looking yard goods. What sort of invention is that?"

Mav turned to his mother, ignoring my question. "Here is one for you, my dear, that you may return to the house undampened. Take care with it, for there are as yet only a dozen like it in existence. I had meant to speak with Tis concerning their adoption by the Bucketeers, particularly in connection with the new liquid method for extinguishing fires. But this accursed murder took place shortly after I had them made up for demonstration, and—"

"Mav!" I interrupted impatiently. A ripple of amused

exasperation was briefly visible in Sathe's fur. "Will you *please* tell me what it is that you are talking about?"

His own fur, freshly dried, crinkled with delight. "Kindly do not speak so to your elders, Mymy, particularly to those rare and brilliant innovators among them. What you see before you now is the latest marvel of a marvelous age—the weatherproof cloak! As you are no doubt aware, the sap of certain cactuses may be distilled into a substance useful in making sealants for bottles, and—"

"As well as eradicating mistakes in penmanship, if I recall aright. What has that to do with—"

"Interrupting again! This same substance may be pressed into a flat sheet and bonded through the use of moderate heat into any ordinary clothing material. In that state, it becomes quite damp-proof and enables the wearer to negotiate in every sort of weather imaginable. Truly, I have found myself thinking lately that a *completely* sealed garment—and some supply of air—might allow a sailor to walk about beneath the water, such as might be necessary to repair the bottom of a ship or to retrieve some object that has been lost over the side."

"Mav, you irrepressible dreamer! Who could possibly imagine wanting to do such a fantastic—" I stopped here, for I realized at once how much I was beginning to sound like Tis.

Mav, too, hesitated, an almost diffident element suddenly present in his countenance. "Well, I, for one, perhaps. Ahum! In the meanwhile, with your kindly cooperation, dear Mymy, let us demonstrate for my mother how this garment is to be donned and worn. That's it, align the eyeholes so that you can see. . . . Now, if you'll permit me, we will fasten these ties about your upper . . . well, perhaps you had better do that for yourself."

Sathe watched these proceedings with amused interest, then began to follow Mav's directions. The cablam, at this point, looked up from his third helping of roast burrower. "I see, guv'nor! Why, I could take my rig 'most anywhere, anytime I wanted—an' beat out all the rest of th' boys doin' it! How much of this here silver will you want for one of them cloaks?"

"For a fellow of your daring and insight?" Mav's fur was positively kinky with delighted pride. "My compliments, and kindly take this one! Hmmm . . . I wonder whether there isn't any surplus fabric left upon that back shelf." Abruptly, he wandered off again, leaving me standing there to feel ridiculously like a nomad's tent. Sathe crinkled a silent farewell and left the stable.

On another hand, with the fastenings done up (a task I believe would properly have required the assistance of at least three dressers), I began to see how my friend's invention might actually be of some utility—on the one or two occasions each year when it rained. I wondered why this thought had not occurred to the driver as well, and then remembered that he was a male, and, like all such, enamored of gadgetry, anywhere, anytime, utterly without regard as to its practicality.

When Mav at last returned, it was with a bolt of his waterproofed fabric, a set of very large shears, and some odd hand tool, which he promptly informed us was intended for setting "grommets," whatever they may have been. He draped the cloth along the ground beside the cablam's resting watu, made a few quick, sliding cuts that might have done credit to the city's finest tailor, and began folding and fastening the fabric into an odd shape.

"Now, my good fellow, if you will kindly hold your animal, I believe that I can offer him the same protection that you will enjoy henceforward in inclement weather. Mind the jaws! Hold him—that's it!"

Together, with much shying and prancing on the part of the beast, they draped the frightened creature in the folds of the material, and Mav riveted tie strings in appropriate places so that the newly fashioned garment, substantially the same as ours, though more voluminous, would not work its way off as the animal moved about. Allowances had been made for the odd, essentially four-cornered configuration of the watu, and soon it was resigned to wearing the cloak, and in fact settled back to picking up its fodder with a claw and stuffing it through a slitted aperture that Mav had thoughtfully provided.

"Capital!" exclaimed my companion. "Please let me know of any difficulties you may encounter so that, in future, I may make corrections. Our new means of fighting fires frightens and endangers the Department's animals quite as thoroughly as it does our gallant Bucketeers. Which reminds me . . ."

He walked across the stable toward a wooden box affixed to one of the roof pillars. Inside, there was revealed a telephone, which instrument he activated, requesting of the operator a number I knew all too well.

"Vyssu? I trust that I am doing you no inconvenience, for I have quite an extraordinary favor to ask. Why, yes, I am quite well . . . yes, and so is Mymy, who is with me as we speak—Vyssu says hullo, Mymy. Why, yes, of course, Mymy says hullo."

I had not.

"Uh, Vyssu, about the favor. Could you send round your steam carriage immediately? It is most impor—what? Of course I know that it is raining. That is why I've called you, for I remember that your carriage is quite weatherproof, and— Of course I am, would I have called you unless . . . Thank you, then, my dear, I'm at my mother's digs in Uppermost, the watu barn, if you'll believe it of me. I'll have a small gift for you and a large gratuity for Fatpa—as well as a substantial jolt or two should he require it after so harrowing an experience as driving in the rain. After all, the poor dear was only a timid highwaylam of old, and—Oh, very well, then, the same to you, and thanks."

"Mav?" I asked, my voice sounding odd beneath the stifling cloak. "Surely you do not intend to— Merciful Trine, I see that you do! And me, too, I suppose? Ah, well, it was not to be hoped otherwise. That's what these raincloaks are for, aren't they?"

He stood watching me with some amusement. "Dear Mymy, we have our work, and a little moisture mustn't be permitted to deter a Bucketeer, must it?"

"Why ever not?" I countered, but I knew, in vain.

The establishment of Doctor Zanyw N'botpemy *Ensda* was situated in a suitably disreputable portion of the city, surrounded by such others as dispense herbs, good luck tokens, and a thousand other varieties of bad advice that operated in direct competition with that which the good doctor himself administered.

His "offices," which bore the look of having once been a greengrocer's, fronted upon a grimy street; two large and rather untidy triangular glass windows (one of them long broken and desultorily repaired with sticking tape) were painted nearly opaque with symbols such as might impress a gullible and superstitious lower-class clientele. The door was firmly bolted and the place unlit from within.

Mav, muffled absurdly in his own invention, stepped from the carriage, insisting, as he did, that I accompany him. Despite my own raincloak, I was regretting that I hadn't worn a sturdier half-dozen walking gloves. Vyssu—for yes, that is who had driven her machine to his mother's place, no doubt leaving her bandit friend before a toasty blaze at home—stayed warm and dry within the machine.

"Curious," the investigator observed, more to himself than to me, "this should be about the time when Ensda begins his day's work; his sort always operates best in the twilight. Still, there is this rain, and— Hallo, what's this?" He rattled at the bolt upon the door, held there by a sturdy padlock that, for the record, I will state was brightly finished and of recent manufacture. "This ancient, worn-out thing seems nearly to have rusted away in the rain, doesn't it?"

"Mav, what are you doing? Do you realize that you are committing a burg—"

SNAP! The hasp twisted off from the door, assisted in no small part by the manner in which Mav had inserted one of his accursed springbow bolts and levered it away.

"—lary? What you are doing is illegal and immoral, insupportable conduct for a Bucket—"

"Do be quiet a moment, Mymy, and kindly wait here for me in case someone comes. I do not believe it will be the good doctor, in any case. Keep your insignia at hand on the chance it is one of our own, will you?" With these words he stepped through the door he'd forced and disappeared into the gloomy interior.

How had I come to this in so short a time? From the bosom of a highly respected and well-bred family, to common breaking and entering? Or at least to being the lookout for a breaker and enterer. So much for Service to Crown and Country: it seems to have some subtle corrupting influence, no matter how earnestly one strives to the contrary.

A wisp of vagrant steam drifted up from Vyssu's carriage. She, too, was acting in the prototypically criminal fashion, instinctively keeping the motor operating were a rapid departure suddenly called for.

Or perhaps the corrupting influence was hers.

In any event, I stood cold and shivering in the driving

mist, quite unaware of what I should do if we were all discovered. Suddenly, there was a sound behind me—I whirled, and . . .

"Mav! You have frightened me out of nine years' growth! Back from your criminal career already?"

He held in his hand a newspaper roll turned back to display an item prominently circled in wax pencil among the steamship schedules. "I was correct, Mymy! That initial telephone call Myssmo placed was routed to this very office! It would appear, my dear paracauterist, that the good doctor has taken it on the—"

"*Mav!*" I jumped again, for suddenly beside me, a small child, soaking damp, had come upon me quite unseen. These raincloaks had a way of limiting peripheral vision. "Why, little lammie, you're all wet!" I said. "Do come inside where it is warmer!"

"An' get braided by th' Bucks fer B&E? Not on yer soggy life, Missur!"

I blinked. Despite rher unkempt appearance, not mentioning the roughness of rher language, the little child was all but irresistible. True, perhaps those miniature surmale features, which all children bear, would someday acquire a masculine or feminine cast. Yet perhaps they would mature as they were set now, and the child would, as I had, remain (outwardly, and, I am chagrined to say, in social treatment) infantile. This would be a very different civilization indeed, did babies but resemble males or females.

"Child," Mav said at once, displaying a coin, "how long have you been standing there in that doorway?" He indicated the entrance to a neighboring establishment, a dealer in vague warnings based upon the shape that kood-smoke assumed.

"Since it begun t'rain, guv. No place else t'go."

"Very good, child, now tell me, did you see Doctor Ensda leave this place a while ago?"

"What, that old faker? What you want with him? I can give you better advice, and"—the child acquired an ugly, venal expression in rher dampened fur—"lots cheaper."

"I've no doubt of that, none at all," Mav replied. "Will you answer my question?"

"What's in it fer me if I do?" Rhe knew, of course, for rher eyes never once left the silver gleam in my companion's outstretched hand.

"A considerable amount," he said evenly.

"Yeah, I saw him leave, hardly a minute before the three of you drove up. Look fer yerself—the pavement's almost dry beneath that steam thingy of yours; that's where his cab was waitin'. Now gimme!"

Mav held the coin back. "Not quite yet, little missur. That's quite a story—and it never occurred to me to examine the condition of the street; I must make a note of that for future application. But we must inquire first into your veracity—*for there are no cabs in this rain!*"

"There are if they get here before the rain starts," retorted the child, "an' they go where you want if you hold a pistol to the driver's head! Now gimme!"

Calmly, Mav not only gave the money to the child, but doubled it. "Go find someplace to get warm and dry." He showed me the newspaper again. The circled item was the planned departure of the freighter *Habo*, and, unlike the city's land-bound traffic, it would not be delayed so much as a second by the weather; it would steam off almost precisely an hour and a third from now.

Mav leaped into the carriage, dragging me after him. "Ensda would appear to be our lam!" cried he, "and could only have gone by way of Commoner's Bridge from here! Let us be off before we lose him!"

Vyssu wheeled away before either of us was quite properly settled. The rain garments dripped and steamed, their bulk making the compartment seem quite close and confining. I was thrown solidly against my friend, who gently aided me in regaining my seat, and we were both rather silent for a long while.

Vyssu, visible through a window that connected her portion of the car with this, displayed great amusement. She had disdained use of the raincloak Mav had offered; it lay dry and neatly folded on the cushion beside her. Her hands seemed preternaturally calm and competent upon the steering tiller, just as they had while knitting or preparing food. I began to wonder whether there is truly anything in this world males claim as their exclusive jurisdiction that can not be accomplished more skillfully (and with less fanfare) by one of the other sexes.

For his part, Mav seemed perfectly content to permit a female to do the driving; I must confess that no few of the corners Vyssu negotiated may have cost me some measurable fraction of my normal life expectancy. We raced through the town in the direction of the river and the port beyond, expecting at any time to overtake the only other moving vehicle on the streets, and thus a fleeing murder suspect. Along the way, we passed many a cab and private conveyance parked beside the road or beneath some sheltering construction.

At last we came to Commoner's Bridge.

"Stop here!" cried Mav to Vyssu. "Surely he could not have come this far with both a recalcitrant driver and a damp and frightened animal! I believe that we have overhauled him—and that we may yet apprehend him here!"

The madness (I thought at the time) of this assertion was soon to be more than matched by Mav's next proposal. At his instruction, a reluctant Vyssu directed her machine to the far end of the bridge.

It is necessary, here, to describe the Commoner's Bridge on which we stood, for it has long since been replaced by a larger and, I think, a somewhat more sensible thoroughfare, firmly rooted at both ends as well as in its middle span. In those days, it was deemed unseemly that the pilings of the bridge should touch upon the island it crossed. King's Island, site of the royal palace (and of the Sound Point Bucketeer station, as well), was to be reached directly by the Royal Bridge, which stretched across the west branch of the River Dybod somewhat further downstream from King's Hall, on the western shore.

For some reason, Commoner's Bridge was placed across the northern tip of the island at what is called Sound Point, but, being *Commoner's* Bridge, was not permitted to encroach upon the island itself. Thus there was a single clear and marvelous span across both river and island, a veritable marvel of engineering, which had been accomplished at great expense and effort for no reasonable purpose. Altogether, I suppose, there was a drop of eighteen or twenty lam-heights from the bridge to the island, and perhaps another nine or ten to the river on either side of the point.

It was at the eastern extremity of the bridge that Mav insisted we park the carriage, in such a manner that, with one quick sweep of the tiller, Vyssu could turn the car and block the narrow roadway so that no vehicle (and scarcely a lam on fingertip) could pass.

He left us there, admonishing us to be watchful, and walked back nearly to the center of the bridge, just above the eastern margin of the island. There, swathed and en-

cumbered by his raincloak, the break in rhythm of his
walking clearly visible, owing to his old colonial injury and
the rain, he stood looking at the iron bracing on both sides
of the bridge and above, then clambered up upon the railing, grasped a pair of crossing stanchions, and began to
climb until he reached the over-roofing cables and beams,
perhaps three lam-heights above the roadway.

With some further difficulty, he negotiated the brace-
works until he hung directly over the center of the road,
and there, with patience and with what seemed to me to be
insane confidence in his theory that we'd passed Doctor
Ensda, he waited in the pouring mist, one hand beneath his
cloak and no doubt resting on the handle of his reciprocator.

I waited, too, until I could bear it no longer. Vyssu
glanced at me, without a word, but with a quizzical look in
her fur, then reached through the driver's window and
tugged at the little tassel I had sprung upon my first
occasion riding in this contraption. She removed the treewood juicing box, whose key was permanently affixed, and
gave it several cranks, then set it firmly before me.

"Thank you, Vyssu, I do not indulge."

"Nor, my dear Mymy, do I—nor do I ordinarily sit in
this car in the rain waiting for the best friend I have to
leap to his death from the top of a bridge. Now put your
fingers in the apertures and pull the catch, for I am in
need of a jolt myself, and soon!"

I looked sharply at her, then at the box. Slowly, with
reluctance and trepidation, I set a finger from each outer
hand into the place provided for it. Not knowing what to
expect, I took a deep breath, held it, and, with my middle
hand, threw the catch.

!!!!!

Someone once said that striking yourself repeatedly
with a hammer has one beneficial consequence: it feels so
good when you stop. That, in a prawnshell, sums up juicing. I will admit that it relaxed me. I will also admit that,
when Vyssu had taken hers, I permitted myself one final
lapse.

Then turned again and watched my friend upon the cables and braces of the bridge.

For bearing down upon us, traveling as fast as it could
go, was a galloping watu with a taxi swaying in its wake.

XII: A Study in Emerald

As the animal and vehicle passed like a flash beneath him, Mav leaped from the cross braces. What further transpired at that instant I can only guess, for Vyssu swung the tiller hard, treading upon the steam valve. I was dashed to the floor once again; before I could regain my seat and the view from my window, the cab was nearly upon us, two struggling figures upon the roof locked in combat as the fear-crazed watu rolled its eyes and galloped onward. Despite myself I shrank back, for I could see the beast had gone quite mad. The lamn atop the cab thrashed at each other as if unconscious of the disaster about to overtake us all.

Suddenly, upon the very brink of collision with Vyssu's steaming engine, the taxi swerved and smashed against the railing. Screaming beast and vehicle pitched over, teetered. Mav and Ensda, cab and watu disappeared into the mist. I heard something huge and awful strike the water below. A yawning hideous gap was left in the rail behind them. I do not remember leaping from Vyssu's carriage; all I know is that in a trice I was balanced on the very edge of the roadway, Vyssu hard beside me. Beneath us on the margin of the eastern shoreline the shattered fragments of the cab, the crushed and broken body of its watu, lay awash.

A groan. Scarcely a lam-height below our feet, two figures clung to a trailing member of the bridge. One, rather, for it was Mav who held on desperately and with his walking legs still grasped the limp and silent body of his captive. He tried to speak again, but only a gasping wheeze escaped his nostrils.

"Mav, for pity's sake," I exclaimed, "do not despair, for I shall save you!" With that, I ripped the ties of my raincloak away, whipped off the garment unheeding of the weather, and stretched out so that it brushed the detective's carapace. Vyssu rapidly understood, braced herself behind

126

me, and, seizing both the upper limbs I stood upon, held me back from tumbling to my own demise. Mav groaned once again, then painfully raised his third—and crippled—set of legs until he had the edge of the raincloak. With a mighty heave that nearly lost me my footing, he dragged himself and Ensda up the cloak until he got three hands over the kerbside. I snatched at him and pulled. He slid onto the pavement and together all three of us drew the lunologist to safety. The river raged below, swollen with the rain—and, perhaps, a surge of disappointment.

Mav did not attempt to regain his feet, but lay for a while upon the underside of his carapace, breathing with some difficulty. Then, summoning at last some superlamviin reserve, he croaked, "Braid him, he is ours!" and sank back, insensible. I felt about within the Inquirer's cloak for his set of lamacles, sorted out the nine locking rings, and snapped them, one by one, upon the suspect's wrists, following Mav's new practice of imprisoning a felon's limbs *above*—yet another point of recent controversy with Tis—the body, so that his jaws might not snap at an officer, instead of in the customary method. I then turned to my friend, regretting for a moment I had not brought my bag from the carriage. Suddenly it was at hand, delivered thoughtfully by Vyssu. I struck a match to find my smelling-vapors.

There, in the flickering globe of light, I saw that Mav lay in a pool of blood.

That endless carriage journey from the bridge back to the Kiiden is one which shall never fade from memory as long as the burdens of living continue to be imposed upon me. Ensda lay upon the floor, trussed up like some wild game animal, Vyssu quiet and intense at the tiller, and I, hovering without daring much to hope over what remained of my dear friend, whose adventure—and mine as well, it was beginning to appear—had ended with that moment at the rail.

Little of consequence passed through my tortured mind during those protracted minutes save remembrances of Mav, a bright image here, a gentle word there, whole conversations with him which I found I could recall almost verbatim and which had taught me much about the world. One such, not coincidentally concerning Vyssu, struck me now, and I felt suddenly very small of mind and narrow

127

for having let it slip past notice and thus misjudging her character considerably.

It had been one recent forenoon, after Srafen's murder, when the detective and I found ourselves en route to the Precinct station, too short a distance of traverse to justify the expense of a cab, yet too long not to entertain ourselves in friendly discourse. We chanced to pass by, on our way through the City, a tiny waif, only just beginning to manifest female characteristics, installed upon a corner, her middle arm supporting a tray of rudely handmade combs sawn from the dried carapaces of watun and ajotiin.

"How touching," I remarked sadly, "that such as she has no warm and loving home to feel secure in and is thus reduced to hawking cheap trinkets in the street." I could see her in my mind's eye, fashioning these selfsame combs with primitive tools by the flickering light of a candle dearly bought, and, weary from her nightly labors, emerging at dawn to dispense them on the street.

Mav paused and tucked away his pipe, examined the child's wares with interest, and, producing a copper coin or three, exchanged it for one of the combs, a dark, striated, pretty thing, despite its homewrought crudity. This he ran experimentally through the fur upon his arm, manifested gratification, bade the pitiable urchin as good a day as she might expect to have, and urged me to continue upon our way.

"Quite to the contrary, esteemed colleague," he remarked suddenly, causing me to search back in my memory for whatever comment of mine had provoked this rejoinder, "while it is perhaps unfortunate that little alternative apparently exists for her at this time, I believe that many a better-placed young Fodduan might benefit from following a career such as hers, at least for some short while."

My pelt must surely have betrayed some hint of scandalized surprise. "How ghastly a prescription!" I cried, imagining myself in that destitute orphan's place. "Whatever could one learn of any value from that, except perhaps despair and some final, terrible degradation at the end?"

"Well, Mymy, there is some small satisfaction in seeing that you are not entirely a child of your class." Mav crinkled, restoring the inhaling tube to his nostril. "You have traveled the ideological distance equal to one full House of Parliament."

I shifted my bag. "And precisely what is it that you mean to convey by such an odd remark?"

"Simply that, given your upbringing, one might reasonably expect that you would take an attitude which most upper-class Pillars of the Empire, not excluding those appointed by the Triarchy to the Lezynsiin—"

"I was not aware that street vendors amounted to that much of a political issue."

Again his pelt crinkled good-naturedly. "You're quite correct, except that our little enterpreneur back there stands representative of everything which is happening in Great Fodduan political economy today, and of choices for the future which are being made, supposedly in our behalf—for better or for worse—this very instant. The Lezynsiin, for example, would view that little comb hawker as a public nuisance, annoying to the populace and cluttering the thoroughfare, possibly or potentially a menace, and on any account to be disposed of with inconspicuous facility by the Bucketeers. I have not the slightest doubt that, as a consequence, she tenders daily some portion of her meager earnings to the officer whose assignment her corner happens to be part of. An informal licensing procedure, to be sure, an ancient and dishonorable one which sometimes appears to be ineradicable and will remain so for as long as the Lezynsiin and those it represents continue to believe as they do."

I halted, beginning to feel somewhat insulted. "And this is the cold, uncharitable view which you attribute to me? Why—"

He held up a hand. "A moment, Mymy—peace. It is the opinion which many of our class express. I said, however, did I not, that you yourself had moved one house away—toward the Nazemynsiin, the Middle House of Parliament?"

"Perhaps that is what *you* think of me. However, *I* believe that—"

"That the child ought to remain at home, being taken care of, or by tragic circumstances failing that, enrolled in some school or institution where what she learns of life may be properly filtered and sanitized—quite unlike what she encounters every second in the real world for herself? I tell you, your House would make the licensure all the more stringent with the object of diminishing the number of such 'unfortunates' as she, reducing them under the absolute motherly concern of the State. And that prospect, my dear, gives me to shudder violently."

And I, as well, until I realized that this was nothing more than his own, simplistic, somewhat distorted view of a complex matter, persuasively expressed. Easy enough for Mav to criticize the upper class from which he also was sprung, or to opine from the security it afforded him concerning the needs and wants of the poverty-stricken. "But Mav, you little realize her bitter struggle—"

"Is precisely the same as anyone's, dear Mymy, to become her own person. For some, that struggle is financial in character, for others it is political or emotional. Cosseting, either on the part of one's family or the government, merely shifts the issue from one battlefield to another."

"And the Mykodsedyetiin—that Lower House upon which you lately set such great store—what would be their view?"

"Quite the same as my own," he said, "as you no doubt anticipated, that our little comb vendor ought to be left alone, both by the criminal authorities whose venue she in no way trespasses, and by those claiming to be concerned for her welfare—who would ruin her life in the pursuit of it. I warrant that she'll not be a tray-hawker long, Mymy. Soon she'll have a pushcart, and, after that, with some thrift and application, a little storefront. Any 'terrible degradation at the end' will be at the hands of meddlers, and that is the plain truth. Left to her own diligence and enterprise, her children will be better off than she is."

I was apalled. "How quaintly naive of you, May! Such a fairy story, this one of yours! Whom do you know to whom this has actually happened?"

This time, instead of crinkling, his laughter was outright and prolonged. When he had once more regained his composure, he answered, "That is the entire matter in a prawnshell, Mymy: 'to whom it has happened?' Ask instead, who it is who has *made* it happen, as our little comb hawker will. The answer, my very dear, may surprise you not at all."

Some years ago (Mav told me as we continued to the Precinct), in Lower Honwath upon the eastern side of the river bordering the dreadful Ipmu Moors district, there happened to be born amongst the meagerest of circumstances a child of—shall we express it 'casual liaison'?—

130

whose unfortunate mother passed away shortly afterward.

You have never been to Lower Honwath, Mymy, I am sure, and it is likely that you shall never have occasion to go there, although the fabled Tesret Hurrier and other trains pass nearby to it; one may look across its humble rooftops and crumbling chimneypots from the trestles if one is of such a mind. It is a place which makes the meanest neighborhoods of the Kiiden seem quite like Upper Hedgerow by comparison, where a helpless stranger to its grimy streets is naive if he expects something other than having his eyes pierced for him before traveling a single block after dark, and where the most revolting of household vermin are the only playthings children may hope to possess.

It is in this grim, impoverished atmosphere that our little female—for that is what she later proved to be—grew up and, in a manner of speaking, eventually prospered and flourished, reared by her mother's colleagues, also cutpurses, street vendors, and thieves. She became something of a mascot to them, and, as soon as she could walk and speak articulately, found herself an occupation of sorts carrying messages for a coin or three, to and fro for the denizens of the alleys, saving them exposure on the streets and the consequent effort of dodging those few Bucketeers our Service provides that area.

This enterprise she soon extended in a flash of native brilliance to nearby Fasmou Common, an industrial enclave between Lower Honwath, from which it draws its factory workers but is otherwise a different world, and Lower Dockside, whose habitues would have to reassess their putative lamly toughness if they traveled but a few blocks inland from the south branch of the River Dybod. The factory owners and managers appreciated the little female's message-running, and she soon had other urchins to whom she delegated much of this effort hither and yon, even to our own side of the river upon occasion.

At about the time when people learn what gender they're to be, our little friend was herself bearing messages for, among others, a wealthy older factor by the name of *Dahwoms* Ott Fiddeu—a trademark I'm sure any gardener would recognize for its synthetic fertilizers—who, aside from pursuing an aggressive string of businesses, possessed a remarkable reputation as a rake of the most unsavory character.

Dahwoms himself soon spied our little Vyssu—for that, of course, is precisely who the heroine of this tale happens to be—and recognized the possibilities: a lovely, innocent, virginal child with little (he thought, for he did not know her as we do) reason to hope for more than a lowly, miserable future existence. A young surmale who worked for her also caught his eye, a lurry who, like our Vyssu and for the same reasons, bore but one name: Obodiin.

In rher own way, this Obodiin was fully as ambitious as Vyssu or Dahwoms, although rhe wanted both the enterprise and innovative thoughtfulness which either of them owned. Rhe worked quite energetically enough in Vyssu's behalf, and, when the elderly millionaire put his proposition to them, accepted without a trace of the hesitancy Vyssu initially manifested. The offer he tendered them was this, that they should live in his house with him, receive a private education and enjoy every luxury, in recompense for which they should keep themselves available to him for whatever purposes he might desire.

Now, Mymy, let your pelt be still! I quite agree, it was a vile and debasing arrangement. Nonetheless, it was openly stated and freely acquiesced to. Dahwoms, at the time, was rather old, and I suspect that even our heroine did not expect the relationship to continue into perpetuity.

In any case, Vyssu and her erstwhile employe came to Middle Hedgerow, although the proposition turned out substantially differently than anyone anticipated. She was, as she is now, a charming creature, astute and graceful, quick, and possessing a natural elegance perceptible even to the least sensitive of lamn. To his surprise and horror, Dahwoms quickly found himself looking upon her as a daughter and treating her accordingly. Obodiin, who I gather shared something of the old lam's less honorable fleshly inclinations, had desired Vyssu for some long while; that, and rher cupidity, led to rher eventual undoing, although precisely how this was motivated, Vyssu wasn't to know for a long time.

For five years, the three of them and numerous servants dwelt in that great old house in Middle Hedgerow in circumstances of complete respectability. Old Dahwoms kept to his part of the bargain entirely, without making any claims upon the children or demanding aught from them but that they grace his table with their presence and other wise grant to him their kind companionship. For this and many other favors, Vyssu came to love him greatly, but Obodiin, dissatisfied, grew bolder as the years of frustration piled one upon another. No amount of genteel company nor polite education would satisfy rher.

One dark night following a birthday dinner party given in rher honor, Obodiin pushed a tipsy Dahwoms down the stairs and, with the household money—no inconsiderable amount—absconded to the Continent.

Still grieving the loss of her adopted father, Vyssu, now become a poised, sophisticated young lady, temporarily set elegance aside, deciding to put the rough teachings of her inglorious origins and upbringing to good use. She followed the ungrateful Obodiin to the Continent, where she spent a full two years alternatively tutoring the children of the rich and powerful—incidentally making many impressive friends in the process—and seeking out the whereabouts of Dahwom's murderer.

Somewhere along the way, I am not sure precisely how, nor am I sure I want to know, Vyssu encountered Fatpa, a highwaylam of illustrious repute, almost a local hero in a region which was subsequently doomed to involuntary incorporation into the Podfettian Hegemony. In those days it was a wild, adventurous sort of place where males carried enormous pistols to defend themselves, females and surmales were often kidnapped and taken to wife as a tradition, and life itself, though dearly bought at times, was cheap as tissue paper in a hatbox.

In those craggy, ill-explored mountains, Vyssu struck a bargain of her own with the robber. There was an outpost watering station for the stagecoach lines where she would catch the express she had somehow learned that Obodiin would be upon. Once the coach reached a place which they had mutually agreed was satisfactory, Fatpa would halt the coach. And all went as planned.

"Stand and deliver—your money or your life!"

The stagecoach screeched to a halt, its frightened watun stamping and foaming about the jaws. The driver reached into his box for a fowling piece long obsolete in any civilized portion of our Empire, but Fatpa was upon him in a trice, snatching away the gun and striking the fellow with it in a stunning but charitably light and otherwise uninjurious manner.

This, Vyssu had insisted upon as a part of their agreement.

The driver climbed down from the carriage into the dusty roadbed, and the passengers, an odd assortment of travelers, vagabonds, and local peasants, followed him. Among these were Vyssu, heavily veiled as is the custom in that part of the world, and a surmale, equally unrecognizable, except that she had followed rher for days in the capital and knew rher true identity full well.

Fatpa quickly deprived all the passengers of their worldly goods, even taking a brace of domesticated sandshrimp from a peasant woman and dangling them across the reinrail of his chariot. Wielding a huge pistol in each of his hands, he bade the group remount, halting Vyssu and the surmale at the last moment.

"Hold on, then, it gets a bit lonely up here in these hills, and I could do with a bit of fun before I let the pair of you go on!" He waved all three pistols threateningly, and Vyssu was appropriately outraged, as was the surmale. However, they complied with his demand to stay behind, and the stagecoach driver gratefully made haste away from the scene of the recent and future crime.

When the dust had settled from this getaway, the pistols turned, leveled at the surmale alone, and one of them was handed across to Vyssu, who shed her veils. "Obodiin, remove your hat so that I may look upon you before you die!" She had not ever shot a pistol before, and it waggled up and down in her hand in a manner far more frightening than any properly aimed weapon would have been.

Obodiin pulled rher hat and veils away, shocked to hear this voice, to see this face from a past rhe thought was long behind rher. "Why, Vyssu, what a sweet surprise to see you, darling, whatever are you doing in *this* awful place?"

"Seeing that justice is done, Obodiin. This is my friend Fatpa, here. I suggest that you hold still, for he is a deadly shot, and even better with a knife, which he can throw with startling accuracy."

"But what is it you want from me? I have done you no harm! Indeed, I have always harbored extremely fond memories of you, my dear."

"Oh, be still! Obodiin, this is scarcely a kood social or even a court of law, so I'll not bandy words with you. You murdered poor old Dahwoms, three of the servants saw you do it from separate vantages and independently came to me to tell me so. I found proof that you had arranged to travel days before your evil and ungrateful deed, and I

134

found the empty cashbox in Dahwom's study, as well. Do you deny any of this?"

Obodiin fidgeted, looked about rher for an avenue of escape, and then said shrewdly, "No, I do not. We grew up together, Vyssu, and did many things nearly as bad as that before we knew what gender we would be. You have grown soft from easy living, though, and will not kill me in revenge—you're too genteel and civilized. As it would be craven to hire the job done, rather than do it yourself—and I see that you believe that, too—you'll not have your ruffian dispose of me. So I believe I'll go, now. It's been pleasant seeing you again after all these years. Perhaps we can do it again, some time, what do you say?"

With that, Vyssu discharged her pistol straight into one of Obodiin's eyes, and the guilty culprit dropped dead at her feet. They left rher body there, riding away behind Fatpa's watun, and the fellow has been with her ever since.

When they returned to Foddu, Vyssu discovered, as haste had not allowed her to before her departure, that Dahwoms had left her all his fortune. It is to be surmised from certain remarks that Obodiin made before the murder that rhe knew of this, expecting Vyssu to share her good fortune, and undertook to hasten its arrival.

Yes, Mymy, I know that an inheritance scarcely constitutes the sort of betterment I described in the case of the comb vendor, but that is not all of the story. Vyssu took what was left to her, no mighty fortune, to be sure, for the properties of Dahwoms were heavily mortgaged and his vices had consumed no little amount, as well. From what remained after his debts were paid, she built a second fortune, vastly greater than the first. You will believe me, I trust, when I inform you that Vyssu is one of the wealthiest individuals in all of Mathas. Given our unspeakable social class system, this will never buy her respectability, but it does buy her respect. The Archsacerdot himself sometimes borrows money from her for various Church enterprises, as do certain members of the royal family.

"I think I understand," said I. "There always did seem more to Vyssu than was readily apparent, but tell me, Mav, why does she remain in the Kiiden, then? What became of Dahwoms's old home in Middle Hedgerow?"

"That place? If you can keep a secret, Mymy—it's highly important that you do, as you shall see."

"I don't know as I should like the burden of so important a confidence, Mav. But you ought to know me well enough by now to realize that I understand when to keep my silence." I felt mildly insulted again, but attempted not to show it.

Mav removed his pipe from a nostril and examined it, a ripple of humor running through his fur. "So you do, my dear, I apologize sincerely. And I shall tell you on any account, for it is quite amazing, really. The place in question is riddled with a hundred secret passages and hidden rooms, having to do with Dahwoms's various unsavory practices. They are all most carefully concealed and connected now with an underground passage to some nearby buildings.

"Dahwoms's house was sold some years ago and is now the Podfettian Embassy—there, you know the place! The tunnels run to Their Majesties' intelligence agencies and there is nothing which transpires inside the building of which we—by which I mean the Government—are not intimately aware! Clever lady, our Vyssu, for it was her idea, and carried out at a considerable profit to her, I might add!"

I interrupted Mav's quiet laughter with another question. "But, Mav, if Vyssu is so rich and, well, worthy of respect, why does she remain in the Kiiden, operating a bawdy house?"

"Mymy, I am shocked that you know such words! Really! Never mind, it is another of her ideas, you see. You know the sort of place she runs, straight forward, no perversions, simple, innocent—if you'll permit the term in this connexion—pleasure? This gives to young females and surmales of the poorer districts gainful employment in an atmosphere protective of their dignity. It also provides Vyssu with a stock from which to draw the matches which she makes for the upper classes, for she educates her employes in all the social graces and finds for them good marriages when their prime is past.

"In her own way, Mymy, Vyssu is a great revolutionary, for, once she is done, the hereditary distinction in this city between upper and lower classes will be illusory in its entirety. What do you think of that?"

XIII: The Innocent Culprits

"I never meant to *kill* him!"

Mav's broken body lay across a trio of hastily assembled cushions in a parlor at Srafen's home, to which we had, an happier times, not before been admitted. This quiet chamber, apparently, had been the late Professor's sole domain, its walls completely plastered up with diagrams and sketches of countless hideous creatures, only the veriest few of which are still extant upon the globe, the majority long extinct, known by nothing more than their scant subsoddean remains.

This vista of dubious esthetic appeal was interrupted only by huge floor-to-ceiling racks for the familiar cylindrical forms of books, their labeled ends revealing that no few of them had been written by Srafen rherself, including— (filed alphabetically like any of the other works here)— rher classic *The Ascent of Lamviin*.

The room was filled agreeably enough with the scent of ancient, well-seasoned cactuswood wainscotting, pereskine shelving, and dozens of free-standing glazed display cases of exotic origin and material—as well as from the hundred or more bizarre biological specimens preserved within them. The place, however, smelled not in the slightest of the carpet-setting resin whose malevolent odor permeated and polluted the remainder of the house, a point most definitely in its favor at the moment. There was, too, a firegrate whose would-be cheerful blaze failed utterly to dispel the gloom which had settled over us all owing to the unhappy fate of my poor detective friend. Considering Mav's fervent desire to finish his effort well, it had seemed both to Vyssu and myself that bringing him here to his old teacher's house had been the most fitting thing we could do.

"I tell you, it was *not* my doing, at all!"

This had been Srafen's faithless husband, Law, who had spoken, his wastrel gaze cast downward as he did so upon

137

Mav's silent, inert form. I had applied what inadequate skill I possessed as well as the impoverished contents of my bag in defense of my dear companion's mortal existence, yet the wound was terrible to behold even now, having bled heavily and darkly through its bandages. It was that very joint, strained in the act of preserving his own and Ensda's life, almost to the extent of being severed, which had, so many years ago, suffered near-crippling damage from the arrow of a savage. It had now been forcefully reopened upon some hidden, poorly healed seam, spilling out Mav's life onto the cobbles of Commoner's Bridge.

I had not been able to staunch the flow; the villain, Ensda, had escaped his own doom virtually unscathed, at the grievous expense of a far better lam than he. I was determined that the scoundrel and charlatan now be brought to stern justice.

Vyssu, the grimmest of imaginable arrangements in her fur, had agreed.

Our return into the city, as I have indicated, marked the lowest point so far in my life. The lunological faker we had tucked neatly between two seats. Had my friend not been there with us, too, gradually losing his already pitiably weakened grasp upon existence, this "doctor" should have seemed most comical a spectacle, rocking back and forward upon the bottom of his carapace with the motion of the carriage, his limbs having been fastened together neatly above his jaws. He cursed vehemently at us, shattering the reverie which had preoccupied me, cursed Mav, cursed the cab which he had chosen for his ill-fated escape, cursed the partners he had chosen for his crimes. He likewise cursed the day on which he'd first begun telling people what to do on the predication of the supposed relative positions of the moons of Sodde Lydfe.

"You cretins!" he exploded, causing me to wish vainly for some means of immobilizing his nostrils—I thought of several drugs, of which I had none, and of my professional ethics which, in Ensda's case, were rapidly evaporating. "How you all would stand on line, clutching your pitiable earnings, eager to hand them over to anyone who would make decisions for you! I actually once spent an entire afternoon sagaciously explaining a lunoscopic chart which, I discovered afterward, I'd inadvertently hung upside-down upon the easel! And yet you stood there by appointment, raptly listening, eyes turned inward blissfully at the comforting prospect that you'd never be called upon again to strain yourselves to generate an independent thought!"

Having virtually resigned myself by now to losing the battle for my dear friend's life, I dully allowed a bit of my attention to drift toward the conlam. "Yet you, 'Doctor,' made your contemptible living from those you mock, explaining the positions of the Martyred Trine."

He gave me a bristly chuckle. "Indeed I did, and every day gave hearty thanks to whatever superstitious clod named them thus—as well as saving a certain amount of gratitude for the happy coincidence that this world of ours possesses three moons! I'll never understand it: have not the public been informed that their precious Martyred Trine in the sky are but three balls of rock whose relative positions are significant of nothing save the way they fall about each other and this planet? I am no philosopher, to be sure, yet this much I, myself, have managed to understand!"

"I am no philosopher myself," I replied, and glancing once again at Mav's motionless body, added, "nor much of a paracauterist. Yet, at this moment, did I but believe, even in the remotest tip of a finger, that some magic might restore my friend to me, I might very well stand in your queue, Ensda, and give over my money. You are a criminal—you prey upon the lonely and the sick, the hopeless and those struck with tragedy. I hope you get what you deserve!"

Again that cynical ripple: "Ah, a sentimentalist! And I suppose that you attend the *established* Church with regularity and listen to *their* brand of counterfeit advice and consolation? The Royally Approved brand?"

"Why, no, as a matter of fact." Nor had I done so since earliest childhood.

"Well, at least in that, you are consistent. We are all in the same business, you know—performing a 'service' for which there is no need. My dear, 'criminals' like myself and like the Reverend Trinist Churchlamn would be out of business in a fraction of a moment if your lonely, sick, hopeless, tragic masses simply took charge of their own lives. No one can make anyone less lonely or ill, generate hope or negate tragedy. Or make anyone else happy, for that matter. Only we can do that for ourselves, by identifying what it is we want and then acting to obtain it. Most people spend their lives avoiding the knowledge of what it is they really desire, and it is these self-evaders who

139

become *my* customers. They deserve me, my dear, they richly deserve me, and I do my best to serve them as they merit!"

I bridled at his cynicism. "By selling them nonsense instead of the advice they really need—the advice which you have just given me?"

"Precisely—by selling them the nonsense which they will accept nine thousand times as willingly as the truth. There is very little money in the truth, my dear, very little money at all. Usually some ugly form of popular execution, instead."

"I only meant to *frighten* him!" Law now insisted for perhaps the thirtieth time in the past hour. "It was this accursed investigation of his! Oh, how did I ever get mixed up in all this? Why ever did I agree to—"

"Silence, idiot!" growled Ensda, freed now of some of his restraints. He rose and began to pace the little room—until he was jerked up short and thus reminded that I had left one of the rings upon a walking leg and fastened another to that of Srafen's large, heavy desk. He stopped and, addressing Law, pointed a finger at Mav: "You will place us both between the Blocks, whether this foul snooper—"

"Gentlelamn," intoned a brisk, familiar voice, "kindly do not speak of me in the third person, for it is neither vary polite nor yet appropriate." My hearts leaped as Mav stirred upon the cushions. "Mymy, my dear, I thank you for your kind ministrations; they were most helpful. If you will observe, the bleeding has now stopped—another benefit of *resre* disciplines. I believe that, with a spot of kood—"

"Mav! If you do not remain still, you will start bleeding again! Kood is a stimulant, which you do not require—it might very well prove fatal!"

"Unlock these fetters," offered Ensda with a hideous leer, "and I'll *happily* get him his kood."

"Your generosity overwhelms me, my good Doctor. I see that I was successful, by Pah, not only in apprehending you, but in preserving your person for the tender mercies of Their Majesties' Justice! Quite gratifying, really, Tis will be well pleased!"

I spoke once again. "Mav, you really must lie still. You have given me quite a turn, you know, and Vyssu, as well—two turns, really, for I thought you surely to be dying, nor do I fully understand this recovery of yours."

Vyssu, very silent for once, nodded agreement.

"Nor do I, altogether, Mymy. I believe that I reflexively began the disciplines whilst hanging from the bridge. I remember nothing after that, except some vague sense that the two of you were highly agitated—oh yes, and your valiant attempts to save my being. Tell me, then, what is the damage?"

I hesitated, not quite knowing what to say. Then: "Well, since you have not succumbed to exsanguination, I should say that, if you will comport yourself with prudence over the next several weeks, you may enjoy greater mobility in that shattered joint than you have previously. It was most amateurishly set, and—"

"Upon the field of battle, if you will recall, my dear. Capital! Now where have you secreted my inhaling tube? And, Law, you will explain your earlier remarks immediately, or face the Blocks for a certainty. What do you mean you did not intend to kill me? When?"

Law cast his gaze about the room and seemed to shrink upon himself. Not a soul present would stand up for him. Besides myself, Mav, Vyssu, and vile Ensda, the remaining individual present had been totally silent, almost hysterically withdrawn; Myssmo's world was disintegrating before her unbelieving eyes and it was fully consistent with her character that she should now deny that world and sink into a dull torpor, a sort of waking *hann*.

Gone too was Law's old-school playboy bravado. He took breath to speak, but Ensda growled again, and, for the first time, there was the slightest whimper from Myssmo. Mav interrupted: "Ensda, threaten him again, and I shall personally see that you are placed within the coldest, darkest, dampest cell in all of Mathas while awaiting execution for the murder of Professor Srafen! Now speak, Law! Perhaps you can save yourself a similar fate!"

There was a long pause, then, in confirmation of what my friend had suspected all along, Law removed the walking glove from his right rearmost hand.

As well as, to all appearances, the hand along with it.

"Why, you *are* the one who attacked us in the Kiiden!" I said, quite unnecessarily, and, from Mav's expression, out of turn. Yes, there they were, the first childlike, tender shoots of regenerating fingers. I knew now that their predecessors lay preserved in my surfather's office ice chest.

"And you," Law answered in a lifeless voice, "are the

141

one who struck my hand off in retribution!" He looked upon his severed limb almost in disbelief.

With a chuckle in his fur, Mav observed, "Quite so, old lam, and what, if I may inquire—which officially I'm obliged to—has become of your accomplice in incompetent thuggery?"

Law winced. "Oh, him? A hireling, merely, picked up by chance at a tavern very near there. He should be gone by now, aboard the very ship on which he came. I believe that they were to steam tonight—the *Habo*, it was, I think. Podfettian: I chose him because he didn't speak a word of Fodduan. Not that he let on, I—"

"Get hold of yourself!" Mav shouted suddenly. "You're wandering!"

Law blinked. "Oh, sorry. Where was I? You must believe me, sir, it was never my intention that anyone—most particularly myself—should be injured in what transpired. It is just that, well, your inquiries were taking you rather closer to my . . . that is, they seemed to endanger me, so I took measures to frighten you off."

"Hmm—I begin to see," replied the detective quietly. He'd found the pocket of the cloak I'd draped him with and was now, despite the strongest warning looks from me, dripping volatile solvents into his silver pipe. Now he stopped and looked at Law quite sharply. "And what has all of this to do with Doctor Ensda, here?" My friend quite suddenly sounded fatigued—I suppose there is a limit to what anyone, however trained and fit, can endure. His fur drooped and suddenly seemed to lose its luster.

With a clank, Ensda struck the limit of his leash again, glared at me, and sat down where he was upon the nearest cushion to Myssmo, who uncharacteristically—but now understandably—shrank backward from him, emitting another little whimper. "I'll tell you what it has to do with me! I'll not be bound over for a killing I had no connection with! I've done time before, and whatever they give me now, I can do it standing on my jaws—but I'll *not* go between the Blocks for the likes of these!" He waved a hand, indicating Law and Myssmo.

"It was a simple enough scheme, but this pair was even simpler, and, accordingly, required my assistance, not only to carry it off, but to think of it in the first place! *This*—" he pointed now toward Myssmo—"actually *believes* in the watu-marbles I dispense as personal advice. Lunology? Rot it all, I cannot so much as calculate the position of tomorrow's *sunrise*! Yet use the proper 'magic' words, and morons like her *always* believe—and pay!"

At this, Myssmo began to wail.

"Oh be still, you silly female, you're interrupting! The problem was that there's a limit to how much she could pay. Her surhusband, the real algae-winner (here he took a long, contemptuous look at Law) of this *happy* family, had placed her on a strict allowance. Little wonder, when you see what she's done to this place since the old surry kicked off! Srafen, I discovered, intended donating as much of rher considerable fortune as possible to the pursuit of rher philosophical flights of fancy. What a waste! Imagine giving everything away just to help a lot of thin-pelts generate even longer words and less-comprehensible theories!"

Well, I reflected, here was something which I had heard before, a point of some agreement between this mountebank, Niitood the reporter, and the Keeper of Fundamental Truth. It seemed a wonder to me that there continued to be any progress at all, it had so many willing enemies.

"In any event," continued Ensda, "I approached 'Lawsie' here, for he seemed to have some personal uses to which money could be put—"

Here, Vyssu surprised me by laughing briefly.

"—it would have done no good at all to discuss anything linear and rational with their wife, here. After some negotiation, we struck a bargain and made a plan. With the help of one of Srafen's solicitors, concerning whom I was privy to a number of embarrassing facts, we began to manipulate the accounts a trifle. Srafen would never know, as what strain we placed upon rher resources would never become apparent until after rhe had passed away—when there would be no free lunch forthcoming for natural philosophers!"

Abruptly, Law sank to the floor and placed a hand over each eye. Myssmo, who was hearing this for the first time, just as we were, appeared strangely unmoved. I kept an eye on Mav, as well, whose thoughtful expression waxed gloomier with each successive word from the lunologist.

Ensda whirled upon them both in turn. "We saw to it that our gullible friend here had some remuneration which might stem any minimal curiosity it might occur to her to exercise. You may see, around this place, the uses to which she has applied it—disgusting!

"And you—get up from there, you soft-shelled weakling! Face what's coming to you like a lamviin! You suffered your share of the spoils quite cheerfully enough when they were the only apparent consequences!

"So there you have it all, my dear Inquirer, a complete confession—to embezzlement! It's readily vertifiable; among other bonafides, I shall supply the name of Srafen's perfidious lawyer. But I see you are confused—why am I doing this? Because, you see, our periodic raids upon rher wealth were only possible as long as rhe was alive; upon rher death, the trust—that delightfully manipulable trust—would be dissolved, all remaining wealth devolve upon the Museum and University, and we would cease deriving any benefit. You have me now for a thief, but never for a murderer—I stood to gain far too much from Srafen's continued health!"

Mav propped himself up a little, leaning more than I liked upon his wounded limb. "I understand entirely, sir," he said very quietly. "And you, Law, fearing my investigation into Srafen's death would disclose this flummery, decided to take violent means against me and my friend." He took the inhaler from his nostril with a discouraged move of his hand and laid it upon a side table.

There was not a sound from Srafen's husband, only an abject cast of resignation in his fur. The set of Ensda's pelt was one of positive contempt. "And thus the fool directed your attention straight toward us!"

Mav fell strangely silent, an expression I could not interpret covering his carapace. He looked toward the window; it was black as pitch by now outside, and, judging by that expression, possibly within his soul, as well. He was not far from the wall, and so reached over and pulled back the drape. "I see the rain has stopped, Mymy. Do be good enough to telephone the Precinct. They'll be wanting Dr. Ensda here, and Law. I believe, for what little good it shall do her, that we may leave mention of Myssmo out of things." His languor affrighted me sorely.

Vyssu rose in my place and left the room, for I could not leave the detective's side, so poignantly did he fail to conceal his bitter disappointment. I feared far more for his life at this moment than I had at any time earlier in the evening, for people must have some reason to go on living, and there was not the slightest trace of that remaining in my friend.

"Mav," I offered, "we have brought two criminals to book, and there is still a murderer to——"

"I know, my dearest friend," he murmured gently, "I have not forgotten. I think now that the only remaining course is to see whether or not, when I have recovered from this wound, I can get myself murdered, as well."

XIV: A Desperate Enterprise

Mav's despondency proved dreadfully contagious. He had spent much precious time and effort and hopes dearly held, nearly expended his own life as well, pursuing matters we now had learned were wholly unconnected (at least in any save the most indirect of senses) with Professor Srafen's murder.

That my detective friend should manifest discouragement did not surprise me. My own attitude, I realized, was one of unrelieved weariness, and I even began doubting, so intertangled and complex did the most ordinary and innocent affairs of lamn appear, whether Mav's shining dream of scientifically untwining the criminal ones was practicable at all. Perhaps such tasks had best be left to Churchlamn and to these new alienists who were beginning to enjoy a certain notoriety.

Ensda turned out, uncharacteristically, as good as his word, for his story was confirmed upon the next morning—I had this through one of the most singular telephonic communications I have ever received—with the apprehension of the criminal solicitor (a phrase Niitood later was to claim is the soul of redundancy) and his subsequent confession. It is positively astounding what the possibility of accusation for a capital offense—and of the Blocks—will do to elicit cooperation from the commonplace thief.

Somehow, in the next few days, Vyssu's establishment in the Kiiden was to become our unofficial headquarters, due partly, I suppose, to Mav's indisposition. He would tolerate no servants in his own lodgings; Fatpa and one or two others such as owed their livelihood to Vyssu anxiously oversaw the Inquirer's return to health. This was something of an annoyance to me, since it was I who had begun his course of treatment and who, in every professionally ethical regard, ought to have seen to its continuance and completion.

Nonetheless, it was upon no medical matter that I was so curtly summoned the next morning to the detective's side. He lay upon a broad satin-covered cushion, the slim wand of his silver inhaling tube tilted rakishly from one nostril, and a wick of some robust and lamly kood filling his female friend's front parlor (which now served as his office and infirmary) with a heartening fragrance.

I set my bag upon the carpet. "Good morning, Mav. I see that you have done well by yourself, as usual. A word about that pipe of yours, however, which will slow your healing by at least—"

He crinkled and looked up at me. "Ah, Mymy, good morning to you, also. If I am not to be allowed my pipe, dear paracauterist, I shall perforce have to turn instead to juicing." Here, he mimicked quite accurately that sudden rigor which current induces in the body. "What effect might *that* have on my health? I am given to understand that you may now deliver an informed opinion on the subject."

"Why, of all the . . . oh, very well, then, make a finish of what Ensda has begun! But before you do, kindly inform me why that strange unpalatable creature Fatpa telephoned my rooms this morning, asking for assistance on your behalf. Have you some idea, after all, of continuing these efforts?" With this unthoughtful utterance, I felt instantly ashamed, for I could understand and sympathize with Mav's vain labors, if anybody could, and with the final resignation of his words last evening.

Mav, however, remained quite cheerful. "Quite so, my dear, quite so, although you have been summoned here somewhat less to render assistance to me than for your own continued well-being. Tell me, Mymy, have you still that little equalizer we took from Law?"

"Why, yes, I believe that I have. It is to be hoped that Law will have little use for it in future. Why ever do you ask—would you like me to return it to him?"

"On the contrary." He laughed. "Do you believe that you can make proficient use of it after just one brief lesson?" He extended a hand, which I took as a request on his part to examine the weapon in question. I rummaged about in my bag, found the gun, and gave it to him, though I hesitated to answer immediately. Much like my earlier exchange with Fatpa, this conversation was making less and less sense to me the longer it lasted.

"I am unsure how to judge proficiency at such things,

147

Mav. I think that I can do as well or better than I did upon the morning of our picnic."

He slammed the little pistol shut. "Splendid. You must have a care, now, and keep this where you can reach it with celerity, for over the next few days I shall have to place your life—and my own, I hasten to add—upon the gambling table, risking all against nothing to ensnare an evil-doer." He gave me back the gun and fell silent for a moment. Then: "Had I not anticipated the self-righteous vigor of your reaction, I would tender the suggestion that you take a room here in this place, where I could be more assured of your safety."

"My dear fellow," I intoned icily, "I trust your anticipations will be satisfied, for the suggestion fills me with that full measure of revulsion you expected! As to my safety, sir, I have been taking care of myself for nearly—"

"Now, Mymy," he said with a sudden gentleness, "there is a genuine concern here. You had no way of knowing, when you arrived, that I am about to publicly announce that I have the identity of our killer. I fear—indeed, I trust—that this announcement will compel him to attempt to strike again before—"

"What are you saying? Why did you not tell me of this immediately instead of—" I sat down heavily upon the cushion beside him, perplexed and in no small degree annoyed that I had wasted so much sympathy.

"I did not say that I *know* who murdered Srafen, Mymy, merely that I intend *announcing* that I do. It is to be hoped, by means of this deception and the killer's subsequent actions, that I will discover his identity and be enabled thus to fulfill my public pledge. Do you follow me?"

My mind was in a whirl. "*That* is what you spoke of yesternight! I took it for a sort of suicidal resignation!"

He laughed, his fur acrinkle to the very roots. "No, not all all, my very dear, not at all! I'm sorry indeed to have alarmed you so. Perhaps the tone I used was affected by my wounds and fatigue. This sally had occurred to me—in fact, I have some notes upon it, made last year sometime—but, when it seemed that Ensda was our lam, I set it aside. Now it is the only recourse I have left, an act of calculated desperation, for all my other traces seem to have evaporated along with the dampness from yesterday's rain."

I inhaled the koodsmoke drifting through the room and

braced myself up again. "I see. And how is it that you intend to make this announcement of yours?"

He reached out to pat one of my hands. "I have already done so, to Niitood, his colleagues and competitors, through a written deposition, copies of which good Fatpa is distributing in newspaper offices throughout the city at this very moment. Would you care to see the original?"

He handed me a scrap of paper that bore, not the Department's sigil, but, in neatly handwritten lines, his own name and the address of this place in which we sat conversing:.

To Parties Interested in the Matter
of the Late Professor *Srafen* Rotdu Rizmou:
Following extensive inquiries into the circumstances surrounding the recent brutal murder of the Curator of the Imperial Museum of Natural Philosophy, I have determined to name the responsible party at a gathering to be conducted in the offices of Battalion Chief Waad Hifk *Tis* three days hence. Those persons whose involvement in the matter is legitimate—and otherwise—may assure themselves that Their Majesties' justice shall be vindicated to the utter limit which Their law provides.
Agot Edmoot *Mav*, Extraordinary Inquirer
Their Majesties' Bucketeers
Fadyedsu Street, The Kiiden

It had certainly by no means escaped my notice that Mav, for the first time in our acquaintance, had placed a hand upon my person in some manner other than is necessary, for example, in assisting one of the weaker sexes into a carriage or in escorting someone across a dangerous thoroughfare. Indeed, the difficulty I encountered finishing that conversation with him comprehensibly was but the first of many equally dizzying events that seemed to tread over our carapaces during the next several dozen hours with such ferociousness and rapidity it now feels quite ludicrous to me that, for most of that period of time, I remember being rather bored.

Mav continued calling into doubt the security of my person were I to stay within my own doors in Gamlo Road. For my part, naturally, I adamantly refused lodging, however temporarily, at a place so notorious as Vyssu's. It was settled upon, finally, and not without considerable and

149

heated debate, that the Department would supply a room for me, *incognito,* in a boardinghouse across the street.

What upward increment in propriety I thereby gained I am not certain, but I had ultimately made the point with Mav that if anyone were responsible for the conduct and safety of my life, it was I myself alone. He had stated many times in the past that any wholly ethical civilization would leave each individual the sole exclusive arbiter of his, her, or rher own being; in his view this was the irreducible premise upon which societal decency must be founded. He had, on that account, no consistent alternative but to cease arguing with me upon the matter of where I was to live for the remainder of this situation. I did not happily antici- pate applying the same line of reasoning upon my mother, but determined to address *that* particular problem as well after the fact as could be managed.

To Zoobon, my duplicitous maidservant, I said simply that I was traveling for the Department under suitable chaperonage—which, in a manner, was true. The boarding- house across from Vyssu's was owned and operated by a sweet little old lurrie of extreme fragility and advanced years who would tolerate not the slightest apparent devia- tion from respectable behavior upon my part or that of any other resident or visitor. Mav or Fatpa must call upon me in the tiny lobby under rher surparental eye and within a narrow set of hours appointed for the purpose, entering never further into the establishment. I must also, when I stepped out, return well before dusk each evening or face immediate eviction.

All in all, it can be said that I—as well as that sense of nicety my parents had gone to some pains to instill in me— was highly satisfied with these arrangements. It was not until some long time afterward that Mav informed me, with the blandest humor rippling through his fur, that the stric- tures in that house were intended (vainly, it would seem) to allay certain suspicions among the local populace and authorities: a "secret" ring of Unarchists habitually gathered deep down in the basement there, under the enthusiastic leadership of my sweet little old lurrie, every second, fifth, and eighth day of the week, around a guttering candle.

This was, I thought, a conspiracy not apparently destined to electrify the world.

At the time, however, I sat complacently ensconced

within my hired rooms up on the first floor, staring down across the street to Vyssu's, relatively well satisfied with things, as I have said. Pah in his wisdom knows there was little enough else to do with myself. Mav's provocative notice had appeared in all the papers, copies of which were scattered about the floor of my own self-inflicted hermitage, every line of every single page read over and over and over again for want of some alternative activity. It was a waiting game that we were playing, I reminded myself every hour with less and less conviction, a game of agonizing ennui with only the vague uncertain promise of some stark and violent terror toward its conclusion as a point of relief. I have come since to understand this as a principle characteristic of all law-enforcement work. Mav compared it to the baiting of a trap for predators with a bit of meat and began referring to it as a "steak-out" until I convinced him that the turn of phrase lacked elegance.

I am glad I am a paracauterist where emergencies are dealt with, for the most part, by appointment.

Having, as I say, then, little or nothing else upon my plate, I decided to increase what little expertise I possessed concerning the pistol with which Mav and I had practiced. Gathering that the landlurry would most likely look askance at my peppering rher walls and ceiling with bullet pocks, and that the other inhabitants of this place might be inclined to complain over the noise of it, I reasoned finally that many of the prerequisite skills might be enhanced with the firing of no actual shots at all: the steady hand, the lining up of sights, the careful and deliberate pull upon the trigger—all of these might well be practiced without benefit of ammunition, sound, or fury (that latter, most likely, from my neighbors). In addition, I thought, the absence of dreadful recoil might indeed prevent any further engenderment upon my part of what Mav had called a flinch—yet another inelegance of his.

Thus I aimed the little gun at lamp brackets upon the walls, decorative cornices of buildings I could see past my curtains, at insects or little accidental whorls in the sand upon the floor; I squeezed the handle, trying to keep the sights aligned until the striker fell. I suppose I must have repeated these exercises, along with practicing the loading and unloading of the thing, nine thousand times or more in the many weary hours I sat alone in that room. Should ever

I be set upon by angry lamp brackets, wild cornices, aggressive bugs, or vicious sandy lumps, I would now be well protected.

Mav's recovery was swifter than I might have predicted, I suspect due to the prospect that he might, at last, be nearing some agreeable conclusion to this soggy and infernal mystery. Several times each day he came across the street, met me belowstairs, and accompanied me back to where he himself had grown accustomed to fidgeting against the possibility of action. How he occupied his time when I was not beside him I would not have cared to speculate; there also was Vyssu, who seemed almost to have given over whatever ordinary enterprises she pursued to this strangely static pursuit of Mav's. Whenever I was there, we sat discussing art and politics, sports and drama, the weather, and every other incidental topic except that matter most at hand. With the failing light, my detective friend would escort me home, his pace visibly much livelier and healthier each occasion. I would then wait by myself until the next time he appeared.

Each such afternoon I protested that I might go shopping, visiting, or simply for a walk. This Mav surprised me by graciously agreeing to—provided I took Fatpa with me everywhere I went! It took me not more than a few seconds imagining that apparition occupying a cushion in my mother's parlor or assisting me with packages through the gilt doors of some respected and fashionable place of retail business, to dismiss the notion and return to those same three walls I had come to know—and to dislike—so well.

I did derive some small amusement at the time contemplating how Tis might react to Fatpa's imposing presence at the Precinct.

The evening of the third day, following yet another of my sociables with Mav and Vyssu, I felt the state of hann beginning to steal over me. This, as one might expect, was far from unwelcome as it would neatly dispose of a weary hour that would otherwise be occupied adding to the callosity on my trigger fingers. I secured the bolt upon the door, sifted the uppermost layer of sand in the hannbox, then settled into it, digging all nine arms as comfortably deep as possible. Drifting, I closed my eyes and—

Suddenly, a great commotion sounded in the street below! With painful effort I wrenched consciousness back into focus, surging upward in a shower of fine, clean sand that spattered on the floor, mixing with the coarser grade that served as carpet in this place. Through the window, I could see a pair of waggons in the lamplight, their trees and traces tangled inextricably, the axle of one of them broken, a watun lying on the pavement, to all appearances sorely injured. The drivers, working-class fellows in crude and dirty habiliment, stood at the conjunction of the vehicles, waving all their arms and shouting loudly enough to rattle the pane through which I watched them. At any moment, it was clear, they would begin to strike each other savagely; despite the hour, a crowd was gathering in cheerful anticipation of such an unscheduled sporting event. All the neighborhood around about seemed compelled to offer, at the tops of their voices, suggestions and encouragement. Somewhere, faint in the background, a Bucketeer's trumpet sounded, promising that there might even be a referee.

From my vantage, a full story above the potential melee, I suddenly espied something no other could have been aware of, and understood the true nature of the scene below: it was a sham. On the roof of Vyssu's, a dark and silent form prised at a trap that would admit him to an upper floor. For some queer reason, the character of his stealthy movements caused me to glance down once more at the waggons—now I recognized one of the vehicles as well as the beast that had drawn it hither. I knew that figure among the chimney pots as well as I knew any other, despite the fact that he was clad now altogether differently than the occasion when I had seen him last.

Finally, finally I say, something was about to happen, and I would not be left out of it.

I seized my little pistol, remembering also to snatch up the billfold with my official insignia, and dashed down the stairs. There the doors were bolted shut already. As I made to unfasten them, the owner emerged from her room.

"Here, now, missur, what's goin' on? You know there ain't no comin' nor goin' after dark—house rules."

I waved my Bucketeer credentials at rher suddenly widened eyes. "Be damned to your rules! Keep still and help me with this accursed night chain, for I am about Their Majesties' business!"

My host complied with alacrity, giving the lie to rher Unarchist tendencies. Even as I charged out into the street, I thrilled at having uttered those stirring words as I had heard Mav do before me many times. I ran around the edge of the crowd toward Vyssu's and pounded upon the door. Fatpa greeted me, flared a nostril as if to speak, took in the weapon in my hand, and moved out of the way. As he did so, I noticed him produce an intimidating knife from somewhere on his person; he followed me upstairs without a word.

There, upon the landing, stood the figure I had seen upon the roof. We very nearly collided, but he drew back in alarm and snatched desperately among the black robes that he now wore. I pointed my pistol at him. "Stand where you are, in Their Majesties' names, or I shall—"

A metallic gleam shone from his hand, sweeping upward nearly faster than the eye could follow. I pulled the trigger. There was a roar and a sharply stinging slap at my palm, both of which I scarcely noticed at the moment. The figure staggered backward, fetched against a wall, raised his weapon again. I fired once more. His arm dropped and his gun discharged into the floor. When the smoke cleared from the air between us, the Reverend Mr. Adem lay in a heap of tangled limbs upon the carpet, breathing his last.

XV: A Criminal Convergence

Scarcely aware of the smoking pistol still gripped in my hand, I crouched beside the fallen lam. He stirred a little, and in great apparent pain uttered a single word, incomprehensible to me: "Danokih . . ." Then, shutting out forever the light of the world, he closed his eyes and expired.

All round me on the landing, doors popped open, eyes peered timidly about the corridor. Dimly it occurred to me that, in each instance, in each doorway, actually, their owners were uniformly three in number, a male, a surmale, and a female. The reason for this even distribution of the genders, when it finally dawned upon my much-rattled sensibilities, swept a shiver of embarrassment through my fur. After all, I remembered, this *was* Vyssu's.

I rose and turned toward the stairs, only to confront an individual known to me, a . . . well . . . a customer of Vyssu's, caught, by me and by the violence of circumstances, unprepared. He withdrew in guilty haste into the room from which he'd just emerged.

"Your Eminence!" I cried in astonished outrage. "Whatever are you *doing* in a place like . . ." I stopped, then, and spoke no further, for I knew all too well the answer to my foolish question—and that, as well, the Archsacerdot of Mathas, my parents' good and respectable friend, was unlikely ever to provide it to me in any case.

Precisely at that awkward moment, there erupted a commotion on the ground floor. As I could be of no further use to my patient, I rushed to the edge of the landing. Belowstairs, Mav and Vyssu, among others of the house, having by all appearances just recently hurried to see what the shooting was about, now were being distracted by an angry confrontation at the entrance. Fatpa, a fellow ordinarily quite capable of handling any threat of this kind, unaccountably was finding himself overwhelmed by a frail and familiar sweet little old Unarchist.

155

"Get out of my way, you oafish churl!" rhe shouted. "You minion of the Statist elite! Begone from my path, I tell you!" Here rhe brandished some metallic object, which I recognized to be the large and heavy ring of keys rhe carried out of continuous and proprietary habit to the numerous apartments rhe rented out. "One of my lurries is in trouble of some kind here! You'll produce rher for me this very instant or I'll have the Bucks on you!"

"But, but, but, but . . ." said Fatpa, dodging the old lurry's substantial brass collection as it whirled viciously about his carapace. "But, but, but, but . . ."

"Madam—" Mav attempted, his tone and pelt nearly as urbane as the fashionable dressing gown he affected.

"Don't you call me that," retorted the landlurry, "not in *this* place!"

My detective friend recovered quickly. "Your pardon, dear lurry, I am Agot Edmoot *Mav* of Their Majesties' Bucketeers. May I be of some—"

"A Bucketeer?" Rhe looked him over carefully. "I might have known! The corruption in high—"

Suddenly there was a resounding *crash!* The front doors, bolted once again by Fatpa, groaned and splintered, then gave way. A squad of half a dozen Bucketeers rushed in from out of doors, the wagon axle they'd employed as a battering ram still in their hands until they dropped it where they stood, grease spattering in the carpet sand.

"Here now, what's goin' on?" Their leader, a short, abrasive fellows wielded a fire ax as his lamn began to search about, undecided, by their attitude, whether they were here to stop a fight or extinguish a blaze. One zealot among them seized upon the landlurry and started locking lamacles upon rher wrists. Rhe shouted angrily at him and began again to swing rher keys. Another, with similar ambitions toward Fatpa, faced that imposing worthy squarely, looked him over, up and down, gave a sheepish ripple, and turned his intentions elsewhere. His fellows now were overturning cushions and ferreting out suspicious wrinkles among the draperies.

Vyssu watched this for a while, shrugged her arms in boredom, and went out to get some kood started.

Mav reached into the folds of his dressing gown as if to produce credentials, but the squad leader, who did not know him, drew his service revolver. "Keep yer hands in sight now! Keep 'em up, I say!"

Behind me, the Archsacerdot, now fully clothed in a voluminous and concealing cloak, eased out of the little room he'd occupied and attempted to sneak past me on the stairs. "Your Eminence," I cautioned, "I would not go down there, if I were—"

My landlurry, freed suddenly by rher startled would-be captor, began striking the poor fellow in earnest with rher keys as he cowered in anguish. Behind rher, through the broken doors, a little unkempt group of strangers entered at a run, spied rher with the Bucketeer, and fell upon him. Unarchists, then, I gathered. Some of the other officers leapt into the fray and soon there was a milling, noisy mass of lamviinity battling across Vyssu's parlor and entryway. I determined then to remain precisely where I was standing, safe upon the upper floor.

Suddenly, behind me, a window crashed and tinkled. An oddly garbed lam swung through the shattered frame upon the end of a large length of rope, collided with a hatstand, and fell over it in a tangle of arms and headpieces. He sorted himself out, leapt to his hands, and tied the rope's end to the metal wall bracket of a converted gaslamp, straightened out his cloak, and reached beneath it to produce a large, long-barreled hunting pistol. It was not until this moment that I realized I still held my own life preserver, both barrels now discharged, and that the spare ammunition for it was somewhere across the crowd-filled street in my medical bag. The fellow saw me and raised his gun, yet before he could so much as say a word, another of his sort slid awkwardly down the rope, and another and another.

The rope went slack an instant, then tautened once again. With a screech and an alarming shower of electrical sparks, the light fixture was wrenched from its place upon the wall and carried out the window, where a blurry form whipped by, his mournfully resigned wail descending both in pitch and position until it terminated with a crash in the alleyway below.

The surviving intruders lay piled upon each other in a heap. Considerable grumbling, cursing effort and much rough diplomacy were required before they separated themselves from one another and the hatstand. As one, they trained suspicious eyes upon me, along with an impressively mismatched array of weapons, making toward the stairs in single file. Here they paused abruptly, jam-

ming into one another once again as they espied the crowd
below, still engrossed in an enthusiastic and deafening
fight. A shout of recognition came from one of the new-
comers and from all. "Third Contraconventionals!" They
clenched their fists and gnashed their jaws.

I buttonholed the last in line, a little fellow carrying a
meat cleaver. "What, pray, is a Third Contraconventional?"

He growled self-righteously, pointing toward my landlurry and rher friends. "Revisionists and traitors to the
Cause! We've run across a nest of 'em, it seems!" His companions, muttering agreement with his sentiments, started
down the stairs. He moved to catch them up.

"A moment, sir, if you will be so kind. May I ask what
you are, in this connexion?"

"A *Second* Contraconventional, of course, an' soggy well
proud of it! Now unhand me, missur, please, for I am
needed by my comrades!" He followed his friends and together they trooped down the stairs—past the Archsacerdot, who clung timidly to the handrail—plunging with a
single, sanguine shout into the battle. I felt a momentary
pang of disappointment, for I greatly wished to inquire further—for example, about the *First* Contraconventionals—
but it seemed that the Seconds and the Thirds were now
happily preoccupied with one another and the Bucketeers
and disinclined to answer questions.

Were there Second, Third, and even First *Con*vention-
als? I must ask this of Niitood someday, I thought. Politics
were growing more and more complex by the moment.

As I turned to give my last attentions to the remains of
Reverend Adem, yet another flurry of shouts arose above
the sounds of violence below. *A shot rang out!* Rushing to
the stairs once more, I saw Mav calmly poking a finger
into a large, ragged hole in Vyssu's parlor wall, where it
appeared that someone had just shot at him—and missed,
fortunately. Across the crowded chamber, Fatpa, now
swinging a screaming Bucketeer from a length of chain,
plunged a heavily muscled hand into a curtained alcove
from which there issued a considerable volume of whitepowder gunsmoke. He retrieved his arm and, with it, the
disheveled figure of a lam held, securely, if without much
dignity, by the fur atop his carapace. Retaining his hold
upon the chain connected to the Bucketeer, Fatpa seized
the weapon in the would-be assassin's fingers. A large-bore

158

shrimp-hunter—Great Merciful Pah (as Mav would have it), it was that fellow, the little gray Middle House bureaucrat from Tis's offce. Why—

FLASH! That from the front door, where Niitood the reporter had just appeared, readying his camera for another shot. *"Imperial Intelligencer!"* he shouted absurdly, striding across the room, dodging bodies locked in mortal combat. *Flash!* He made another photograph. The leader of the Bucketeers turned, swung a vicious blow at the correspondent, who danced back, protective of his camera, and *flashed!* another picture.

Fatpa had a hand now upon each end of the shotgun, having turned a length of chain tightly about the bureaucrat's upper limb and hung both him and the unfortunate Bucketeer whose chain it was from a chandelier, where they swung and crashed together, punching at each other vigorously. Vyssu's bodyguard gave a grunt clearly audible even from my vantage and bent the gun almost in two, its stock splintering in his hands. He tossed it away, and before it landed on the floor, it struck one of the Unarchists—a Second Contraconventional, I believe, but it may have been a Third—upon the carapace. He sank groundward in oblivion.

Behind Niitood, a crowd of roughly dressed strangers barged indoors to claim their own place in the meelee. Some of these I recognized from the crowd outside, likely disappointed now with what had turned out to be the bogus fight Adem had no doubt arranged to entertain and divert them. One picked up a sizable lounging cushion and threw it in my general direction the length of the room, staggering the Archsacerdot, who'd made it to the bottom of the stairs. The cleric stumbled, narrowly missing Niitood's camera, and fell across the half-disrobed carapace of one of Vyssu's females, who screamed and promptly fainted.

As if that were their cue, a freshly arrived troupe of stern and dignified individuals in sacerdotal robes nearly tripped over the form of their august superior, who was by this time crawling toward the door between the legs of the combatants. Someone struck one of the priests with yet another cushion, and the group of them was somehow absorbed into the fighting before they realized what had happened to them. These worthies' heels were nearly trod upon by a character in Imperial Navy uniform, his dress sword dragging upon the floor and the rest of his attire in careless, unmilitary disarray. I suspected this was Hedgyt, Srafen's old friend whom Mav had interviewed, for he carried in his arms some ungainly and complex device half-draped in a ragged length of sailcloth. The elderly Navy surgeon looked about, bewildered by the riot he'd blundered into, spotted Mav, and started toward my friend, clearly intent upon conversing with him. Through some fanatical transformation I have sometimes noticed in inventors, he quickly became oblivious to his surroundings once he had engaged the detective.

Despite the obvious perils of negotiating the intervening distance, I thought at once to join them, there being nothing further I could do for Adem, and took a measured step again toward the stairs, when I was pushed violently from behind and lost my balance, tumbling down several steps, trampled over by a dozen of Vyssu's female and surmale employees, followed closely by a fresh squad of Bucketeers, who'd likely come in by the roof trap. As I regained a vertical attitude and orientation, yet another wave of hurrying lamviinity overwhelmed me; Vyssu's customers and yet another Departmental brigade. By the time I had recovered my full sensibilities a second time, I somehow found myself at the bottom of the flight; those who had used me so unkindly were now indistinguishable from any of the others fighting with one another (for reasons they'd apparently forgotten long since) in Vyssu's front hall and parlor. Indeed, the melee had extended itself to the kitchen and to every other nook and cranny upon this floor. There was a surge and sally that threatened to spread deliberations up the stairs, the way I'd come, as well. I ducked out of the way, only to trip over the Archsacerdot, and fell sprawling with him. The unconscious trollop he'd tripped over had caught a cheap and garish bracelet in his cloak; he'd dragged her with him until they were both directly before the front door.

I shook myself again to stimulate a sorely bruised apprehension of reality. Two trines of walking hands appeared before me, looking somehow familiar; I glanced up. There, of all the people in the world to choose among, was my vile, perfidious maidservant, Zoobon, and beside her, my mother, father, and surfather. A flying cushion struck my male parent between the eyes. He swayed, by dint of doughty character remained standing, straightened his hat

160

with an angry wrench, and glared down at me, his nostrils quivering with reproof.

"Good day, Papa," I preempted. "Mama, Sasa—Zoobon, you're dismissed this very minute—won't you join us in some kood?" A heavy ring of brass keys whirled across the room, striking Zoobon on the ear. She slapped a palm over the orifice, cried in anguish, whirled to confront her attacker, and got a cushion of her own for the trouble of it. She lacked Papa's stern disposition; it knocked her over and she was instantly trampled by a passing gaggle of Bucketeers and Unarchists. Sasa stepped back out of harm's way, seizing Mama, but the Bucketeers leapt upon my father, clamping all his legs in irons despite his most vociferous and threatening protests.

Despite my better inclinations, I giggled, glad that I had lived to see my father's dignity deflated just a little. There would be a reckoning for this, I knew. I hoped that I would live to see that, too.

FLASH! Niitood caught Papa in a most embarrassing condition, all his arms and legs bound up together above his jaws (Mav was having some influence, it would seem). Someone heaved a vase at the reporter, but he ducked, once again narrowly preserving his camera, and the object took Fatpa on the jaws. When his eyes cleared, Fatpa picked up a Bucketeer at random—also the two prisoners he was attached to—and in retaliation threw the whole lot back at the vase-thrower. There was a splendid *crash!*, but I could not quite make out where, nor upon whom, this trio of unfortunates had come to rest. Mama and Sasa huddled close beside the front wall to the left of the entrance, where they remained safe when the pair of original combatants, those watu-drivers, tumbled in, still entwined in deadly struggle—their sham dispute, it would appear, had somehow been transformed into an honest duel—and bleeding copiously from a dozen minor wounds apiece. One of them tripped over the Archsacerdot, the other stumbled dangerouly close to Niitood and his precious camera. The reporter danced and ducked away.

This whole affair was rapidly assuming the shape of an outrageous nightmare. The next time I dared to look up, my father, rocking on his carapace, was preparing to swing one single liberated fist at the person next to him, who turned out to be my own Battalion Chief, Waad Hifk *Tis!*

Two brightly liveried footmen I'd not seen before now grappled with Fatpa, who held someone in gentlelam's attire above his carapace, preparing to throw him across the room. The Lord Ennramo shouted ungenteelly until the former highwaylam was persuaded to release him—which transpired at the extremity of Fatpa's swing. Ennramo flew some distance, where he smashed into the Archsacerdot, who had only just regained his walking hands. The pair lay insensate in a lump together.

A momentary pathway among the fighters cleared along the line of the Lord's flight, and I could just see Mav and Hedgyt, the physician, still deep in conversation. Every now and again, some ruffian intent upon involving them in the violence would approach with a rush. Almost absently, Mav would stretch out a fist, strike a preemptive blow, and then return to his consultation with Hedgyt. The doctor scarcely seemed to notice. Vyssu stood nearby with an exceptionally elongated inhaling tube in her fingers, offering occasional comment of her own.

WHEET! Above the thundering chaos, a whistle sounded brilliantly, distracting the combatants from their labors and attracting their attention (and mine) to the entrance of the parlor. Leds, the old Museum guard stood in the doorway, and beside him, Sathe. There was a murmur, then a groan, which circled about the room as each enthusiast began to appreciate the extent of his strains and injuries.

Sathe, surveying the erstwhile field of battle, waited patiently as Mav interrupted his conversation and waded among the damaged carapaces toward her. He paused but once, to retrieve a ring of keys from the floor and return it to the landlurry.

"I say, Mother! How good of you to come! What on Sodde Lydfe brings you down here to the Kiiden?" He took her hand and nodded to old Leds, then noticed Tis, who had somehow acquired a set of female undergarments, which were draped over his jaws. This apparition Mav tactfully disdained to acknowledge, very likely winning, in the process, a friend in Tis for life.

"Good evening, my dear," Sathe replied with equal aplomb. "Why, I read your advertisement in the newspaper and thought to ask you how matters were developing." She looked around her once again, taking in Ennramo and the Archsacerdot. The Bucketeers had begun to sort things out but were running short of lamacles. "It would appear that you have had results."

"By Pah, I think you're right! Have you met Vyssu— and Doctor Hedgyt? And can you stay for kood?" Mav caught the eye of a Bucketeer who seemed to recognize him. "That's quite correct, dear fellow, take *everybody* in— they're all murder suspects, every one of them. Get up from there, will you, Mymy. There's a good lurry. I believe your skills will soon be needed at the Precinct."

Outside, there was the grumbling of bad weather once again, and rain began to fall. Through the parlor window, miraculously unbroached by the fighting, I watched a cab draw up, its watun and driver protected by Mav's new waterproof garments. "Anybody needs a cab?" he shouted smugly.

"Mav, will you kindly tell me something?"

"And what might that be, Mymy?" He fussed with the lapels of his dressing gown and began to dribble fluid into his pipe.

"The meaning of a word—the Reverend Adem's last, that is. And perhaps Podfettian, from the sound of it. The word is 'danokih.' "

"I see. How very interesting." He shook the little flask impatiently and held it once again over the end of his inhaling tube. "It isn't Podfettian, although it's close. It's Old Fodduan."

"Whatever does it mean?" I asked.

Across the room, Niitood *flashed!* a final photograph, glanced out of the window at the lone cab, and moved briskly toward the door. He took a step, tripped over the Archsacerdot, and fell, crushing his camera.

I believe the word he uttered then was Old Fodduan, too.

"You wouldn't want to know," Mav answered, glancing in disgust at both his empty flask and Niitood. "You wouldn't want to know."

XVI: Mathas Behind Bars

Someday, I am confident, there will exist a rational process for determining which victims of mass tragedy, such as an apartment fire or railroad accident, ought to be assisted urgently, which succored at comparative leisure in hospital, and which invited to depart, as it were, under their own sail and rigging. At present, these crucial judgments, inevitably made in haste and never without error, constitute an esoteric art, absorbed by its practitioners pragmatically, and doubtless at the cost of many lives. Perhaps it shall be I who ultimately establishes the principles for this procedure. If so, then I shall have also become an inventor of sorts, like Mav, Niitood, Hedgyt, Law, or any hundred of my other acquaintances, along with nearly everybody else who lives in this highly stimulating epoch of Great Fodduan progress.

That being as it may, the evening of the Kiiden Riot (as it afterward came to be called, typifying the general reliability of history) there existed for me no recourse but to allow our Bucketeers to escort away those persons capable of carrying themselves, a contingent suffering minor fractures, lacerations, and similar indignities.

This left a residuum of serious injuries at Vyssu's establishment, which occupied my attention for a considerable period. May Pah be praised, with the exception of the Reverend Adem (whom I, myself, had despatched, I recalled again in shocked disbelief!), no further fatalities evinced themselves, this likely owing to the substantial number of pistols, knives, and bludgeons present, these artifacts occupying hands that might otherwise have been employed in the more deadly practices of ripping joints, gouging eyes, or tearing jaws from their carapaces. Thank Heaven's Desiccation that the gentlelamly insistence upon weapons has filtered downward even to the lower classes!

A Bucketeer had fetched my bag and I attended to the

wounded, who, excepting the extremest cases, were carted off to Hedgerow over the disgruntled objections of Bucketeers from other Precincts who comprised the majority of the law-enforcement delegation present. Tis was the highest ranker on the premises; had he not been, Mav, as the Inquirer, would have given precisely the same command.

So off they went in chains, a gay and colorful procession, from the pair of watu drivers to the battered Lord Ennramo, who, upon regaining consciousness, vowed imperiously first that Mav would do his future investigations upon some ice-bound island weather station—then, on hearing his own words, began to laugh and, with his hands in irons, clapped my friend upon the carapace and strode aristocratically through the door into a waiting kood waggon appropriated for the purpose, heartily shouting, "Well done, good Inquirer! Do come and share a lamly jolt when this is over!" Frightfully decent of the fellow, I thought, until I noticed Mav, a thoughtful aspect to his fur, making further entries in his notecase.

Thus, with the final insensible victim—or coperpetrator—hauled away, I was left quite by myself. Nor was this excluding Vyssu, who had, upon her own insistence, also been arrested. Sporting of her, everyone admitted; Mav took obvious delight in making sure the lamacles upon her wrists did not chafe. This policy of hers manifested a certain good business sense, for her clientele and admirers cheered and clapped and rippled comradely appreciation of her mettle as she followed in Ennramo's handsteps. Of such gestures are legends born, particularly profitable ones.

Thus nearly everyone departed in a spirit of good fellowship, as if to a celebration rather than to gaol (sparing Mav and his subordinates a deal of logistical difficulty in the process), and I followed sometime afterward.

"Oh, I say, Mav?" Our Precinct's "clientele" had overflowed from the small shabby office over the gaol into the watu barn, where there had been set up a table for the filling out of appropriate paperwork. This ritual was being accomplished by what was at the time a novel means: those transported here from Vyssu's, practically without regard to rank or class, were formed up in three winding queues before the table; meanwhile, paracauterists trafficked up and down applying bandages and liniment. Upon completion of the forms, each "prisoner" was remanded to another crowded corner of the stable, where kood was being served.

"Hullo there, Mymy, I am happy to— *Blast the thrice-accursed desklam who composed these questionnaires!*" He sat behind the table, attempting to record data my erstwhile landlurry supplied within a number of spaces far too small to write in. This amused the elderly Unarchist, who, on that account alone, perhaps, was being unusually cooperative.

"Your full name, if I may ask— Mymy, there are para-cauterists aplenty here. Would you mind greatly doing me a favor?"

"*Minymmo* Pemmopan Viidawasiivyt-Koed," replied the lurry cheerfully, little brushmarks of it tracing through rher fur.

I said: "Not if it means filling out these forms in your stead. How many have you had arrested, anyway?"

He rubbed dispiritedly at the misspelled first half of rher last name. "Your *unmarried* appellation, if you please— No, Mymy, I've something altogether different in mind; I'd appreciate your knocking up Tis and telling him— *Wet!*" The eraser had torn through the cheap and pulpy paper. "Now I shall have to begin another—"

"Koed-Viidawasiivyt," offered the landlurry. "Married a third cousin on me father's side. That's four I's, Inspector darlin', an' a Y. Tell me, where'd they take me keys?"

"Pray continue, Mav. What is it I must tell Tis?" I watched another of the queues: Fatpa stood on line in front of Hedgyt, the latter clutching his invention. Behind Hedgyt stood the bureaucrat with whom he argued over who was next. "What is it Hedgyt has there, a bomb?"

Mav chuckled. "No, my dear, a clock; it is his fancy that people might enjoy to read the time in numbers, as they're written, rather than off the face of a dial. Ridiculous, but beautifully conceived—and executed: I'd know the model maker anywhere, simply from the cut of his lathe turnings. Now where was I? Ah, yes: dear lurry, your lawful occupation?"

"But, Mav, you haven't said why I must go to Tis's office."

Rhe looked down thoughtfully at the space provided. "Hostelier and Chaperone to Young Surmales of Good Character." Ripples spread throughout rher fur again.

"Landlurry." Mav began to write it down upon a dotted line insufficient for even those nine letters.

"Hostelier and chaperone!" the elderly person insisted. "Sayin' less is hurtful slander, most particular in th' Kiiden!"

"You may have a point," conceded Mav. "Mymy, I'll get to you if you'll be more patient!" Here his pencil snapped in two; he breathed heavily, then took up his inhaling tube and flask, rediscovering that the latter was still empty. "*Damp!*"

"Mav?"

"Hostelier and chaperone to young surmales of good character!"

"Young fella, won't you have a drop or two of mine?" Hedgyt had finished with his Bucketeer. Standing now beside me, he set his experiment upon the littered table, fumbling in his tunic for a well-used bronze Navy flask.

"How good of you . . ." Mav stretched across, then withdrew his hand. "*Now* I recall! Mymy, please ask Tis for a sample of that Continental spirit, which he offered me. Hedgyt here, in recompense for inconveniences he has suffered, might appreciate it, too. Also"—he turned the ruptured form upon its back, scribbling a lengthy note— "by rights this ought to be my resignation, and is likely yet to be. However, take it to the old fellow, and read it on the way as it concerns you in part." He rose and gave the pencil stub to a recruit. "I am waterlogged if I'll fill out another of these forms!"

I took the message and left him with the surgeon, pausing to read upon the spiral stairs:

My dear Tis:

Kindly, in about two hours' time, authorize release of all whom I have detained, excepting:

 a) 2nd C'conventional Unarchists (*not* 3rd);
 b) Ypad P'dits *Fatpa*, Esq.;
 c) Rewu Uomag *Niitood, Imp'l Intelligencer*;
 d) C'dr Zedmon Dakods *Hedgyt*, Imp'l Navy;
 e) that gormless little Nazemynsiin creature, I've forgotten his name, the one who shot at me;
 f) His Grace, the Lord Ennramo.

Tomorrow at third hour, if you will gather these together (save the Unarchists, who may go directly to gaol), with Law, Myssmo, and Ensda, I shall clear up this matter once and for all. Please take special pains to

167

obtain the presence of Law; this may be most important. Meanwhile, I am

Yr. Ob't. Svt.,
Agot Edmoot *Mav*

There were two more present upon the next morning: I, after pleasant hours in my own flat (Mav having asserted that, with half of Mathas in our gaol, most likely our murderer was as well); Vyssu, who had not remained, but had returned to her own house in thought of restoring it to its previous elegance. This was well; news of the rioting had greatly enhanced the number of curiosity-seekers through the Kiiden, and thus her clientele.

I often despair of the lamviin race.

My parents were now somewhat mollified by not having been incarcerated with "half of Mathas"—and, to appearances, impressed that this should be so on account of a few words to the "authorities" from their own little surdaughter. They had spent their evening at home as well, and in future I was to have more confidence and independence of them—and no maid servant.

Yesterevening's rainfall had been brief; the sun was streaming into Tis's office windows, yet there were many more than could be accommodated there with comfort, and we moved out into the hallway with a large, imposing Bucketeer at the stairwell to control admission and egress.

I, to my great satisfaction, was back in uniform. Mav, not wishing to abandon any precedent that, despite words to the contrary, had been thus established, wore civilian garments fully equal to anything the Reverend Adem had displayed, and far more tastefully selected. Vyssu, who arrived with him, had adorned herself conservatively, reeking of expensive restraint. Tis was his habitual wrinkled self; Niitood, having spent a second night in gaol, looked even worse. He had received another camera by messenger, however, and was happily preparing to make use of it upon a moment's notice.

Seating cushions formed a loose triangle in the broad corridor: one for Tis at an apex, Mav's beside it, Vyssu's next to his, then a very large one for Fatpa. He alone looked better for a night behind bars; it struck me that all this might be reminding him of a vigorous youth. Niitood took a place between the former highwaylam and another Bucketeer who occupied a second corner of the triangle. Upon the other side, there was a cushion to which I was directed; Hedgyt was set next to me, then Leds, and then the nameless civil servant. At this corner bulked another Bucketeer. Across the final side were placed Ensda, Myssmo, the Lord Ennramo, and Law. I had pondered through the night over Mav's written words concerning the young inventor; for the life of me, nothing about him now seemed of special interest. Well, I would learn soon enough.

Behind Tis, a very large window looked down upon Kevod Lane and caught the morning light, brightening the otherwise dreary scarlet-painted hall. When everyone was seated, Mav ordered a wick, whose service he had placed inside the triangle rather nearer Ennramo than Tis.

"I apologize that some of you have spent an uncomfortable night. I trust this morning's results will compensate you all—all save one—for, as I promised in the newspapers, I am about to reveal the murderer of *Srafen* Rotdu Rizmou, Professor and Curator of the Imperial Museum, my good friend and teacher." He produced his pipe and flask, prepared the little tube, and thrust it into a nostril.

"Before proceeding further, there are questions I should like to ask some of you. Principally, it is important to ascertain your motives in appearing yesterday at Vyssu's. We shall begin with Niitood, as I was there for obvious reasons, as was Vyssu, it being her house, and Fatpa, who is employed there. Niitood?"

The reporter hesitated, fidgeting with his camera. "I say, old sandshrimp, I'm a correspondent, after all. I read your advert, waited till the news was well spread through the city, then came to sniff out what had developed."

Mav's pelt indicated satisfaction. "This seems to have been the motive of fully ninety-nine percent of those who attended our little party yesterday. I shall have to think over this newspaper advertising scheme again, very soon. Very well, Law we shall pass over, for he did not appear that afternoon. M'Lord, why is it that you came?"

The fellow likewise took a while in answering. "As you are aware, sir, I represent some highly placed interests of the Empire. Equally, you surely know that these parties have had an eye upon this affair from its inception. I wished, on their behalf, to observe the consequences of your effort in the newspapers, and—"

"Pardon me, Your Grace. Vyssu, have you a comment?"

The lady had not indicated so, but I knew Mav's style.

This must have been prearranged. I watched him watching Ennramo carefully while appearing to listen to Vyssu, who flared a nostril as if to speak—

"*Very well, then!*" Ennramo suddenly declared. "It was also the address you gave, sir, in your notice! It has been well and truly associated with . . . er, with *discretion*, in the past. I was ordered—but I can say nothing more, as you must understand."

Mav took a puff upon his pipe. "Indeed, and we will speak of it no further here in public. Be prepared, however, for I shall possibly have need of private answers later. Myssmo and Ensda failed to appear yesterday, despite the fact that the latter, like Law here, had been released for other matters upon bond. You, sir, from the Nazemyn-siin—what in dampness is your name?"

The little fellow, swathed in bandages from the drubbing Fatpa had administered, replied, "Mrrmh Hnnrhnn *Frnnhnnhnn.*"

"How is that again?" Mav leaned closer.

"Mrrmh Hnnrhnn *Frnnhnnhnn!*"

"I observe that anonymity can become habit-forming. Very well then, Mr.——, sir, *you* appeared at Vyssu's yesterday to shoot a shot at me. Would you mind very much telling us why?"

The bureaucrat sat sullenly for long minutes. Tis got his pipe, followed by Hedgyt and Ennramo; the place began to fill with fumes, which made the kood seem sour. Fatpa shuffled on his cushion; Niitood continued playing with his camera. Mav's fur began to bristle. "See here, lam, this will avail you nothing! I know that you had orders to terminate my investigation by terminating me, and, for following them, you alone will be most severely punished. Some mitigation may be forthcoming on condition that you volunteer the names of those who gave the orders!"

The bureaucrat tensed. In response, the Bucketeers and Mav stirred as if ready for battle. Even Niitood raised his camera and Ennramo reached for a sword that wasn't there. Tis and Hedgyt, two old campaigners, likewise showed combative eagerness. Were lamviin energy electrical in nature, we should all have been quite thoroughly juiced.

Yet the bureaucrat remained silent. "Very well, then," Mav said in a rather dangerous low tone, "you may inform our masters—when opportunity next presents itself in twenty or thirty years—that they have failed to subvert justice to political expedience. The philosopher whose mind they feared shall be avenged, whatever the public reaction! Leds, what brought you yesterevening to Vyssu's?"

The old guard looked uncomfortable. "Sir, 'twas your own mother telephoned me asking how you were getting on. She'd misunderstood somehow, thinking you were still investigatin' at the Museum, so I asked whether she wouldn't care for someone t'come with her if she was goin' into th' Kiiden."

Mav sat back upon his cushion. "Quite correct. That is how I have it from my mother. Accuse me as you will, I shall not consider her a suspect, and, since she initiated good Leds's presence, I believe that he was there in innocence. Doctor Hedgyt, please explain how you came to the Kiiden that afternoon."

The old Commander straightened up again upon his cushion, shook himself, and, eying those seated across from him with something akin to distaste, answered, "Well, I saw your advert in the paper, younglam, and since I'd no other address for you and had neglected demonstrating my digtial chronometer for your benefit, I— Merciful Pah, I never expected to drop anchor in the middle of a free-for-all! Reminded me of younger days, a fight in every port, me in ratin' uniform so's to enjoy it without sullying the officer corps! Srafen certainly—"

"Thank you, Commander, I'm quite sure rhe did, and I find your clock most intriguing. Mymy, you were there upon my insistence, and that completes the tally—*except for you, sir*." He addressed this last to Tis, who blinked twice and rocked back upon his seat.

"Me—I? Mav, whatever in Pah's name can you be thinking? Naturally I was there—a murder case under way on my responsibility, and also a disturbance that set station semaphores wagging over half the city?" He huffed and grumbled further until he came to a complete stop.

"I see," answered Mav. "Sir, the disturbance wasn't properly within your jurisdiction. Why is it you—"

"Because of that soggydamp newspaper ad of yours, that's why! The *case* is in my jurisdiction—now get on with it!"

"Yes," echoed Lord Ennramo. "Who committed this vile act?" There were several other parallel expressions, which Mav allowed to pass. Then he stepped out into the center.

171

"Gentlelamn, lady and lurry." He held up a hand. "I sympathize with your curiosity and impatience. I can tell you that in many respects I spent a night as uncomfortably as you did. But I know now precisely *how* the murder was accomplished and, on that account, as I have always believed possible, the identity of the killer."

There was a stir.

"The question in my mind has always been that Srafen was killed with a bomb, but *where was it placed?* Secreted in Srafen's lectern, which, too, was utterly destroyed by the blast? It was Mymy told me where the powder charge must be. . . ."

I blinked all three eyes. "I?"

"Indeed, my dear, in the finest, most revoltingly anatomical detail: the distribution of wounds among the spectators as well as the nature of the wounds themselves. Fragments of Srafen's body showered out into the audience; a lectern bomb would have thrown them in the opposite direction.

"Yet blood and carapacial fragments covered the rear walls as well; ergo Srafen had been carrying the bomb, a thought that disturbed me sorely, as I hadn't believed rhe was the suicidal sort. A bomb so powerful must have been relatively weighty and could not have been placed among rher clothing without rher knowledge." He recharged his pipe and began pacing as he spoke.

"There was no lack of indication how the bomb had gotten where it did. This springbow bolt"—he reached into his cloak for the exploded weapon, holding it aloft—"lay upon the stage where Srafen was last seen in this world. It is of the explosive sort, apparently shot through an ancient, rotting door. Mymy and I found supporting evidence in the next room, although there remained certain puzzling contradictions. Would you mind explaining, Mymy?"

"I had not anticipated . . . Very well, then: the first is that the bolt could not have been shot through the door without exploding *there*. Second, upon testing it, Mav found the springbow so deteriorated with age it could not have propelled the bolt through the door at all. Oh, and there was something about wood fragments within the powder cavity. I believe that's the lot, isn't it?"

He gave the bolt a casual toss. "Except that there was also the problem with the alarm system, which went off *after* the springbow was apparently used to murder Srafen! Finally, I determined to my satisfaction that no one could have been in the adjacent room before or during the lecture. What does that suggest to you, dear paracauterist?"

"That the murder couldn't have happened in the manner we believed?"

"Very good!" A gratified ripple spread through his fur. "I clung to this blasted theory of mine too long, yet it produced a general principle to the effect that, having eliminated everything clearly impossible, one must perforce examine the merely improbable. The culprit left the evidence behind *after* the murder was done."

"What?" This from half the people present, including myself.

"A ruse to drag us off the evidential trail. However, it left a trail of its own, and that is what eventually solved this case. Wherever the location of the bomb, however it was ignited, it was *afterward* that the miscreant, taking advantage of the confusion, slipped around into the Weapons Hall, drove his pre-exploded bolt through the door, smashed the display case so we would think exactly what we did, and returned to the auditorium!"

He cast an eye about the room. "You see, when I went to have some experimental bolts made, I found that others were having them fabricated, also. Close examination proved this to be of recent manufacture, artificially tarnished so as to appear ancient. Someone had blown it open, brought it to the Museum, and, at the crucial moment, drove it through the door, using a war hammer mounted on a nearby suit of armor. See the bright spots on the nether end? There are corresponding marks upon the hammer, as it happens. When I lifted the bow from its case, I observed something I did not think about until last night: large splinters of glass on *top* of the springbow, which could not have been there had the weapon been used! Thus the murderer never touched it (and did not realize its weakened condition) but simply smashed the case to mislead us, probably before he drove the arrow, permitting the alarms to cover up his noise."

Here Mav stood a moment breathing deeply, exhilarated. "All of this I had reasoned out at various times. I might as well confess, however, that until last night, I had not the faintest notion of who had done these things or how. In fact"—he now extracted a paper from his pocket—"I was prepared to ask Mymy to present my resignation to Tis, had actually begun to speak the words, when something struck me and I realized that I could solve the murder after all, by the precise means I had always believed applicable. Thus I departed in some haste, looked into a number of details, and now I know!"

"Who was it?" Tis demanded, simultaneously with several others, including one Bucketeer who had gotten caught up in the spirit of things.

Mav pointed a finger. "It was *you*, Niitood, who killed Professor Srafen!"

The reporter leaped to his hands. "Impossible, old sandshrimp! You yourself cleared me! I had no reason, nor the means. My only crime was being there!"

"Nonetheless, *old sandshrimp*, I will prove it before we leave this room. There is one small complication: you didn't know what it was you were doing, and, on that account, are completely innocent."

The reporter sagged back to his seat. "Whew, glad to hear it—you almost had me convinced!"

Mav rippled. "Sorry, Niitood, the story you'll take away will assuage you. Srafen was indeed carrying a bomb, although rhe didn't know it, a complex device with whitepowder and various other parts that rendered it most sensitive to the electromagnetic influences of your flash attachment. I have learned that an electrical arc generates a correlative ethereal vibration, which may be employed for numerous purposes—even as the trigger for a bomb." Once again he pointed his finger. "*Isn't that correct, Law?*"

Srafen's husband blinked surprise. "I suppose you're right, Inquirer. I never believed that you, a mere inventor of raincoats, could figure out such a thing. My congratulations, and I hope you'll carry on for both of us, inventing, while I am in gaol."

"Or between the Blocks!" cried a sanguine Tis.

"They don't send someone to the Blocks for embezzlement," Mav said mildly, "which is all that Law is guilty of. Dear fellow, I believe that you'll be out quite soon enough. Your inventor's expertise has confirmed my theories, and for that it will appear upon your record that you assisted justice."

Mav turned now and raised the finger of guilt once more. Niitood rose as well, for this was the very moment we had come to witness. "The actual criminal is—"

Hedgyt leaped up, holding his clock before him. Before anyone could act, he was behind Tis. "Stand where you

174

arel This is a bomb, and I shall— *NO!*" Niitood advanced upon him, readying his camera. The surgeon retreated to the window in horror. Tis slid in a faint to the floor before his cushion.

"NO!" Mav shouted, and I, too, realized what was about to happen.

BRROOOM!! As the picture flashed, the object in the doctor's hands exploded, dashing him through the window, filling the room with smoke. Tis's cushion back burst into flames. There passed a long time before the Bucketeers brought sand to put it out. I swear that every building in this city is safe from conflagration except our Precinct station.

All adroop, Niitood looked down at the fragments of his camera on the floor.

Mav went to the shattered window. A shudder running through his pelt told me what it was he saw below. There would be nothing I or a dozen of the finest physicians in Mathas could do for our old colleague.

A crowd began to gather; Bucketeers came from the station doors to hold them back.

At last Hedgyt and Srafen were united. In death.

XVII: A Science of Intuition

"Another round, good Tamet!" Mav exclaimed as Niitood slid quietly to the floor of the Hose & Springbow. The victorious detective was determined that we all should join the journalist before this afternoon was done.

"A moment, Mav, before your sensibilities have vanished altogether?" I was becoming equally adamant concerning certain answers Hedgyt's precipitate demise had denied me. "Kindly stay your hand, innkeeper, for first there's a reckoning due that has little connexion with gold or silver."

The retired Bucketeer and landlord looked from Mav to me in some confusion, made up his mind, and wound the juicing box, then stepped away, narrowly avoiding tripping over Niitood. There is a saying to the effect that Pah looks after children and inebriates; besides, Niitood had no new camera. Mav reached toward the box, hesitated, then pushed the infernal contraption across the table at me.

"Mymy, will you *kindly* take a jolt and calm yourself? Tis was satisfied that we found our culprit this morning, as was the Lord Ennramo—and thus certain August Personages better left unmentioned. Myssmo asked no questions, nor did Fatpa, Leds, nor, most especially, Law and Ensdal And look at Niitood here—"

"That's easily explained," said I. "He is a journalist and makes up all his own answers as he goes along!"

Vyssu charged her long inhaling tube from Mav's flask. "Well, I, too, have questions, dear, and I'll be put off no longer. Mymy, we shall keep the scoundrel here until he confesses—how it was he actually solved the murder."

"Indeed," I agreed, "it seems to me that progress requires communication among those who create it. That would be scientifical, would it not?"

"Oh, bother the both of you!" snapped the detective, a sour look in his pelt. "In any event, there was very little 'scientifical' about it, as least in conscious application, which is why I am reluctant to discuss it. Oh, very well, then, I'll supply your moldering answers. Much good they may do you!" He took the little flask from Vyssu's fingers. "When Hedgyt, whom I'd grown to have some feeling for, offered me inhaling fluid on the very day I'd deliberately made myself a target for a murderer, I found myself looking for an excuse to refuse politely. Why? I hadn't the foggiest notion at the time! How do you like *that* for scientifical reasoning, Mymy?"

Vyssu chuckled. "So there *is* a male intuition, after all. I've often suspected as much."

I added, "Perhaps you have an instinct for detectiving, Mav, or at least for discovering the guilty."

" 'Intuition'! 'Instinct'! As Tis would have it, 'Balderdash and damprot!' These expressions would imply that we are born with knowledge in our minds, when, to the contrary, my dears, we come into the world completely ignorant—which is our blessing, Srafen often said, because it means that, unlike animals fixed to predetermined patterns, we can learn and change whatever is around us in a manner unanticipated by nature."

I looked at Vyssu; she looked at me; we both shrugged.

"Yet, for no good reason, I suddenly mistrusted Hedgyt. The alienists are right about one thing: the lamviin mind is of two parts: the conscious, shrewd and dirigible; and the unconscious, naïve, but very quick. And, as thoughts are to the conscious mind, so are feelings to the unconscious."

"Are you saying," I asked, "that we should be guided by our feelings as much as by our thoughts? Scarcely a philosophy for—"

"No, lamviin are a thinking race, and we should be guided by our thoughts, and by our thoughts *about* our feelings. Buried more or less deeply within me, I knew, were perfectly good reasons why I shouldn't complacently be enjoying Hedgyt's spirits. It took me but a moment to discover at least one; can either of you guess what it was?"

Silence from the pair of us initially, then Vyssu spoke: "He was a physician and such a professional might think of poison as a likely weapon—and have access to it."

"An inventor also," countered Mav, "and that is what betrayed him. Unbeknownst to me, I had unconsciously observed and associated his model-maker's worklamship with that of the springbow bolts I'd had made up, and the mention, at the craftslam's shop, that others were requiring springbow bolts, as well. We both thought it a new popular fancy.

"The tarnish on the arrow I connected to that corrosion one often encounters at dockside—which is very likely how Hedgyt artificially aged the projectile. All of this I rediscovered in the moment I hesitated to accept his fluid Later, I remembered Hedgyt mentioning that he had seen to Srafen's medical needs whenever he was in port, and—"

"Stay a moment, Mav!" I cried. "What has that to do with—"

"Do you not yet see, my dear paracauterist? Where might a bomb be placed without the wearer's knowledge? Why, within the carapace itself, by a highly skilled and inventive surgeon! I recalled Srafen mentioning that rhe had undergone an operation, and later when rhe complained of suddenly gaining weight, although I never connected either of the statements with Hedgyt until last evening."

I blinked. No wonder I had never thought of this; it was as alien to me as any harm done to a patient could be. "That would explain the physical evidence, right enough. Tell me, how did Hedgyt know to appear at the Museum—wouldn't any camera have set off Srafen's bomb?"

"Only those designed by and made for Niitood. You see, they all knew one another, Hedgyt, Niitood, and Srafen's husband, Law. They all belonged to the same inventors' club, which each of them invited me to join. I would surmise it was from Niitood or some friend that our murderer learned of my involvement in the case, there upon sending his anonymous messages to me and to your parents, Mymy. Thus Hedgyt, who was experimenting with wireless telegraphy, knew of Niitood's flash camera and of Law's tinkering with whitepowder. Perhaps he hoped that one of them might take the blame, perhaps he merely thought to confuse us utterly—which he very nearly did."

Vyssu crinkled her fur in thought. "Why did he bring the bomb to my house, then?"

Mav said, "We'll never know. I believe he meant to make a gift of it to me, in hopes it would destroy me at some time when he was safely absent. It could be that he planned on triggering it himself, perhaps through a window."

"I see," I ventured, "and when he came and saw the riot,

178

he became confused and decided not to give you the clock, but held on to it jealousy through the entire evening so that it wouldn't be examined."

Mav rippled. "I believe that you are right, my dear. It must have been a shock to see Niitood there this morning. Hedgyt knew, before the end, that he had fashioned his own destruction."

"But why on Sodde Lydfe did he do it at all?" I persisted. "Surely, after all those nonades, he couldn't have harbored a resentment because Srafen had rejected him for marriage? They were friends."

Vyssu drew upon her tube. "I believe that I can answer that one, Mav. It wasn't that rejection, Mymy. It was that Srafen had remarried recently, and to as disgusting a pair as were possible to imagine."

"Don't be too harsh on Law, my dear," said Mav, "for he is a good inventor and will likely prove of use to society someday, despite himself. The peculiarly humorous thing is that despite rher apparently irrational fascination with them (an affliction the likes of which none of us are entirely immune to), Srafen knew quite clearly what rher mates were. When we arrived rher solicitor, we discovered Srafen's will—in which rhe states that rhe married the pair in part to preclude their fastening themselves upon some unfortunate who *didn't* understand them!"

"So I suppose that Srafen had the last laugh, after all," said I.

"Indeed," my friend replied, "and rhe would have liked it that way."

I understand old Leds passed away a few weeks ago. I cannot bring myself to be too sad, for he lived a very long and adventurous life. It has reminded me, however, that, in preparing this memoir for the records of the interstellar vessel *Tom Paine Maru*, I have been asked by *EdWina* Olson-Bear to relate what has become of each of us in the twenty-nine Sodde Lydfan years since we lived through these events.

Tamet, the innkeeper, has acquired a chain of public houses, which he has recently converted into places that serve bad food very quickly to people parked outside in watuless carriages of the sort Law was working on, which I had hoped would not prove popular. Thus individuals may poison themselves and one another at the same time, in

179

which, I suppose, there is a sort of admirable efficiency.

Speaking of pollution, Myssmo eventually became a celebrity of sorts, appearing in moving pictures (which were being experimented with during the time of the Srafen investigation). I understand that she is very rich and that her house reeks every moment of sand setting-resin.

Law went on to invent a good many things, as Mav predicted, yet I fear that his brief association with Hedgyt did us all more harm than good, for he is the creator of the very bomb that figured so highly in the recent war with Podfet—the one that can destroy a city and leaves a cloud behind shaped like a peresk tree.

I don't believe that this is what Mav means when he speaks of progress.

Doctor Ensda never was convicted of embezzlement, having this time found a solicitor nearly as clever as himself. Nor did he give up on fortunetelling, but simply moved on to another area of specialization. The last I heard, he was an economic adviser to Their Majesties' government.

Fatpa, too, has got a civil service position, and one not too unlike the one that he enjoyed during his younger days upon the continent as a highwaylam. He now heads Inland Revenue, collecting taxes.

Sathe? Well, I saw her yesterevening, and every year she grows in dignity and gentle influence. She has it in her to undo the damage wrought by a hundred Ensdas, and her parties, at which many powerful individuals may be seen, are gradually diverting our civilization into a saner, healther direction. I hope she lives to see her son's philosophical garden bear fruit.

Niitood is often one of those whom Sathe has invited, though he is more cynical and nihilistic than ever. Neither she nor Mav will give up hope of his rehabilitation, however, and only partially because he is Editor-in-Chief of the *Mathas Imperial Intelligencer*. He is also an old friend.

Vyssu, of course, retired from her dubious profession shortly after the solution to the Srafen murder and married Mav. They have three lovely children, one who may become Great Foddu's *second* private consulting detective, one who threatens to follow in his mother's handsteps by becoming a politician, and one who, I am pleased to say, plans on studying medicine under the tutelage of his surfather, *Mymysiir* Offe Mav (née Woom), which I suppose gives away the ending of my personal story and that of Mav. I indeed finished studying, dividing my time between the Bucketeers and my surfather's practice, which I eventually inherited—not in the usual tragic manner, but because dear Sasa desired to retire and travel with my other parents.

Mav, on another hand, resigned from the Bucketeers shortly after our adventure with the murderous Navy surgeon and became, as I have said, a private practitioner in his own right. This career he has pursued until this very day, except that he participates, as well, in politics, taking up an end of Srafen's work, which rhe might not have expected. Mav opposed the war with Podfet and has been highly instrumental in making something of the peace. It is his view that politics, like life itself, has three major aspects: there are those to whom tradition and paternal figures are central, who speak of law and order and focus their attention on the Upper House and Triarchy; there are those who somehow concern themselves with people in aggregate, with suffering, and with making others suffer for the sake of those who were suffering in the first place, theirs is the Middle House and a false equality among lamn their fetish; finally, there are those (of whom my husband is one and I another) to whom there are no aggregates, but only individuals, who may be liked or disliked, but only on the basis of what they are or do as individuals. To us, liberty is the central issue, and, although we tend to see the Lower House as useful in obtaining that end, we place little faith in any political process and more upon the people whom we know and trade with, love and live with.

I believe that this philosophy is vital, particularly since, in twenty-nine years, the Podfettian Hegemony has grown from an irritation to a constant threat. They, too, appear to have the kind of weapons Law provided us, and so the world may be destroyed unless we learn to overlook language and nationality and look instead to what people are as individuals. *Tom Paine Maru* has helped us, since rher highly varied crew has lived through times like these in the history of their own world.

But in the end, only we can win peace and freedom for ourselves.

I see that I have somehow overlooked one individual. Tis, that grumpy old fellow, retired eventually to Tesret and yearly comes on holiday to Mathas, where he invaria-

181

bly complains of the food, weather, prices, and accommodations.

Some things never change, despite everything that lamn such as Mav can do to bring about progress. I sometimes wonder why they think it's worth the trouble.

About the Author

Self-defense consultant and former police reservist, L. Neil Smith has also worked as a gunsmith and a professional musician. Born in Denver in 1946, he traveled widely as an Air Force "brat," growing up in a dozen regions of the United States and Canada. In 1964, he returned home to study philosophy, psychology, and anthropology, and wound up with what he refers to as perhaps the lowest grade-point average in the history of Colorado State University.

Neil recently completed his second stint on the Libertarian Party's national platform committee. In 1978 he ran against an entrenched Republican Speaker for a seat in the state legislature, earning 15 percent of the vote on a total campaign expenditure of $44.00.

ALAN DEAN FOSTER

takes you to
the outer reaches of space
in suspense-filled adventures.

Available at your bookstore or use this coupon.

Flinx of the Commonwealth
**The saga of a space orphan, adventurer
and genius.**

___I. THE TAR-AIYM KRANG	29232	$2.25
___II. ORPHAN STAR	29903	$2.50
___III. THE END OF THE MATTER	29594	$2.25

Come to Tran-ky-ky!

___ICERIGGER	29454	$2.25
The frozen world of Tran-ky-ky yields an unforgettable story of survival!		
___MISSION TO MOULOKIN	29661	$2.50
The stunning sequel to *Icerigger!*		

BB **BALLANTINE MAIL SALES**
Dept. AL, 201 E. 50th St., New York, N.Y. 10022

Please send me the BALLANTINE or DEL REY BOOKS I have
checked above. I am enclosing $.......... (add 50¢ per copy to
cover postage and handling). Send check or money order — no
cash or C.O.D.'s please. Prices and numbers are subject to change
without notice.

Name————————————————————————————

Address———————————————————————————

City—————————State—————Zip Code—————

08   Allow at least 4 weeks for delivery.   AL-6